WITHERSHYNNES
CAT'S CRADLE

SUSANNA M. NEWSTEAD

HERESY PUBLISHING

First Published in 2021
by HERESY PUBLISHING
Newbury RG14 5JG
www.heresypublishing.co.uk

Cover design by Charlie Farrow

A CIP catalogue record for this book is available from the British Library.

ISBN 978-1-909237-10-0

Based upon the map of Bedwyn 1820   Some names are older or later

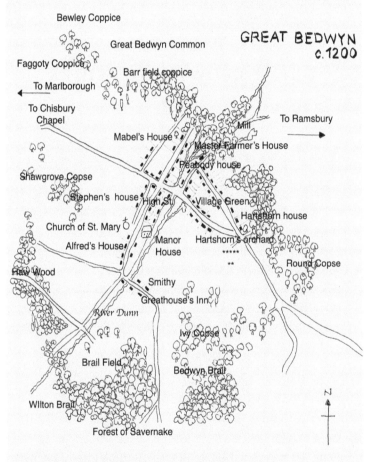

Bewley Coppice

Great Bedwyn Common

GREAT BEDWYN
c.1200

Faggoty Coppice

Barr field coppice

To Marlborough

To Chisbury
Chapel

Mill

To Ramsbury

Mabel's House

Master Farmer's House

Peabody house

Shawgrove Copse

Stephen's house High St

Village Green

Hartshorn house

Church of St. Mary

Alfred's House

Manor
House

Hartshorn's orchard

Haw Wood

Smithy

Round Copse

River Dunn

Greathouse's Inn

Ivy Copse

Brail Field

Bedwyn Brail

Wilton Brail

N

Forest of Savernake

Not to scale and not intended in
any way to be totally historical.

© Susanna. M. Newstead 2021

PREFACE
GREAT BEDWYN WILTSHIRE
1212

It was at the thirteenth hour of the thirteenth day upon her thirteenth birthday that Mabel Wetherspring had realised that she was very different from her friends and what was left of her family.

She had dropped out of the village ring dance because she'd begun to get too hot, nauseous and dizzy. John Swineherd had hold of her right hand and Stephen Meadow her left, she recalled.

She'd let go of them and spun off into the trees.

Those trees were tall silver birches, their white bark glowing in the moonlight. It grew dark early in December and the only light was from the full moon and the bonfire which they'd lit. As she stumbled on, the light diminished.

'Oh... I have had too much mead,' she'd said to herself. 'I will have an unholy headache tomorrow.' But somehow she knew that it wasn't true. She hadn't drunk enough to piss into a thimble.

She was so dizzy. It was so dark. And to combat the feeling of the forest spinning around her, she stood as still as she could with her arms out, her eyes closed and spun withershynnes three times whilst saying to herself, 'Oh how I wish I could be a little black bat and see in the dark.'

She liked bats. She still did. They were clever little things. They could hang upside down and the blood never rushed to their heads.

She'd tried it a few times herself, her knees hooked over a low branch of a beech tree and blood *always* rushed to her head, making her ears thump and her face turn red.

Suddenly her ears were thumping, but differently.

She felt her eyes widening even though she had not told them to do so.

She'd straightened out her arms and felt the sleeves of her kirtle stretching tight. She'd watched as her fingers changed shape and colour, lengthening and darkening and growing a webbing between them. Her ears wriggled through her hair. She hadn't been aware of them until that moment when she picked up the sound of something small rushing through the undergrowth.

Her shoulders pulled back, her arms twisted and the stitching of her kirtle snapped with a popping sound. Her elbows doubled up and her teeth lengthened. She ran her tongue along them. Oh how sharp they were suddenly.

Then all at once she was on the ground and everything around her was much, much bigger.

Her body was tiny; her arms were enormous and where her sleeves should be, were membranous wings. She tried to take a hand to her ears; there was a strange buzzing in them, but her arms wouldn't reach.

She tried walking. That was very difficult because her legs were so short.

Eventually she clambered up onto a sarsen rock, many of which were littered around the countryside, and launched herself from the edge.

The air held her up. She flapped. She twisted. She gained height.

She flapped some more.

"Wheeee!" she yelled at the top of her voice, only her voice was tiny.

"Oh. My. God" she said. "Mabel, you're a bat!"

CHAPTER ONE ~ THEFT

Upon the eighth hour of the eighth day of the eighth month, Mabel Wetherspring was flitting through the air on gauzy blue wings which beat dozens of times every heartbeat.

Her large azure eyes resembled two polished agates and her segmented sapphire body was patterned with black bands. Her delicate legs were tucked underneath her; she wondered how she would ever stand on such elegant appendages.

She flitted in and out of the reeds by the river and smiled to herself, as much as a dragonfly can smile, pondering why she had never thought to become such a creature before.

Mabel was a shapeshifter. She was able to change her form at will and become any animal she wished.

She had discovered this skill quite by accident on her thirteenth birthday and ever since that day she had used her power to transform herself to any creature she'd wanted.

Yes, she remembered the day well. However, oddly in eight years she had never become a dragonfly.

Skimming the surface, Mabel was inches away from the water but, despite the fact she could not swim as a human, as a dragonfly she was not afraid.

She lifted higher on wings which purred softly and saw beneath her, the river with its reed beds, splitting into several tributaries.

She saw other insects too; the water boatmen out in force on the river surface, scuttling along on their long legs. She took in the clouds of midges over the pools where the trout lay, basking in the late August sun.

She mentally licked her lips. 'Ooh. Shall I just have a snack?'

'Ah no, Mabel, you are a woman, not really a dragonfly, you don't eat insects.' But that fat fly buzzing towards her, totally oblivious of the danger, did look tasty. Mabel shook herself. Again she had to remind herself that she did not eat insects.

Time to go home. Home was the small village of Bedwyn, deep in the Forest of Savernake, close by Marlborough town, in the county of Wiltshire.

She turned about and flew straight and true down the middle of the water and veered off when she reached the mill.

She landed on a tall stem of decaying meadowsweet, growing behind the building where she knew she would not be overlooked and turned deosil, with the direction of the sun.

"I wish to be a woman again," she said.

Pulling down her kirtle and straightening her hair, she marched around the wall of the mill and made for home.

Master Miller was just exiting his building.

"Hello Mistress Wetherspring, been for your walk have you?"

"Yes. Yes I have."

Little did he know that she'd actually been flying.

Mabel had put it about the village that she went walking out now and again. It was one way to explain her absence from her home and place of work, the manor house.

"It's such a lovely evening, don't you think?"

"It is indeed," though Mabel thought it would be an even nicer evening if the man with whom she was falling in love could be with her too.

Sir Gabriel Warrener had ridden out with their lord a few weeks ago, returning to another manor owned by their Lord, Sir Robert Stokke in a distant part of Wiltshire.

The few short weeks since she had last seen him, had been tormenting.

He had promised to write but as yet, Mabel, who was literate, had not had any letter.

She gave a mental shrug. Men! They weren't good letter writers unless they were writing about war or weapons. Or money.

She approached her cottage; a snug little thatch with a patch of garden at the front and a vegetable and crop plot at the rear and noticed the small clump of scarlet pimpernel or weather flower close by her hazel hedge was flowering again. It was cheery and bright and lifted her mood.

In her house, a one roomed affair with a central fireplace, Mabel walked to the table to pour herself a beaker of milk, which she'd left there in a jug earlier that day.

Her eyes raked the board. It wasn't there.

"I am sure I left it here," she said out loud. She was accustomed to talking to herself, for living alone, she usually had no one else to talk to. And, to be truthful, she got more sense that way.

She stood in the room and swivelled her eyes around. The white pottery jug was nowhere to be seen.

"How odd."

Was there anything else missing?

She couldn't see anything obvious.

"Hmmm. Well. I am a member of the senior manor staff and should be able to have some milk from the manor kitchen if I want. In all the years I have been housekeeper here—was it really four years— she had never really asked for anything in particular.

Somehow it grated to go and ask for milk without taking something in return, so Mabel took one of her little pottery jars of honey from her own bees and tucked it into her fist.

The cook's assistant smiled.

"A second lot of milk, Mistress Wetherspring?"

"I beg your pardon?"

"Did you not send Little Johnny Chatterwell for some this morning?"

"I most certainly did not," said Mabel. "I bargained with my neighbour Master Farmer for some of *his* milk. Now I find that it's gone."

"Gone?"

"As in disappeared. Even my jug is gone."

"You must have drunk it,"

"I have been saving it, sir and I think I would know if I had drunk it."

"You must have forgotten."

Mabel was getting cross. "Master Platt, there is nothing wrong with my memory. I can recall my day perfectly from morn till night. I do not let strong drink befuddle my senses."

The cook coughed. His bright red nose told the story of his devotion to ale.

"Then you'd better take some more. The green jug there will do you."

"Thank you."

Mabel carried the full jug back to her home.

Sitting in the doorway to watch her friends the bats flutter over her garden, she looked up at the darkening sky, took a sip of her milk and thought about the man she loved.

"I hope Sir Gabriel's all right," she said to the heavens. "Please look after him."

She saw him in her mind's eye; his wavy blond hair, his speedwell blue eyes, his muscled body and the terrible livid scar which had deformed his cheek; his otherwise baby soft cheek. She had never kissed that cheek but she knew it would be soft. Oh how she wished she had kissed it when she'd had the opportunity. The memory of it would keep her warm at night.

'Oh Mabel... are you really so witless? He is a knight. A nobleman. You are a bailiff's daughter. You might be the housekeeper to this grand manor but you are of ordinary stock. You will never see him again. He won't be bothered by you. He won't count the days since he last saw you... like you do him.'

"Forty eight days, fourteen hours and four heartbeats." She wasn't entirely sure about the heartbeats... but it sounded good.

"Oh Gabriel! I hope you are looking after your face and using the healing unguent I gave you."

Shortly after they'd crossed paths, Sir Gabriel had met with an unfortunate accident which had scarred his handsome face beyond retrieval. A rogue shape shifting wolf had raked his cheek with its sharp claw from eye to mouth and Mabel had sewn him up as best she could.

She sipped the creamy milk and looked back into her cottage. She frowned. She never locked it. She possessed very little. No one in Bedwyn ever locked their cottages. The neighbours borrowed or bartered from and with each other but no one ever stole.

But there was no doubt, someone had stolen her milk jug!

*****

"You what, Master Thoroughgood?" said Mabel, half hearing.

"I said that someone has stolen my wagon tack."

"The reins and...?"

"Yes... to my wagon. I can't hitch Gedeon up to go to market."

"When did you notice it missing?"

"This morning when I went into the shed."

"But you still have your horse?"

"Oh Aye...'e's still there, right as the adamant."

"Well, you must report it to the steward."

"I'm telling you, Mabel."

"You want me to tell Master Steward?"

"Well, I don't want to speak to the pompous ass." Master Thoroughgood turned about and marched off up the slight incline to the barn. "You tell 'im."

What was going on? It wasn't long before Mabel had met another someone who had lost something.

"It was my mother's, you see."

"Ah yes, Mistress Peabody. Are you sure you haven't just mislaid it."

The woman widened her eyes. "It's too big to mislay, Mistress Wetherspring."

"And it's quite big to purloin, Mistress Peabody."

"Eh?"

"A large skillet. It's not easy to conceal."

"No, I suppose not. But this morning when I came to use it, it was not where I always leave it."

"Well maybe we shall get one of the young lads to have a look round."

By the end of the day, Mabel had learned that a pair of shoes, a small barrel of salted fish, a rather nice bone comb and a silver paten from the church had all gone missing. Things were getting serious.

*****

It was no good, Mabel needed to have a good look around the village when no one was aware or at least when no one knew she was there. They might be looking straight at her but they'd never know it was her. Mabel would be in disguise. Mabel would change herself into an animal.

Early next day she sauntered up to the village green and standing behind the preaching cross in the churchyard, she let her arms rise out to her sides. She turned withershynnes three times and spoke.

A swift footed mouse named Mabel, darted between the barrels in Master Thoroughgood's yard. She poked a twitching nose out from the base of the wood and steadied herself with her long tail.

6

There was Gedeon, Master Matthew Thoroughgood's small pony. He seemed quite pleased that he hadn't got to draw the cart out to town that day. Thoroughgood was sitting on top of a small barrel, leaning on the barn wall with a mug of ale, his eyes closed.

Mabel scurried into the shed. It was true, she could find no horse tack; it seemed Master Matthew had no spares. The nails upon which it hung were empty. He would probably have to borrow some from his neighbours.

Back to the preaching cross and Mabel turned withershynnes three times. She became a prowling cat. Her nose grew and turned from the pink of a small mouse to the black of a tabby cat. A long striped tail grew behind her which she swished from side to side. Little paws lifted silently one by one and this time she slunk off up the road to Mistress Peabody's house close by the river. The woman was on her knees by the washing stones doing some laundry and didn't see Mabel as she swiftly trod into her house.

Up onto the table she jumped, her green eyes taking in all the details of the cottage. It hadn't changed since she'd been here a mere month ago. There on the wall was a space where the large skillet had been hung. Now there was simply a grey mark on the daub.

Mabel sniffed. Could she smell milk? She was a cat and of course she could smell milk. But it was not contained in her own white jug.

Off she ran before anyone saw her and into the next house. This was the cott of the owner of the missing pair of shoes. Before she could really have a good look, Mistress Chatterwell came in and shooed her out with a broom. In the garden plot, Johnny Chatterwell, eight, and the youngest child of a large family, was weeding in bare feet. Now Mabel knew who the missing shoes belonged to.

The bone comb, it seemed, belonged to Mistress Houndstooth because she was bemoaning its loss to her friend, Emelia Farmer, Mabel's nearest neighbour.

"Oh, I am right put out by it," she said. "Well of course I got other combs but that one was especially nice and my mother gave it to me on the occasion of my marriage to Farmer." She wagged a horny nailed finger, "If I find out who's taken it, I'll beat them black and blue, so I will."

"My fish!" squealed Alys Brockman. "What am I to do now for supper?"

Mabel sloped nearer.

"It's Friday and I have nothing which we're allowed to eat."

"Oh, Alys... you can have some of ours," said a kind Mistress Peabody, sauntering up. "Tom has brought us some eels, nice and fresh today. I got enough for us and for you and yours." Friday was a day when they were not allowed to eat meat.

Mabel ran for the water mill and watched as the miller began to move the sluices of his pond to change the direction of the water flow.

The miller stood over his pond and leaned on the wall. Mabel jumped up. "Prrrrp—meouw."

"Oh hello ol' Pusskins. How are we today?" Master Miller liked cats. He liked them because they kept his grain stores free of vermin. Mabel liked Master Miller and she stroked herself along his floury apron.

He seemed a little distracted and stared out into the distance.

Mabel mounted the watermill steps three at a time. Master Miller kept a little caged bird, a greenfinch, in the mill and when Mabel was a cat the urge to go and stare at it was overwhelming. Sometimes the animal behaviour took over for a short while.

But the bird in its cage was gone.

Mabel sat on the shelf and swished her tail angrily. "Where had it gone?"

"Ah yes, Pusskins. You've noticed. Someone has stolen Chloris. How could they do that eh? Poor Chloris. He'll be so upset." Master Miller sniffed. By all accounts, Chloris wasn't the only one upset. Mabel had always thought it strange that Chloris was a male bird when in the stories she'd heard, Chloris was a she but she decided that Master Miller just liked the name.

8

Mabel turned deosil behind the mill and marched out into the sunshine, waving to the miller.

Most peculiar. It was all very odd. Strange things had disappeared. Things of worth in many ways, only to the person who owned them.

The only real thing of value was the silver paten from the church. Mabel spoke to one of the church wardens. They didn't know exactly when it had gone missing, for the church was locked by order of the Pope and no services could be performed. However the silver was still being polished and it was not there when they last took out all the pieces.

Mabel walked slowly to the manor rubbing her lips with the back of her hand, in contemplation.

'Was there anything missing from the manor?'

Mabel took all her keys which were always on her belt and began to check the storage cupboards and chests.

Everything that was locked away was present and correct. But she noticed that her inkwell, which had been on her table yesterday, was missing. It was made of ivory and rather a nice piece.

She found the key to the manor lord's office and opened the door. Everything was present and correct. So the person who was doing the stealing did not have keys. That was a relief.

Mabel got on with her work. There was not so much to do when her lord, Sir Robert Stokke was not resident at the manor. She checked her stores, a job which she did every Friday. She went to the kitchen to discuss with the cook the state of supplies for the following week and came to a decision about what they needed to order after discussion with the steward.

She took a mug of ale with the cook who was responsible for, amongst other things, the sweets, desserts and comfits, when the Lord Stokke was at home.

"Sugar!"

"I... I beg your pardon?"

"Sugar. Our big block of sugar."

"Oh?"

"I keep it in the pantry there. It's large and cumbersome. And very valuable."

"It's gone, I take it?"

"It's gone. Not a grain left. You know what that block weighs?"

"No. I don't know exactly, but I know that it's heavy."

"How is someone going to lift that and hide it?"

"I don't know, Maurice."

"It will cost an arm and a leg to replace and I bet it's my arm and my leg which is to pay for it."

"Oh no surely."

"In my kitchen...! My responsibility."

 Mabel felt sorry for him.

"I'll see what I can find out. When did you last see the thing?"

"Oooh, probably last Sunday. I took just a slither off for Master Steward's dinner. To make a sauce."

"And it was large and in its place then?"

"It was."

"When did you notice it was gone?"

"Only this morning, I'd gone in to get some raisins and there it was... gone."

"You have not been talking to anyone about it... discussing...?"

"What do you take me for Mabel?"

"No... no I don't mean."

"People know it's there but I haven't been mentioning it in particular."

"Not even to your undercook?"

"To Alban. No."

"Well, he would be the one to bash off a bit for your cooking. You don't do that personally."

"No, I certainly don't. Why keep a dog and bark yourself, I say."

 Maurice's eyes grew huge. "You think...?"

"I don't know. Why would he want to steal the rest of the things which are missing?"

"He's odd, but he's not that odd. He comes from Bath, you know."

"Oh, as far away as that?"

"They're all a bit odd from over there."

"I'll have a word with him," said Mabel with a chuckle.

*****

Alban Sweetcheeks, undercook, was a small almost bald man with terrible taste in clothes. Or rather in the colours of clothes.

That day he was wearing a bluish lilac with a rusty yellow super tunic and his hose were bright green.

He looked like one of Master Miller's caged birds.

Mabel watched him from her hidden vantage point up on the beams of the small kitchen.

If she was spotted, she'd be chased out. Where there was food preparation, no birds were allowed, if they could be kept out.

If one looked carefully, one would see a tiny wren blending into the brown of the cross 't' of the roof. It squatted silently and made no movement.

Alban was alone.

He was whisking something in a metal bowl. Mabel thought that it was egg whites. They needed a lot of effort.

All at once he set them aside, washed the whisk, the usual type, a collection of twigs and secreted it in the front of his tunic.

Now, was he going to take it somewhere or was he simply keeping it back to use later for some other purpose? Odd... yes that was odd behaviour.

Mabel watched him carefully. He set aside the egg whites to keep cool on a marble slab and marched out of the kitchen with great confidence, throwing off his apron as he walked.

Where was he going?

Mabel flew out of the high louvre which allowed the smoke from the fires to escape the kitchen and quickly skimmed the thatch.

Ah, there he was. Making for the edge of the village where the smaller outlying trees of the Forest of Savernake crept up to the fields of the village of Bedwyn.

He disappeared into the trees and was soon lost.

Mabel needed more speed and so, as she'd done many times before, she changed quickly into a wood pigeon. Her nose elongated and became a yellow hooded beak. Her arms grew feathers of a pale grey. The wood pigeon was a rather unnoticeable, common bird but one which was a fast flyer. She tucked up her scaly pink feet, fixed her black bordered yellow eye on the place where Sweetcheeks had last been seen and over the treetops she flew.

She dipped down when she reached the first large glade in the trees and perched to look round.

Alban Sweetcheeks was ducking down to the forest floor and retrieving a sack which had been buried by leaves. Into it he stuffed the whisk. Mabel heard the chink of something metal and something more solid like pottery. She couldn't see a cage though. No Chloris.

Alban disappeared again whistling a tune which Mabel thought was bravado and was soon lost. She knew where he was going. Back to Bedwyn. What she wanted to know was why were all these things hidden in the forest?

She snuggled up to the trunk of her ash tree and prepared to wait.

Other birds came and went around her. Further wood pigeons; a green woodpecker looking for insects in the bark of the tree, joined her. He was noisy and Mabel sent him packing with a clatter of her wings and a jut of her beak. He decided that his usual home of the grass under the tree was safer. There he hunted ants for his dinner.

Then out of the forest came a man. Mabel craned her neck to see him.

She searched a little too diligently for she lost her balance, wavered and let go of her grip on the branch and clapping her wings in a noisy clatter, she gained her perch again but not before the man had looked up and seen her.

As quickly as a diving otter, he had loaded a catapult and had stretched it tight.

Mabel lifted off from her branch turning as she did so but she was too slow.

The stone came hurtling through the air and struck her.

"Ouch!"

Down she fell, trying desperately to flap her wings to stop her from falling to the ground. A nasty pain coursed through her side.

She saw the man scouting where she was heading. 'Oh no you don't.'

As Mabel fell through the tree branches, she managed to turn withershynnes again and become a spider. She quickly fed out a thread which held her and she stopped abruptly about six feet from the ground, bouncing on her lifeline.

"Phew!" She scurried for a friendly leaf.

The man was looking round for his missing supper and after searching for a while shrugged and recovered the sack.

Throwing it over his shoulder, he picked his way carefully over the forest floor and dived into the undergrowth.

However, Mabel had seen his face. And she knew him.

His name was Simon Scarepath. And he was a very bad man.

*****

Holding her side, Mabel staggered home through the forest trees. She'd tried but had found she couldn't fly at all. She'd look at the damage when she got home.

Never had she been so glad to see her small cott as on that day. She fell in the door and sat down quickly.

It took her some time, against the pain, to peel off her kirtle and find the damage.

A huge bruise disfigured her side. She thought she'd probably

13

broken a lower rib. Or had one broken for her by Simon Scarepath. She'd have something to say to him when she saw him.

Ah... no, she couldn't, could she? She had to keep her ability to shapeshift a secret. And so far she had. No one knew about her special skill, no one but Sir Gabriel Warrener.

The thought of him suddenly made her tearful and to stop herself from becoming mawkish she bathed her hurts and smeared some 'cure-all' onto her ribs.

Simon Scarepath, eh?

He was a known criminal who had lived in Marlborough. He'd been a specialist in housebreaking and in stealing from churches. At last they'd got him for some crime or other and he'd been sentenced to a thorough thrashing and to have his ears clipped. Then he'd been sent packing from the town.

Everyone knew about him because he had been so unrepentant and brazen.

And he was still in the forest. Had he become a wolfshead, an outlaw?

Why was he still there? Had the Warden of the forest and his men not chased him out or arrested him. They usually did. The forest was huge; it stretched from Marlborough in the north to Collingbourne in the south, Avebury in the west and Hungerford in the east. Even though it was well patrolled, maybe they hadn't managed to find him.

Well they would now. Mabel would make it her job to find him. And pay him back for her bruises!

CHAPTER TWO ~ THE POACHER

Why was Mabel so nosy? She tried to convince herself it wasn't nosiness; it was being community spirited. She simply wanted justice. She didn't like people getting away with things. They had to be found out.

And she was in a unique position, she thought, to do that. Find out.

Meanwhile, she had to go to work in the manor.

That day she was to work in the still room.

Mabel was adept at making remedies for illnesses and with the onset of autumn, there would begin to be many such ills in the folk of Bedwyn Manor. Medicines for coughs, stuffy noses, chilblains, sore eyes; remedies for chapped hands and sore skin from the icy winds. Mabel knew all the recipes. Most of the ingredients had to be gathered in the spring and summer and then chopped, diced, boiled, dried and distilled into syrup, drops and unguents and stored. It was a busy day.

Luckily she'd have an excuse to go out into the countryside later that day to gather some herbs and roots. Let's see if her sharp peregrine eyes could spot anything untoward in the forest.

She took her basket with her and wandered off, waving to a few folk as she disappeared into the trees.

Once she knew she couldn't be overlooked, she hid her basket, twizzled three turns to withershynnes and became a bird.

The peregrine dashed over the treetops, its sight ten times better than Mabel Wetherspring's.

Up to the glade where she'd last seen the felon, the peregrine soared on sharp pointed wings. Her yellow beak opened to give a screech. 'Mui... mui... mui...' a high pitched penetrating yell which echoed over the forest.

She'd let him know she was coming for him.

Alighting at the top of a tall ash tree, Mabel used her acute sense of sight to peer in amongst the tangle of branches. Something was moving up ahead. Something large. It was light brown and making headway through the dense foliage.

Ah no. Not a man but a fallow deer. There were many such in parts of the forest, all of them owned by the King. Woe betide anyone caught poaching.

Mabel watched the gentle creature as it delicately traversed the glade below the tree.

All at once an arrow sped out of the base foliage and bracken right under where she was hiding. The poor thing didn't stand a chance. Skewered right through the neck, the deer fell, thrashed once or twice and lay still.

Mabel swallowed. She had been a deer a couple of times and knew how the creatures felt. They lived their lives in almost perpetual fear. Ah well, no more fear for this one.

A man in brown dashed out from the bracken.

'AHA! Not only is Scarepath a thief, he's a poacher too,' said Mabel to herself. 'There's a surprise.'

She watched for a while as the felon began to paunch the deer and then when he was well engrossed, she flew down closer to him and stared at him with her evil yellow rimmed eyes.

Somehow he realised he was being watched and turned slowly. His face was small and rather squashed as if at some time in his childhood someone had sat on him. His eyes were deep set and dark; it was hard to fathom by looking into them, what he was thinking. His head was almost completely bald—he'd made a poor attempt at shaving his head. Well, maybe living rough as he probably did, it would be hard to keep tidy, lice and flea-free. She could see he'd had his ears cropped—both. He was grubby and dishevelled and thoroughly horrible to look at.

"HA! Do yer own 'unting!" he yelled at Mabel and turned back to his task.

Mabel cried out, 'You're breaking the law! Again!' but all Scarepath heard was 'Mui, crarrp, crarrp.'

Over his shoulder he threw a piece of the beast's liver, still warm. "There... now go away!"

Mabel turned up her beak in disgust. Raw liver! Never.

She turned three times deosil and making sure she could run off if necessary, she said, "I don't like raw liver."

The man froze. Then he turned his head over his shoulder.

"You'd like it if it was all you could get."

"You realise that you are breaking the law... again?"

"You goin'a tell the authorities?"

"I might."

He stood, and brandishing the bloodied knife he said, "If you survive."

"Master Scarepath, you are a housebreaker and thief. Now I find you are also a poacher but I don't think you're a cold blooded murderer. Well... not with your own hands anyway."

"Oh, you don't? One way to find out."

Mabel took a deep breath. "You've been getting Sweetcheeks to steal things from Bedwyn for you, haven't you? And for all I know others elsewhere as well."

Scarepath wiped the knife on a patch of grass. "Of course I haven't."

"I think it had better stop."

The man screwed up his already screwed up face. "How do you know?"

"I just do. I followed him."

"You're a brave girl."

"Stop it and return what you have and I will say nothing about your illegal presence in the forest."

He grinned. His teeth were yellow and covered in ugly crusts. Poor diet, thought Mabel.

"And what will you do if I don't?"

"I will tell the authorities where to find you."

The man laughed and his voice soared up into the tree canopy.

"You won't find me, girlie," he said. "I move about."

"Oh Master Scarepath... you have no idea. I will find you. How do you think I found you today?"

The grin left his face. He looked over to the untouched piece of liver.

"Who are you?"

"One from whom you've stolen."

"Who are you?"

"Oh Master Scarepath, you think I'd tell you? " Mabel moved around him in a circle. "So you can send any of your family... your boys after me?"

"Boys? I have no boys."

"Three sons I believe. All living in Collingbourne... ah no... one is now in Hungerford isn't he? He didn't want anything to do with you, did he? Once you'd had your ears cropped."

"You are remarkably well informed for a girl."

"Woman. And word gets round. I just have large bat ears." Mabel tried not to giggle. Well… sometimes it was true.

The felon wiped his hands on the grass, made for a tree at the edge of the glade and thrust his hand into a hole in the trunk. He pulled out the sack she'd seen before.

"What belongs to you?"

"A jug, white pottery."

He rummaged and brought it out.

"There, now go away."

He laid it in the grass a few feet from her and retreated.

She picked it up.

"Oh dear, it's chipped."

He sighed swiftly through his nose. "Can't help that. Got no money with which to recompense you. Well, not here anyway." His tone was haughty.

"Leave the sack. I will get things back to the owners. And get out of the forest."

Suddenly she thought of something else. "How were you getting rid of the things you'd stolen?"

"I didn't admit to stealing them."

Mabel pulled a face. "You have the goods."

"I found them... in this sack, all of them in the forest a few days ago. No harm in taking them for myself. They'd obviously been thrown out."

"I didn't throw out my jug. It belonged to my mother. I wouldn't."

"Ah well. Maybe it's this Sweetcheeks you're talking about."

"I do believe he's your cousin."

"You are well informed." He hawked and spat. "Anyway, I've retired."

"Retired?"

"No more housebreaking for me. I live simply now."

"Simply? By poaching and getting others to steal for you?"

"A man must eat." He folded his now dried, bloody hands under his armpits. "You must have heard, since you have ears like an owl..."

'Oh Master Scarepath, you have no idea,' she said to herself.

"...That I have retired and am recommending it as a way of life to all my friends... my previous friends."

"Felons never retire, sir," said Mabel with a slight chuckle.

The man screwed up his eyes again and gave her a long stare. "Who are you? What are you?"

She shrugged.

"Anyway. I have never really been a felon..."

"Pah!" Mabel could not help but laugh out loud. "Your ears proclaim differently."

"A terrible miscarriage of justice!"

"A just punishment for a life of crime."

"Oooh—harsh mistress!"

Mabel smiled. She was trying not to like this objectionable man but found herself sort of warming to him.

"Anyway. My needs are few." He waved his hands around the trees. "I have a manor and a lot of land. I am well respected, even feared by my subjects." He gestured to the deer. "And I no longer have a need to stoop to crime."

"Ah... sir. The deer is proof of poaching. That is a crime."

"Again, girlie, I came across it already dead."

"Ah I see. You shot a dead deer with that bow there?"

"You cannot have seen me. You have no evidence."

"Oh I saw you," said Mabel forcefully. "But I am willing to turn a blind eye if you quit the forest."

"Madam... I retired... How long ago now, four months ago? The day they cropped my ears for a crime I did not commit."

"I believe someone, at the same time, also injured you?"

"Ah yes... Someone loosed an arrow at me and damaged my leg. I thought that God was probably telling me it was time to retire."

"It seems to me that one of your victims or associates was settling an old score. Isn't that the truth?"

"You may believe that if you wish."

"I think they said it was a man called Fisher."

"You have got a good memory."

"As good as a raven's, sir," she answered.

"Aye, they're clever birds."

Oh my! Again he had no idea. "And he was found shortly after, floating in the river in Devizes, wasn't he?"

"Ah yes. Devizes is such a violent place."

Mabel smiled, despite herself. "Not your doing then?"

"You'd certainly find felons... felons and criminals galore in Devizes."

There came a rustling in the undergrowth and Mabel turned to look but she could see no one there.

She hugged her mother's jug to her.

"Well... remember what I say. No more criminal activity. I'll return the stolen things to..."

"AH no... No! They're mine." Scarepath hovered over the sack with his knife.

"Then at least let me return the silver to St. Mary's. Perhaps then, your soul will not be carrying the heavy sin of stealing from the church."

After a further long stare, Scarepath threw her the paten.

She turned to leave.

"Thank you. I never want to see you again. Oh, and I'll overlook the milk which was in my white jug. You're welcome to it."

"Ah dear girl... that will have been Sweetcheeks. I cannot abide milk."

Mabel chuckled and left by the nearest track.

*****

She didn't go far. She hid the jug and paten in a tree bole; three turns to withershynnes and her body shrank, black feathers sprung from her and she gazed out from a glossy black eye. Mabel was a raven.

She watched from the top of the ash tree as Scarepath scanned the bushes at the edge of the glade.

"You can come out now, she's gone."

A woman scurried out like a little mouse.

So that was who Mabel had heard.

"Who was she?" said the woman in a worried tone.

"Some woman."

"What was she doing here?"

"She seems to think it's her job to take my ill-gotten gains from me and prevent me from further sins."

"Who is she? Where's she from?"

"I have no idea," said Simon Scarepath. "But that's something, my dear you might be able to find out. If you have a wish."

The woman gave Scarepath a passionate kiss.

'Ugh...' thought Mabel, the raven. 'Those teeth! How can you? He must have a mouth like a privy.'

At last she let go and Mabel hopped down a few branches to have them in better sight.

"My dear Wymark, you are very... ardent... today."

"Why should I not be? It's been days since I last saw you."

'Ah... here we have an amorous partner.' Mabel did remember one mentioned when the man lived in Marlborough town so perhaps he did have a lover or a wife.

They kissed again.

"Here I brought you some food." She looked round the glade. "But I see you've been obtaining your own."

He raised his eyebrows. "A man must fend for himself..."

The knife came into play again as Simon butchered the carcass.

"Here... for you."

The woman smirked and took the meat.

"And the rest I shall hang here until I can recover it in safety."

"Do you fear that woman?"

"Nah... but I fear the warden."

"I've told you, that's all organised. He'll not be bothering you. I've fixed that. We've bribed the local agister."

He pinched her cheek.

It was then that Mabel got a good look at this woman.

She was buxom with a heart shaped face and dark blue eyes, perfectly groomed eyebrows and hair the colour of a pale flame. She was very beautiful.

'Now what is a decrepit old fellow like him doing with a lovely young woman like her?' Mabel asked herself cynically. 'She's at least twenty years his junior and... well... what's he got to interest her?"

They went off arm in arm and Mabel wondered if she should follow.

No. She needed to find out about this woman.

Wymark. It wasn't a common name. Someone somewhere would know her.

Mabel made for home and the one person who knew all the gossip in the forest and surrounding area.

Master Buttermere, the Bedwyn Manor steward.

*****

She found him in his office groaning over accounts—the likes of which Mabel would make mincemeat in a heartbeat.

"Ah... just the lady."

"And I could say the same of you, Master Buttermere."

"Oh?" His eye glinted.

"I need your help."

"AH."

"And it seems you need mine so shall we barter?"

He gestured her to a seat.

"Wymark. It's not a common name in the forest. Do you know anyone who owns that name hereabouts, Henry?" She smiled. She rarely used his personal name and he noticed.

"Well, now then." He smoothed a string of fine mousey hair over his bald pate and leaned back in his chair.

"Wymark... There was a woman out towards Hungerford."

"How old is she?"

"She was about forty when she died."

"Ah no..."

"She died, I believe, of..."

"It's not her."

"Not. Her." He pursed his thin lips. "Wymark?"

"I don't have any other names or information save that she is probably in her late twenties with flame coloured hair and she is rather beautiful."

"Why do you need to know?"

"Do we know any woman associated with the felon Scarepath?"

"What? The housebreaker?"

"Him."

"Well, he had a lover I believe, before he received his punishment and went away."

"And her name was Wymark?"

"Oh, most certainly. She was adamant that the judgement had been false and that he was innocent."

"How come?"

"Love is blind, Mistress Wetherspring."

"Ah... that kind of certainty?"

"She made a great fuss, I believe, when the deed, ahem, was done."

"What, the cropping of his ears?"

"It was his second. The first was for..."

"Yes. Where does she dwell... Do you know?"

Master Buttermere's face had turned up to the roof and he had gone... somewhere else.

"She was a very striking woman. Beautiful even. Her face was like..."

"Did you ever wonder why such a woman had struck up with a man like him?"

"Mistress Wetherspring, of what interest is this to you?"

"Accounts, Master Buttermere, Henry? Accounts?"

Buttermere ran his finger along the neck of his brown cotte.

"Ah yes... accounts."

"Where is she living now?"

"I'm sorry but I can't help you there. All I know is, she lived in the town."

"In Marlborough?"

"It was when her lover lived there too, before..."

"His ears were cropped."

"Just so. Mistress Wetherspring, I cannot possibly see what such an upright young lady such as you, might have to do with either of these unsavoury people."

"Nothing. Nothing at all Master Buttermere."

Mabel turned to leave.

The man coughed.

"Mabel... ahem. The... erm accounts?"

"Ah yes."

*****

Mabel got a lift to the town on the tail of a cart driven by the new village blacksmith. He'd moved up from one of Lord Stokke's other manors to take over the smithy left empty and cold by the death of the previous smith, who'd met a terrible end by asphyxiation. The man had been stung by a bee several times and no one had known that he had been mortally susceptible to such stings. It was very sad.

Alan Shoer was a large rubicund man in his twenties with a tiny wife and three children, with another on the way.

He had been very happy to come to Bedwyn for a forge of his own and a large house to accommodate his growing family.

He spent the journey telling Mabel all about his trials as an under-blacksmith in Rutishall.

Mabel's brain immediately recalled that this was the village to which Sir Gabriel Warrener had moved earlier in the summer.

"And when you were there, did you meet one of the Lord Stokke's knights? A man called Sir Gabriel Warrener?" Mabel broke in over his long monologue.

"I surely did, mistress."

"And... how did he seem to you?"

"Miserable as a wet day in December, if you ask me."

"Ah no." Mabel's heart sank.

"Of course, I suppose I might be as miserable if I looked like he does."

"Oh yes?"

"That horrible disfigurin' scar. Enough to make any man have an expression like he'd just lost a pound and found a penny!"

"Ah yes. How is it doing?"

"He told me that there was some kind and very clever woman in Bedwyn who had patched him up."

"Did he?"

"And that he would forever be in her debt."

"Ah…"

"But Lordy me! I don't think she done a very good job, like what he said."

"Oh?" said Mabel tartly.

"All red and puckered it is. And it drags down his left eye something shocking. And it looks as if he's permanently frowning with his mouth."

"No!"

"That's probably why he's as sombre as a soggy Sunday."

'Oh poor Gabriel.' Mabel wished she could have encouraged him to stay here in Bedwyn. She could have treated his wound and made it much less ugly.

Mabel was very quiet for the rest of the journey.

"I'll meet you back here as the bell strikes for vespers," said Shoer.

"Alan, I think that it will be a bit late to get home in the light."

"Oh… right."

"Let's meet at the priory gates as the bell rings for nones."

"If you say so, Mistress Wetherspring."

After instructions from Mabel, he drove off in the direction of the forge on the Marsh from where he had arranged to buy some smelted bog iron.

Mabel walked the wide High Street wondering how she might discover where the woman, Wymark lived.

Mercers. A woman always needed a mercer. They would know everyone.

Mabel ducked into the cloth merchant's shop and began to stare at the bolts of cloth.

There were no other customers and so Mabel received the undivided attention of Master Mercer.

"Oh no... I'm not in need of any cloth, Master Mercer. I weave most of what I need myself."

The man looked her up and down. "That, mistress, is very obvious."

"I beg your pardon."

"Well... the erm... yellow of your kirtle."

"There is nothing wrong with the yellow of my kirtle. It was dyed by Mistress Dyer of Bedwyn."

"Ah yes... and it shows. You see..."

"I am not in need of advice about cloth. I would like to know, if you can tell me, if there is a woman by the name of Wymark, living in Marlborough and if so where does she dwell?"

The man was rather brought up sharply. Most young women did not contradict him in mid-sentence in such a way. Most young women were in awe of him. He was a good looking man with a certain presence and he knew it. He had a way with the ladies, as they were oft to say.

"Wymark?"

"It is not a common name, I wonder if..."

"Yes, I know where she lives."

"Where?" asked Mabel quickly.

"Now if I could just show you the quality of my linen thread, mistress, I am sure we could come to some sort of an arrangement..." The tone of his voice left nothing to be guessed at. She'd have to buy in order to learn the whereabouts of Wymark.

She looked around the shop. She hated to be bullied.

Another matron of Marlborough had entered the building and Master Mercer went off with an oily voice, "Mistress Partridge, it is an honour to have you here."

Mabel ducked behind a large display of fabric and twizzled three times.

Her skin began to grow long white hairs. Her nose turned black and wet. A long pink tongue lolled from her mouth and dribbled spittle most horribly.

Her ears pricked up and her eyes grew round as plates and a dark brown colour, as dark as a peat bog.

She ran around the shop, tangling in everything and knocking the displays evading every attempt at capture. Master Mercer ran after her. Mistress Partridge stood leaning on her stick laughing.

"Is this your dog, madam?"

Mistress Partridge clutched her middle. "Ah no, it's not but I almost wish it was!"

Then as quickly as it had come it disappeared.

Mercer was breathless.

"Master Mercer, the address of Mistress Wymark?"

In his haste to deal with his other and much more prestigious customer, and the mess left by the dog, he blurted out, "Martin's Lane. House with the crucks at the triple gable."

As Mabel left the shop, Mistress Partridge winked at her. "Love your little dog," she said. And pointing down the road, she giggled like a little girl, though she was seventy if she was a day.

Mercer was tutting... "Oh the hairs... the white hairs... just everywhere!"

Mabel chuckled as she made her way down the marketplace. She stopped one child to ask where Martin's Lane was and was told it was up the hill between The Green on Barn Street.

The house was easily found for it was quite a large building on a single plot and stood out from its neighbours.

Mabel stood before the door and discussed with herself how she should approach this.

Would the woman be at home? Would she speak to Mabel? That

was doubtful. Would she even allow her into the house knowing who she was and what she wanted?

Mabel's practised eye rode over the building in front of her. An upper window, no more than eight feet above her, was open. Below it was a hurdle fence. Mabel quickly skirted around and turned three times withershynnes.

She became a tabby cat and sprung for the top of the hurdle. Hardly touching it with her soft paws, she leapt for the window and padded down inside as gently as an alighting butterfly.

There was no one in the upper room. It seemed to belong to a scribe for there were parchments and ink everywhere. A gown of black was hanging on a peg on the wall. A man's gown. This was a clerk's room, for there was his writing slope. Mabel tried the door latch by leaping up and knocking it.

Eventually after a few tries she managed to open it and she padded out of the room quickly and into the next.

This was a woman's room. A woman who was quite wealthy. Here was jewellery; rings and a rather nice brooch. Kirtles were strewn about on the bed as if the occupant had not been certain what she'd wear that day and had tried them all on. A chest was in the corner but it was firmly locked.

Mabel wondered what lay in there.

Out through this door which was open a crack, she found herself looking down onto a central hall and three more rooms of the same sort on a gallery at the other end.

The woman had a fine house and it seemed she rented rooms.

Mabel was staring, cogitating when the front door opened.

In came the woman she'd seen in the forest and a man she knew to be the town reeve, Master Barbflet's man. His name was Greaves and he was one of those who kept the peace in the town.

"Mistress Honfleur, I need to speak with you."

"Why do you need to speak to me? You know everything I do. Everywhere I go. You follow me... I've seen your silly men."

"It's about Master Scarepath."

"I have already told you. I haven't seen him for months."

"Mistress, you might like to sit down."

"Why should I want to sit down? I'm not infirm!"

"No, but..."

"I have nothing to do with Scarepath since he left town. I am a respectable woman who rents out my properties."

"Properties which once belonged to Master Scarepath?"

"Of course they didn't. You think that half-wit would know how to deal with property?"

"Mistress, it is my sad duty to inform you..."

"Oh, for goodness sake!" The woman stormed off and poured herself a drink from a jug lying on the central table.

Mabel squeezed her head through the beams of the gallery above Wymark Honfleur.

"... To inform you that the body of Master Scarepath was found on the lane to Faggoty Coppice in Bedwyn this morning. His throat had been cut."

Mabel let out a cat-like, 'Errrp?'

She backed out from the bannister but her head got stuck.

She hissed and growled.

"How did that infernal cat get in here?" yelled Mistress Honfleur, peering up with no reaction to Greaves' words.

Greaves looked up and chuckled.

"Get after it. Get it out, you oaf!"

Reluctantly Master Greaves ran up the stairs but not before Mabel had extricated herself by twisting her cat head sideways. She bolted for the window and was gone.

But as she ran, she was in no doubt she had heard what Greaves had said.

Simon Scarepath had been murdered. "Oh my God!" she said out loud.

"Meeeeow!"

CHAPTER THREE ~ THE MISTRESS

As a cat Mabel scampered through the crowds, thinking furiously.

The man was a wolfshead. Had someone killed him in order to claim the reward? No... the reeve's man hadn't said that the head had been removed and brought to the office for money. Just that his throat had been cut.

No one was going to bother about his death because he was a man outside the law. Or was he?

He'd been convicted of his latest crime and he'd paid for it. He'd been banished from the town and it had been his choice to go into the forest and—as he'd said—retire. No one knew, she was sure, about his poaching or recent thieving in Bedwyn. Or did they? Had they reported him? That was a crime. That could make someone believe him a wolfshead and allow them to remove his cranium.

Had he been declared as such? Or was his removal to the forest simply, as he'd said his 'retirement'? It was odd. What was he really up to?

She needed to find out more.

She crossed the road making sure she didn't end up under the wheels of a cart and dashed down Crooks Yard where lay the town's large watermill. At this time of day, Master Barbflet, the town reeve, should be there as he was the town miller.

She watched and waited.

At last, swinging down the lane came Master Greaves. He'd just completed his business at Mistress Honfleur's house and would now be wanting to report to his master.

Carefully negotiating the mill equipment and the feet of the millers working there, Mabel crept into the office after Greaves. It was a good job he didn't look behind him as he closed the door or Mabel would have been shooed out or chopped in two by the heavy panel.

She dived for the cover of a large chest.

"Ah Greaves."

"Master."

"What happened?"

"The woman broke down."

"As we thought she might."

"In tears and wails, sir."

"Ah."

"Firstly she was quite composed and said she hadn't seen the villain in ages. Then when she knew he was dead, she cried a lot."

"Hmm. She must have seen him. How else would they carry on their thieving?"

"We haven't been able to follow her to the forest, sir. We always lose her. It's hard to... We can't prove that she's involved in thieving. But we do know that Scarepath hasn't been to the town."

Mabel sat down and began to lick her paws and clean her whiskers.

"So somehow they were still managing it."

"It's hard to see how, sir."

'Scarepath and Honfleur were suspected of thieving in the town. It was still going on', said Mabel to herself.

"Sir, are you absolutely sure it's him?"

"Absolutely."

"But might it not just be another man?"

"Taken over from him you mean?" asked Barbflet.

"Yessir."

"No. I feel it. It was still him. Them."

"But we have no evidence."

"We'll get it, Greaves. We'll keep looking."

Greaves sighed. "Yessir." He paused at the door.

"The weapon, sir. We'll have a devil of a job finding it."

"First find our culprit, Greaves."

"Did you tell her when the doctor thinks Scarepath was killed?"

"Yes sir. The hour after vespers."

"And where was she then?"

"At home... alone, sir. We saw her in the window dressed in her wimple and veil."

Now why were they so interested in this man? They believed he was still operating in the town as a thief. But how? Mabel didn't think that Scarepath would have come to town. He was too conspicuous. Was he operating his business from the forest?

"The woman came back to her house where you found her. Where had she been?"

"We don't know, sir."

"You didn't ask her Greaves?"

"Er, no sir."

Mabel jumped straight past Master Barbflet and out of the window behind him. She'd find out where the woman had been.

She misjudged the width of the bank and narrowly missed ending up in the river!

*****

Mabel decided to go back to see Mistress Honfleur's house and confront her. She might find out something she could pass on to the authorities.

She didn't change into herself until she got to the house. It was

33

easier to lope along as a fast cat.

She called at the door. "Mistress Honfleur! My name is... Cat. I want to speak to you."

She wasn't going to give her real name.

The door opened tentatively and the woman, dry eyed, spoke. "Ah! You!"

"Can I come in?"

"What do you want?"

"To talk about your lover, Simon Scarepath."

The woman's eyes narrowed. "You'd better come in then."

As she closed the outer door Honfleur looked around to make sure there was no one else there.

"You keep a caged bird, Mistress Honfleur?"

Mabel's eye was drawn to a cage hung in the window at the back of the hall.

"Not a crime is it?"

"No." But it might have been, as Mabel recognised Master Miller's greenfinch, Chloris, in its distinctive cage. Or it was a huge coincidence.

"I spoke with your lover…"

"Please…"

"Master Scarepath... I think you probably saw me."

"Probably?"

"And I found that he had... or someone had, been thieving in his name from the village of Bedwyn."

"SO what?"

"Now I hear that he is also suspected of carrying on his 'business' in the town."

"How can he? He's not here. Hasn't been here," said Wymark nastily.

"He can't now. He's dead."

"I didn't know anything about Simon's businesses!" the woman blurted.

Mabel wasn't impressed with her attitude.

34

"What will they do with him... with his body?"

"He'll be brought into town and you can inter him as you wish, once the coroner and constable have seen him."

"Who are you? How do you know so much?"

Mabel heard the wood pigeons at their cooing and clattering, in the back garden. It reminded her of who she was.

"I am a simple girl who's interested in justice."

"Justice for the likes of Simon. Don't make me laugh."

"Can we talk?"

"How long for?"

"I'm sure it won't take long if you answer me truthfully."

The woman collapsed on a stool. "Why did they have to single out Simon?"

"They?"

"Whoever it was."

"You have no idea?"

"It's just not fair!" She burst into tears.

Mabel came forward. "Life consists of many things, mistress, fairness isn't one of them."

She looked up at Mabel and took in the homespun dress, the worn shoes, the work worn fingers.

"What do you want?"

"Justice. I told you."

"Ah... don't make me laugh."

"It's true. I... have special skills with which I can seek out unfairness and... Put it right... if I can."

"And that is supposed to fill me with awe is it?"

"Not at all. But you do want to know who killed him don't you?"

"Of course I do. But I doubt you can do anything. Look at you. Where do you come from? Who are you? What gives you the right to question me?"

"I think God has."

The woman laughed and all her tears evaporated.

35

"Tell me mistress, do you have a lover?" said Mabel swiftly.

The answer came back equally quickly, "Of course I don't. Not since Simon."

"Forgive me for asking."

"No!"

"I have a reason for asking, Wymark."

The woman bridled at Mabel's use of her first name.

"It's just that it seems the town reeve and his men have been watching you."

"Yes, I know."

"And every so often you manage to lose them."

A smirk started at the corner of Wymark's mouth.

"And the conclusion I must draw from that is that you were able to go into the forest and meet up with Master Scarepath... or someone else."

"You know that to be true. You saw us, I'm sure."

Now it was Mabel's turn for a sardonic smile. "I did."

"The reeve's men are idiots! They couldn't follow their own shadows," said Wymark.

"Well, I knew you were either connected to these thefts in the town, or you had a lover other than Simon. Or both. And it's perfectly possible you get someone to impersonate you to throw the reeve's men off your scent."

The woman crossed her arms over her breast.

"What did you do when you left Simon Scarepath in the forest?"

"I walked home."

"And then?"

"I prepared something to eat."

"And then?"

"I don't know what I did!" screamed Wymark. "I can't think."

"I suppose you will tell me that you loved Simon Scarepath?"

"Of course I loved him. Now get out!"

Mabel came closer. "The town reeve's man said that he was found on the road to Bedwyn. You heard him tell you that?"

"He did. But how do you know…?"

"Who found him, do you know?"

"No!"

"How did you meet Scarepath?"

"I can't remember."

"Oh, I'm sure you can. The love of your life. I would certainly remember where I'd met mine."

'Ah yes… I certainly do,' said Mabel to herself. 'He came to the manor to protect me from harm and I ended up protecting him!'

"It's just that he is so much older than you… and forgive me, not a good looking man."

"At the church."

"St. Mary's?"

"Yes. And… mistress… Cat… it happens. It often happens."

"That you fall in love with a much older man who happens to be wealthy… then. He was wealthy then, wasn't he?"

"Mistress." The woman was very still. "I can't be bought. I can't. His wealth meant nothing to me."

Mabel wandered around the room. "Did you kill him?"

Wymark turned quickly to watch her. "Of course not."

"Then I would be very careful, Mistress Honfleur."

"Why?"

"I would watch your back because… if you didn't, it could be your turn next."

*****

Mabel rushed to the forge where she knew that Blacksmith Shoer was doing business and no doubt taking a drink to while away the afternoon with Master Smith.

"Alan… I shall make my way home. Don't worry about me."

"If you're sure, Mistress Wetherspring."

"I have finished my business. You stay and enjoy your... conversation. I can get a lift." She nodded to Master Smith and turned to walk out of the forge.

"Take great care on the way home," Shoer smiled sweetly.

Mabel was about a quarter of a mile from the main road when she turned three times withershynnes and became a pigeon, fast flying the rest of the way.

She needed to speak to Alban Sweetcheeks.

He was in his kitchen, busying about doing nothing much and she entered silently behind his back.

"Master Sweetcheeks. Are you the only one here today?"

The undercook jumped as if guiltily engaged in something.

"Ah Mistress Wetherspring. It looks like it. Master Maurice is having a lie down before making supper."

"Well that's good because it's you I wanted to speak to. Alone."

"Me?" The man took up a wriggling lamprey eel and began to bleed it by the mouth to thicken the sauce which would be added to the dish. And then another... and another.

Mabel grimaced in distaste. She'd never been a lamprey eel but, poor thing, this didn't seem a kind way at all to kill an animal. Then the undercook began to boil the poor things almost alive.

She turned away. She would never eat them again.

"Yes... about your cousin, Simon Scarepath?"

"What of him?" She swore his hand shook.

"Did you know that he's dead?"

Alban Sweetcheeks left his lampreys and stared at her. "D... d... dead?"

"He was found yesterday, I believe, on the path from the forest to Bedwyn. Faggotty Copse. His throat had been cut."

The cook let out a small scream.

"Oh, this is news to you? I am so sorry to be the one to have to tell you. Somehow I thought you'd know."

"How would I know?" He began to stir his lampreys.

"Well, you were, forgive me, as thick as thieves with him, weren't you?"

"We were... what?"

"Since you were both thieves, I suppose that makes sense."

"Thieves?" Now he was definitely shaking.

"You used to steal things he could sell... oh only little things... like whisks and dishes and jugs. He could sell them on for a little money to keep him going, out in the forest. Maybe in one of the villages."

"How did you...?"

"Know?" She smiled in a sort of friendly, but serious, way. "I saw you one day take an item from this kitchen and along with others, deposit them in a glade in the forest."

"You... followed me?"

"Yes. I am sorry. One of those things was my mother's white jug. I couldn't let that out of my sight. It's of special... sentimental value to me."

The man licked his lips. "Mistress Wetherspring... please... you won't speak of it to anyone... please."

"Oh, I don't think you killed him, Alban. I think you're too... timid to kill a man like that." She thought carefully. "But then... what do I know?"

"He bullied me. He has been awful to me since we were children..."

"In Bath, I believe?"

"We were born in the village of Corsham. Yes, I suppose you could say it's near to Bath."

"You have been in this village working for the lord for about five years, I think."

"I have and that was when I learned that Simon was close by in the town. Oh I can tell you... I wish I'd never come anywhere near him."

"He bullied you into stealing for him?"

Alban nodded and beads of perspiration flew off and into the lamprey pot.

'I certainly will never be eating this dish again,' said Mabel's little voice in her head.

"Well it won't happen again... not with him dead."

"He frightened you didn't he?"

"He did. He was a vicious man."

"I think you can be fairly vicious, Master Sweetcheeks."

"I beg your pardon?"

"The efficient way you have just killed those poor lampreys." She looked into the steam of the pot. They were now dead.

"But mistress, they are animals. Food which we eat. I couldn't kill a man."

"Not even a man who terrified you. Made you do things you didn't want to do."

"No. Not even that," said Sweetcheeks, wiping his forehead on his sleeve. "I don't want to hang."

Mabel walked away to the door. "Did you ever meet his mistress, Alban?"

"The beautiful Wymark? Yes, once or twice."

"What did you think of her?"

"Cold as a floating fish and twice as hard as old oak."

"You believe she was associating with him simply for money?"

"What do you think?"

"Hmmm." Mabel opened the door. "I'll say nothing. To anyone. It's over. I got my jug back."

"What? How...?"

"I caught Simon in the forest and I asked politely for it."

"You... what?"

"Took it back from him, yes. And the church paten you stole. Now you may rest easy for you have not committed a sin against the church and your conscience and soul are clear, Alban."

As she turned to leave, she thought she saw a look of admiration pass over his face.

*****

40

She was tired that night. She sat in her doorway in the fading sunlight with a little pot of ale and her netting. She was making a small crespinette for her hair. The pale linen threads showed up well in the fading daylight and her fingers worked quickly in the intricate patterns.

She wondered if she might be able to make something larger. From hemp thread perhaps, or nettle.

She put her work aside and walked into her garden. Late bees were still buzzing amongst the few flowers that she kept for medicinal purposes. Bats were flying overhead and chasing flies which gathered under the oak tree in her plot.

She watched them for a moment. She loved being a bat, almost more than any other animal. The freedom they had, the speed, the agility. The amazing senses they owned. The ability to fly fast through obstacles and never ever touch them. Their power to rest upside down and never let the blood go to their heads. She knew this for a fact because she had been a bat many times since she was thirteen. In fact, a bat had been the first animal she had changed into. So was it any wonder she had a particular love for them?

She turned back to her cottage wall.

Might she grow something up the wall? A plant? One which clings. If she made a sort of net and attached it with pegs to the wattle and daub, she might manage to twine a honeysuckle or woodbine up there and she'd have lovely perfume through the summer.

Hmm... she'd have to think about it. It would take quite a lot of thread and a deal of time. Well she had some time.

She went back to her needlework and thought about her day.

Very satisfying. There was just one thing missing—Gabriel was not here to share her success with her.

Her mind went out over the trees, over the downs, through valleys and spanned rivers, like the bat or the owl or the dragonfly which she could choose to be and her spirit, (she supposed,) hovered over the village where Gabriel now lived. Or, would live for the next few months. How those tormenting months would be—so terribly empty.

She had no idea where the village of Rutishall was. She must find out. She knew it was in Wiltshire and was owned by the Lord Stokke. Perhaps it was possible to get there and back in a day. She might be able to fly there, meet Gabriel and fly back.

Oh, but it would have to be in secret. She couldn't simply appear and disappear in an unknown village. Damn her special power! If she couldn't change and move so fast, she would not even think of going and her heart would not ache with the thought of what she might be able to do in order to see him.

If she were a normal girl, she would not even contemplate it. She'd stay here and...

But then if she were an ordinary woman, she would never have met Sir Gabriel Warrener and none of this would be possible at all.

She shook her head as she sat down again to ply her needle.

The darkness crept in around her.

She lifted her head. She now couldn't see the oak tree and the bats had gone.

Mabel took up her work, picked up her stool and prepared to lock and bar the door for the night.

Had she been a fox, or a night bird, she would have seen who it was who came rushing towards her with evil intent.

As it was, she only felt the rush of air as the person hurtled around the gable end and, as Mabel turned into her home, brought down something very heavy onto her skull.

She did not even feel the ground as it came up to meet her.

CHAPTER FOUR ~ RECOVERY

It was Master Farmer, her nearest neighbour, who found her slumped and bleeding on her doorstep a little while later. He had been coming back from dealing with his cows for the night and had noticed that her door wasn't closed. Her light clothing was what made him see her, he'd said.

He took her into her house and yelled for his son to go and fetch the manor steward and Mistress Little, who was the village cunning woman.

They patched Mabel up as best they could and then waited. She had a large lump on the back of her head.

Master Steward took it upon himself to write immediately to his lord at Rutishall, for it was obvious that this was an unprovoked attack designed to murder his housekeeper. He sent a swift rider off to the Lord Stokke along with the letter.

Mabel lay in her bed, breathing shallowly but not regaining consciousness. And Master Steward would not let her be alone for one moment. Two people stayed with her night and day. If it were to be known she had survived the attack, then someone might decide to finish the job. Of course, they had no idea why she should be targeted in this way.

Upon the dying of the daylight on the following day, Mabel had a visitor.

He came creeping into the house quietly and nodded to Mistress Peabody and Mistress Miller. They jumped up immediately and curtsied, for they knew who he was.

"She has not stirred, sir," said the miller's wife, at a whisper. "She has been out of her body since she was found and a while before, we think."

Mabel lay with her head bound with a bandage and some sweet smelling herb packing the wound.

"I have come from our Lord Robert Stokke. He wishes me to make an investigation into this attack. Thank you. If you wish to go home now, you may leave her in my care."

"But, sir... one of us must remain at all times. The steward has said..."

"And forgive us m'lord, but you are a man and there are things which only a woman may do for a woman."

"If I need you... I will call for you."

The two women looked at each other in the poor light of the darkening day. They remembered this young man and they knew that Mabel and he had formed an attachment when he'd last been here—a friendship, however unusual.

After lighting a couple of lamps, they left, closing the door slowly. He was a nobleman and they could not gainsay him.

Gabriel Warrener removed his supertunic and hauberk and sitting in his gambeson, he took Mabel's hand in his.

"Well, I leave you for forty odd days and look what happens."

He gave her a kiss upon her forehead, much as he had done when he'd left her just over a month ago.

He began to speak to Mabel as if she could hear him. Well, he did not know that she couldn't.

"When the Lord Stokke knew what had happened he was all for jumping on a horse and coming back to Bedwyn. But I told him that I could reach you easily and quickly on my own and work out the lie of the land. And so here I am. I am sworn to write to him daily, giving him a report."

He pulled up the blankets which were laid over her and tidied her hair spilling out over the pillow. "And now I am here, you can get better and we can investigate together to find the vile creature who hit you over the head with intent to kill you."

He watched her face for any reaction.

Nothing.

"What have you been doing Mabel, that someone wishes to silence you?"

In the following quietude there was a rustling in the thatch and Gabriel looked up swiftly with a worried expression. No, it was unlikely that there was another shapeshifter in the village. It was merely a real animal, a mouse perhaps, running across the reeds.

Gabriel looked for ale and found some at the bottom of a jug. It was stale. But there was some of Mabel's elderflower mixture and he poured a generous measure of that.

He wrapped himself in a blanket, poked the fire a little into life and sat by the bed.

He was sitting there thinking when at the darkest part of the night, Mabel stirred. Her eyelashes fluttered.

"Ooh."

She opened her eyes into the relative darkness of the cottage and into her vision came the scarred face of Gabriel Warrener.

"Oh... am I in Heaven?" she said a little slurred.

"If you are in Heaven, then so am I, Mabel."

"I have not died?"

"No. I am really here."

"Am I at home?" She tried to turn her head but it was impossible.

"In your own bed and I am here with you."

"Oh, Gabriel."

He kissed her forehead again. "Sleep is best for you and then we shall talk."

"What happened?"

"You don't know?"

"No... I don't recall."

"Someone hit you over the head intending to mortally wound you but your head is too hard and you have been out of your body for almost two days."

"Oh... no..."

"Whom have you annoyed Mabel?"

"Several people."

"Ah, good old Mabel. Don't peeve one where you can peeve several."

"Have you come with the Lord Robert?"

"No, he sent me. I have to write him a report every day."

"You promised to write to me and I have had nothing for over forty days."

"Ah well," said Gabriel a little shamefacedly, "I am here now, in person."

A tear escaped her eye. "I am so glad you are."

"I am glad too. Even if I did have to ride through almost the whole day to get here and go without supper."

Mabel closed her eyes. "There is supper in the pot. Just put it on the fire to heat."

He nodded.

"Your face... your poor face" said Mabel suddenly. "Oh Gabriel!"

"Ah, it's alright. It's healing nicely thanks to you."

"But Master Shoer said that it was awful."

She tried to examine him in the semi-dark but her eyes merely danced and blurred.

"Nah! It's fine. Once it's really healed, it'll be no more than a white scar, I'm sure. Master Shoer exaggerates."

"I don't know him well," she said. "He's new here."

And then she slept once more.

*****

Mabel's head must have been very hard or the object with which she had been hit was not hard enough for she suffered no terrible lasting damage and within two days was fit to walk about the cott, even though she was still a little wobbly.

Mistress Peabody came in to help. She gave the excuse that Mabel has helped her greatly in the past and had saved her life. The cunning woman also returned and took off the bandage, pronouncing the wound clean and healing.

Now Mabel and Gabriel could sit in the sun, fitful though it was through the cloud, and discuss what had been happening.

"And so you accused the undercook of theft?"

"Er, yes. And consorting with a known felon in the forest."

"And you have made a sort of enemy of a woman in town who was mistress to this known felon, a man who has since been murdered?"

"His throat cut."

"Well, not much then!"

"I did not think either would try to kill me."

"This woman..."

"Wymark Honfleur?"

"Do you think she might have done the deed? Or perhaps has someone who would do it for her?" asked Gabriel.

"She seemed very loyal to Simon. Ah..."

"What?"

"The town reeve said that they had been watching her for a while to see if she was involved with the thefts in town. Of course I know that she was still seeing Simon and that he was, rather than being retired, still at his old job."

"Meaning?"

"Meaning that he must have had people working for him. People the town reeve has no knowledge of."

"Where was the woman when the man Scarepath was killed?"

"She was nowhere near, but there may have been another."

47

Mabel yawned. She felt so tired. "She lives in a building up on St. Martin's Lane. There are several people in the house. Perhaps we can speak to them? They might be able to give us an idea about her."

"Ah, a list of tenants would be a good idea," said Gabriel.

"Oh... can we do that, though?"

"Why not?"

"I'd have to ask the woman's permission. It's her house after all. And we do need to get in to speak to her. I don't think she'll let me in again."

Gabriel was quite surprised. "She owns the building?"

"She does."

"AH... She owns property paid for by theft, I expect," he said. "Do we know if she has any other business dealings?"

"We can find out."

"Ah... no. I can find out. You are to stay here until you feel absolutely well."

"But I do feel well."

"Who is the knight around here?"

Mabel pouted. "Go on then. Go out and use your knightly charm on her. She's very beautiful and no doubt very dangerous. To knights."

Gabriel scoffed.

"We need to find out if there is a great deal of money in the house. That will tell us that she, or they, were selling the things which were stolen and stockpiling the money," said Mabel. "And there is a large locked chest in one room. That needs investigating."

"It might be a good idea to see if this is the only house she owns in Marlborough. There may be others."

"Or maybe others in different places," added Mabel.

"Right, while I'm away, get one of your friends to go with you to the kitchen and confront the undercook. See what he says and how he says it."

"It's not him Gabriel. He's too much of a coward."

"Well then, see if he'll tell you anything."

She sighed. "Trust me to get the boring job!"

*****

Gabriel was admitted to the Honfleur house without argument.

Little did the knight know that he was followed by a large tabby cat, who jumped up to the wattle fence and then into the window on the first floor. It was a matter of heartbeats before Mabel was sitting in the shadows on the gallery boards.

"Madam." Gabriel bowed nicely.

'He'd no need to do that!' said Mabel to herself. 'She's only a trollop.'

"It's kind of you to see me."

"Not at all, Sir... Gabriel, isn't it? What can I do for you?"

"I am looking into the death of the felon, Simon Scarepath. I am told that he was your lover."

The woman affected a sad face. "He may have been a felon once, sir, but of late he was a hermit living in the forest. He'd paid his debt. He no longer carried on his... old business."

"That's as may be, madam, but where are the profits of his thefts? Where's the money he made? I am led to believe that he was still accruing money by selling stolen goods. Where is it... here?"

Mabel nodded her approval. 'Straight to the point, Gabriel.'

The woman tried to deflect him. "Can I offer you some wine, sir?"

The cat watched as wine was poured and Gabriel raked his eyes, appreciatively over the figure of the woman pouring it.

"You may search the house, sir. You'll find nothing. No large amounts of cash. Only the piffling sums I need to live."

'Ah, she's very confident that nothing will be found here,' said Mabel in her cat brain.

Gabriel was already asking her to guide him through the house.

"Might you furnish me with a list of your tenants, Mistress Honfleur?"

"Why? Why do you want that?" She turned on him abruptly half way up the first set of stairs.

"I would like to speak to them. They may be able to tell me something."

The woman scoffed very unprettily. "They are all respectable people, Sir Knight. I cannot have my..."

"It will be a polite and cordial conversation with them, mistress. I will not alert them to any... irregularities, even if I find them."

She grimaced. "You will find nothing."

Gabriel searched the woman's room. "And madam, do you have the key to this chest?"

Mabel, peering around the edge of the door, could see that Wymark had considered lying and not producing the key, but had thought better of it.

Gabriel opened it and scanned the contents.

As Mabel had expected, there was no large amount of money, no stolen goods.

"That all seems to be in order." Gabriel looked particularly authoritative in his hauberk, covered by his long, pale blue tunic with the arms of Stokke stitched onto it.

He swung his sword out behind him.

"And now madam, might I look at the rooms of your tenants?"

Wymark grimaced. "I can't do that, sir. I do not have the keys."

"Not all rooms are locked." Gabriel gestured to the room through which Mabel had entered.

"This one seems to be open."

"Ah, that is Master Scrivens. He is the gentleman responsible for writing up the reports for the Marlborough court. He never locks his door."

"That's interesting."

"How so?"

"A court official living in the house of a lady, forgive me..." Gabriel nodded deferentially to her. "Who is a known consort of a notorious felon?"

"That cannot be proven, sir."

"I think if we dig deep enough we can prove it. Madam. By your own admission, you were his lover."

"After he had... retired from felony."

"So you say." Gabriel took the remaining stairs two by two. "Let's have a look."

There was nothing in the scribe's room—just parchment, pens, ink, the black gown still on the peg on the wall and a satchel of papers. Gabriel glanced through them. They were not in the slightest bit interesting.

Mabel cat scurried down the stairs and up to the further gallery. She'd seen a room open there.

"And who dwells in that room?" said Gabriel, pointing into the room which Mabel had just entered.

"Oh, that is Madame Cecile Clanchet."

"A Frenchwoman?"

"She was married to an Englishman until he died. Then she took back her own name. She came here three years ago and hardly ever leaves her room. I never see her except when she pays her rent."

"The monies which you store in the large chest in your room?"

"I do. I have expenses, the same as anyone else."

Suddenly there was an almighty screeching and flapping of wings. And a woman's voice rising above it all.

"Aw... get out! Get out you nasty creature!"

As Gabriel and Wymark hurtled up the stairs, a tabby cat streaked past them and exited from a back window on the ground floor.

"Oh, that damned cat!" said Wymark. "That's the second time it's been here. Attracted by the birds I suppose."

Gabriel gritted his teeth and closed his eyes. "Is it indeed?"

An old woman came out of the room on the gallery. "Mistress Honfleur, you promised... you promised. No cats."

Wymark hurried up to her and took her shoulder. "And yes, yes...

there will be no cats," she said. "I have no idea how the beast got in."

"No... I cannot have it," said Madame Clanchet. "My birds... my birds..."

"May I look, madame?" said Gabriel in perfect French.

The woman pursed her lips and gestured to the room.

When he entered, the birds in their cages had calmed a little. There must have been twenty of them. Tiny feathers floated in the air and the smell was not pleasant.

Gabriel gave a small smile but under his breath he said, "Well done, Mabel!"

He turned to Wymark Honfleur.

"That list of tenants?"

"You may write it yourself, sir."

Back in the room of the scribe, Gabriel took a small piece of parchment and a piece of charcoal.

He drew a rectangle and divided it into six.

"This is your room?"

"It is."

Gabriel wrote, 'WH'.

"And this, Master Scrivens? He lives here?"

Mabel had managed to get back into the house and was peering at them around the door.

"And there?" He'd walked out onto the gallery.

"Master Philip Savary. Does something administrative at the castle."

"Next to him?"

"Master Paul and Mistress Blanche Bux."

"That's an unusual name."

"He is a box maker."

"Ah, where does he work?" asked Gabriel.

"Somewhere in town. Again I hardly ever see them."

"And lastly... there?"

"That is the room of Mistress Spinner. As you might guess she is a spinster and works for Master Tredder."

"A woman... alone... with a job such as hers. She can afford to live alone?"

"No sir. She lives with her daughter who is also a spinster. It is my smallest room."

"Ah."

Mabel was proud of Gabriel. It seemed he was on top of this 'investigating'. She had thought he'd be pretty useless, but no.

They moved downstairs again.

"I will return to speak to them when they're all here."

"Why do you need to do that?" said Wymark, seeming a little tetchy.

"It's amazing what people see and hear, in a house like this, Mistress Honfleur."

'Oh well done Gabriel,' said Mabel. 'You have her worried now.'

"Well if that's what you want. The Spinners are here—they work from home. And Madam Bux will be home now. She doesn't work."

Gabriel smiled. "Thank you, I'll begin with them."

Mistress Honfleur retired to her room.

The two spinsters were very reticent, almost frightened of Sir Gabriel. There was a lot of bobbing curtsies and silences. Mabel, from her hiding place behind one of the upright looms, the two of which took up a good third of the room, thought maybe she'd try these ladies again when Gabriel had done with them. They would speak to her, she was sure.

Madam Bux was a lively woman of twenty four or so, who answered the door with flour all over her hands.

"Ah Madam Bux. You like to cook?"

She laughed, a sparkling sound. "I cook every day, for my husband, sir. What can I cook, I mean do for you?"

"I am investigating the death of a gentleman who used to be connected with this building..."

'Pah! Gentleman!' said Mabel to herself. It came out as 'Prrp, psss, mrrp.'

"May I come in?"

Damn. Gabriel made sure that the door was closed and Mabel couldn't hear well.

"A man called Simon Scarepath. We believe he was a notorious housebreaker in the town."

"Oooh yes. I have heard about him. I must admit…" The woman cleaned her hands of flour, "I am a terrible busybody."

"Then that is good for me," said Gabriel with a smile in his voice. "Did you know him?"

"No… not really. He used to stay here now and again… before… a while back."

"Ah yes."

"And I used to hear him shouting."

"Shouting?"

The woman came close to Gabriel and lifted the edge of her veil. She brought it up to her mouth and whispered… as if it would muffle her words. "They had rows."

Gabriel chuckled. "Scarepath and Honfleur? Even though they were not married… I thought it was only married couples who fought."

"Haha, my lord. I wouldn't know. I have only been married a matter of a few months."

"Congratulations, madam."

Outside the door Mabel fumed.

"Do you or your husband have much cause to go to Bedwyn, in the forest?"

"None at all. We have no family there. I come from Ramsbury and my husband is a Hungerford man."

"And you now live in Marlborough."

"It was a matter of finding work. He is a carpenter by training, of course, but he saw there was a need for boxes of all kinds. Box making is a specialist trade, sir. Paul wanted to begin his own business and this town was perfect."

"Does he travel about?"

"Oh yes. He doesn't keep regular hours. He works when he can."

"He has a workshop somewhere?" asked Gabriel.

"He does, sir. On the square which is half way up Chandler's Lane. You can find it easily, for there is a sign outside his door. A box suspended from a chain."

The door opened again and Mabel skittered around the corner in order not to be seen. Gabriel saw the end of her grey tail disappearing as he left.

"I may need to speak to you again. Thank you, you have been most helpful."

"Might I be permitted to help further?" said the Bux woman.

"Of course."

"The old woman with the birds. She is an even bigger busy body than me. And she has lived here longer and known Mistress Wymark longer. I am sure she can help you further. She's not quite as silly as she seems."

"Thank you."

At that moment a man came into the central hall.

"Ah. Master Savary," said the woman as she closed her door. "Good day."

The man wore a long red cotte of good wool and a belt studded with metal. Gabriel noticed they were made in the likeness of small crowns. Here was a man employed by the King at the castle and who liked to proclaim it.

"How fortuitous, Master Savary," said Gabriel, dropping down the stairs.

"Oh?"

"I am Sir Gabriel Warrener and I am making inquiries about the murder of a man who is connected to this house...."

"I know nothing at all about Simon Scarepath and I have no wish to know," said the man angrily.

"Ah, you know about it. You met him?"

Master Savary widened his stance. "Once was enough. I knew he was a wrong'un' when first I saw him."

"And your landlady, Wymark Honfleur? It's said that she has been his mistress for some time?"

"That's her lookout and you'd better ask her."

"Oh, I have. She does not deny it."

"Then why are you asking me? I am an important man at the castle. I do not associate with thieves and whores."

"She is your landlady. Surely…"

"I shall be off soon. For better, less… dubious lodgings, sir. As soon as I can."

"Ah, yes. I see. You cannot have your good name associated with…"

"Quite so."

"Then I shall not keep you."

The man unlocked his portal, swished into his room and banged the door.

Gabriel was left alone in the hall.

"Mabel. I know you're here."

The cat did not appear.

"It is you, isn't it Mabel?"

Not even a whisker peeped around a wall. Gabriel began to wonder if he was wrong.

"I am about to go and talk to the old bird woman again. I don't want you to come frightening her birds. If you want to come. Come as something else. Or yourself," he hissed.

The old woman was feeding her birds. One by one Gabriel watched her tip seed into each cage and croon to them.

"Good morning, Madame Clanchet. Your door was open," said Gabriel in French.

The old woman looked up. "Oh it's you again."

"Can I ask you? Do you know what happened to a man called Simon Scarepath?"

"I know there has been a death."

"Did you know him?"

"No, not really. I saw him now and again, on the stairs or in the hall. He was always very kind to me."

Gabriel smiled at her. He felt she was a little simple.

"Was... is... Mistress Honfleur kind to you?"

"She keeps away. I don't see her often, except when I give her my rent."

"Ah, I see."

"She's always been like that. Even when I lived on London Road. When my husband was alive."

"You've known her for a long time?"

"Oh yes. Before that man gave over his properties to her."

"That man? Scarepath?"

"Yes. He owned three houses, I believe."

"As many as that? My, he was a wealthy man," said Gabriel.

"And now she is a wealthy woman."

"Where are those other two houses, Madame Clanchet, do you know?"

"Off the London Road."

"It's a long road."

"There's one on Horsepath."

There were no houses on Horsepath.

"Thank you, madame."

Outside the door he chanced to look down to the boards.

A horrible cockroach had just scurried into the crack by the top step. He lifted his foot to deal with it. Ah no... it might be Mabel after all. Just the sort of thing she'd do. He'd better not.

*****

Gabriel threw down his gloves. "So how did I do?"

"Whatever do you mean?"

He walked about Mabel's cottage keeping his eye on her the

whole time.

"A cat?"

"A cat?"

"A cat who listened at doors."

"That is one very clever cat."

"Oh, come on, Mabel, I know it was you."

She laughed. "I thought you were very thorough. Yes, you did well. We now know where Wymark might be keeping her money... Simon's money."

"We need to find the other properties."

"Not today. I'm tired."

"Aw, I suppose it takes quite a lot of energy to change from a fast bird which gets you to the town before me on Bertran, to a cat to explore Mistress Honfleur's place and a cockroach to hide after I'd told you not to be a cat any longer!"

Mabel's face turned pink. "A cockroach?"

"It wasn't you?"

"You think I'd make myself into a cockroach?"

He leaned over her. "Yes. I think you might. Who's going to engage with a cockroach?"

"Sir Gabriel. A cockroach is an unclean creature. Horrible. Ugh! Really!" She turned and smiled to herself. "I'm not surprised the place has cockroaches. All those birds..."

"Hmmm."

"What do we do now?"

Mabel took her pot and filled it with water, then she hung it up over the fire.

"I think dinner might be a good thing.'

"Oh no, not more pottage."

"You don't like my cooking?"

"Er, Mabel... you throw anything you have into a pot and call it dinner."

"What's wrong with that?"

"Cabbage, turnip, onion, apple, bread, berries."

She sat down and stirred the boiling water. "If it's all I have…"

"I tell you what. I will go to the kitchen and beg something for our dinner. And at the same time make myself known to that Sweetcheeks fellow. I think I'd like to frighten him a little."

"Oh, beg some bread, will you? I have some honey which I think you'll enjoy."

Gabriel did beg some bread and managed to obtain a nice piece of beef which had been destined for the steward's table. He'd not miss a tiny bit.

Alban Sweetcheeks was very nervous around the knight. It was just as Gabriel had wanted.

"Mistress Wetherspring told me that you had given up your life of crime, Alban."

"Oh?" The portly little man began to sweat.

"You should be very grateful to her. She has saved you from having your ears cropped, at the very least. Imagine what the punishment would be for stealing a piece from the church?"

Sweetcheeks swallowed.

"Excommunication, I believe, is customary."

The undercook crossed himself. "She said that she wouldn't tell. How come she's told you?"

"Because we work together, Alban. What she knows, I know and what I know, she knows."

The man licked his lips.

"Imagine what the punishment would be for murder, Alban… or attempted murder."

The man squealed. "I haven't killed anyone."

"No, I don't think you have. You haven't the courage. Have you?"

He was silent then, "So who did you tell?"

"Tell what?"

"Who Mabel was and where she lived."

The man began to tremble.

"Because you did, didn't you?"

"No!"

"That's how whoever it was who tried to kill Mabel, knew where she'd be and that she'd be alone."

"No!"

"Ah well... never mind. There are only a few people tangled up in this cat's cradle and sooner or later one of them will reveal themselves. They'll know who is who. And they'll know who to target next."

Again Alban swallowed.

"You thought your cousin was terrible didn't you. You did what he said because you were afraid of him. Who else are you afraid of Alban?"

The man stuck out his chin. "No one."

"Ah well... perhaps you should be."

Gabriel marched off out of the kitchen door.

"Good evening!"

CHAPTER FIVE ~ THE BOX MAKER

When Gabriel returned to the cottage, Mabel wasn't there. In an irritated mood, he decided to try to cook the dinner himself. It wasn't something with which he had any great experience... but... how difficult must it be?

Whilst he was trying to get to grips with building up the fire and working out how to cook the beef, (oh, why had he not brought his servant with him?) Mabel was winging her way across the trees of Savernake and into the small yard between the High Street and Back Lane, in Marlborough. She obviously wasn't as tired as she had said.

She perched on a fence, looked round and hopped three times withershynnes.

Her nose fined down to a lethal point. She'd lost the pigeon plumpness and became sleek with light brown, spotted plumage. Her wings and tail were pointed and when she hovered the tail became fan shaped.

Mabel, as a kestrel, soared above Chandler's Lane and hovered. She realised no one would take any notice of her as a bird but she found she couldn't really see very much. So at last she dived down into a little patch of green between the workshop of a leatherworker and Bux's small woodyard. Being a kestrel was all very well but hovering was hard work and she couldn't see everything.

Turning three times to withershynnes, she became a cat again.

The tabby jumped up over the fence and entered the working yard. This must belong to Master Bux. The pieces of wood were not too large, not as large as those needed for building and they were all stored neatly under cover.

Mabel sat on the top of a box which looked as if it was made to store arrows—indeed it was one destined for the fletcher a little way down the lane.

In no real hurry, Mabel watched the comings and goings along the yard, with her bright green eyes. She saw the little mouse which darted through the stored upright planks. Her muscles tensed but no, she decided she was not interested in pursuing him. She watched the kite overhead soaring on russet wings. She noted the peacock butterfly, who hovered about the few weeds growing in the yard.

Master Bux came out of a lean to and sorted through one or two pieces of wood.

Mabel found herself peering through the window slats of a small workshop building, sitting on yet another box, one destined for an artisan of the town. Here, were all the tools of the man's trade—benches, clamps, saws, little wooden pegs and pots of glue. In various states of completion were boxes of all sizes—some with lids, some without, some round, some square.

Mabel wondered if the man had an apprentice or a co-worker but the workshop was tiny and it did seem as if Bux worked alone.

She watched him planing a piece of wood for a while. The smell of the wood shavings was lifting up in the afternoon air.

She decided to go back to her patch of grass and become a woman again.

"Master Bux. I am sorry to interrupt you."

The poor man nearly jumped out of his skin, "Oh!" His hand went immediately to the place where his heart lay. "One moment there was a cat peering at me and the next, you... goodness me mistress, you made me jump!"

"I am so sorry. It wasn't my intention to surprise you."

"It's of no consequence."

"I did see the cat. I think it went off looking for mice in your woodpile," lied Mabel, with a smile.

"Well, it's welcome. Such destructive things, mice."

Mabel picked up a nice round bentwood box, exquisitely made with a tight fitting lid.

"What can I do for you?" he asked.

"Oh, I'm here to make inquiries about a box… for my mistress."

"You have come to the right man."

"Much like this one… only bigger." Mabel knew by a sharp eyed look around that there was not a ready-made box of the size she requested.

"We can do that for you… yes."

Mabel looked over his face. "Forgive me… but have we met somewhere before?"

"Have we?" said Bux. "I think I would have remembered."

The man was about thirty with short dark curly hair and was clean shaven. He was of middle height and no doubt because of the profession he pursued, a little stooped in the shoulders. Always bending over his work, Mabel supposed.

He had dark brown eyes and very long eyelashes, Mabel noticed, enviously, all together a very good looking man. "Ah well… I have probably seen you about the town. You live up on St. Martin's Lane, do you not?"

"I do. My wife and I rent a room there. Do you live thereabouts?"

"Ah yes. Barn Street. That's probably why I seem to know you."

Mabel picked up another small box. "You live in the house owned by that terrible villain, Scarepath, don't you?" she said with ghoulish glee.

"You are mistaken, mistress. The man Scarepath gave the house to Mistress Honfleur a while ago. She is my landlady."

"Ah, yes of course." Mabel leaned forward and whispered, "The man's mistress."

"Where have you learned that?" he chuckled.

"Oh, here and there."

"Then you must travel about, mistress, gathering gossip."

"You too must travel about, Master Bux. Your goods must be delivered here, there and everywhere, I suppose, in the locality."

"I do deliver, yes. I have a small handcart to the side here, for the purpose. Are you requiring something large to be delivered?"

"Perhaps."

"Ah. Well, rest assured that can be done for a very small additional cost. Anything you cannot carry yourself can be delivered."

"Might you be able to deliver to Bedwyn, in the forest?"

"Ah, that's a lot further. That delivery would cost you much more," said the man with no change in his voice or face.

"Ah… Do you make safe boxes, sir?"

"I thought you wanted a round box?"

"Oh, yes we do. But also require a chest type box for money. A secure one."

"Then you must ask a carpenter. I make boxes. Not chests."

"Oh, forgive me. It's just that an acquaintance has one, a chest to put valuables into and I wondered if it had been made by you, since it lies in the house in which you live?"

"This friend is?"

"Mistress Honfleur."

He looked at her with a skewed face. "My landlady?"

"Yes. I know her quite well you see."

"Well no. I did not make it."

"How well do you know her, sir?"

He didn't answer immediately but half turned from her. "I... know her very little. We pass on the stair of the house and we pass the time of day when I hand over the rent for our room."

"Ah."

"Why do you want to know? Who are you?"

"No reason. Really. It's just that I have heard that she was the man, Scarepath's mistress and that she might have... you know... killed him for all his money."

He lost his kind attitude. "That is gossip of the most horrendous kind, and not worthy of a friend, mistress... what was your name?"

"Cat."

"The lady in question, as you will know if you claim to be a friend, is a fine woman who could not stoop to... such things."

"Ah... you do know her then Master Bux?"

"As I say... not well, but well enough to trust her to be an honest woman."

"And you do not think that she killed her lover, Master Scarepath?"

"I am sure she could not. And anyway, why should she?" He stood up and moved towards her.

"Did you know him?"

"Who?"

"Simon Scarepath?"

The box maker sighed. "Why would I know him?"

"He once owned the building you live in. I wondered if you had passed him on the stair sometime?"

"Look here. What is this?" He began to get agitated. "Do you wish to order a box or not?"

"I think perhaps I will turn it over in my mind for a while. I'm not sure I need one. Thank you."

She turned to leave.

"Good day, Master Bux."

*****

When Mabel returned to her cottage in Bedwyn, there was a terrible smell of charred meat.

Gabriel was standing looking down at the pot, with his thumbs in his belt.

"Whatever have you been doing?"

"Ah! At last! Where have you been?"

"Talking to the box maker. I repeat, what have you been doing?"

"I... erm ahem... tried to make us some dinner."

"What happened to it?"

"I think I burned it."

"And my pot into the bargain. What were you trying to do?"

Mabel fished out the charred piece of meat from the bottom of her pot with her knife.

"I think the fire was too hot," said Gabriel.

"Did you put no water or oil into the pot?"

"Was I supposed to?"

Mabel rubbed her forehead. "Let me see if I can resurrect it."

"What did you learn? And you should have told me where you'd gone. It's dangerous. So much for you being tired. It's not long ago you were lying on this bed, senseless."

"I learned Master Bux was incredibly nervous when spoken to about Mistress Honfleur. And he defended her very chivalrously."

"As was Sweetcheeks. He was very nervous. He's frightened of someone, I'm sure."

Mabel poured water into a pot and began to add this and that. "We think we know that Scarepath transferred all his businesses to Mistress Honfleur so that he would no longer be suspect. The town reeve had been watching him and his lover for a long while but could never get enough evidence to arrest him."

"Until recently."

"Oh yes recently, he got a little bit too clever and..."

"Cocky..."

"Yes." Mabel stirred her pot. "Cocky. And he was tried and found guilty of some petty crimes for which he was punished. But he carried on, even though he wasn't in the town any longer."

"Why? Why did he remove himself?"

"I think he was saving up the profits from his bigger thefts and businesses and was going to take himself off elsewhere. Out of harm's way. And there was no doubt that he had enemies. He removed himself to what he considered to be safety."

"Where to? Where was he going?"

"Oh, anywhere."

"And he was killed before he could achieve this?"

"Before he could abscond with the money."

Gabriel sat down and watched as Mabel busied about the house, throwing odds and ends into the pot.

"You realise this is going to be pottage again?" he said sadly.

She grinned at him. "What might Mistress Honfleur think to that, do you think?"

"Pottage?"

"Him going off on his own."

Gabriel shrugged.

"But... and it is a big but... I want to know what the man was dealing in? The things stolen from the houses and removed by Master Sweetcheeks were piffling. How was the REAL wealth made and where is the money?" said Mabel.

"You think Mistress Honfleur has it?" asked Gabriel.

"Without a doubt. But she is too clever to let us know where it is hidden."

"So you must think that she killed him?"

"Ah no... you'll remember, she was at home when the deed was done. Master Reeve's men saw her."

"Ah yes. She was seen at the market doing her shopping as the bell for terce was ringing at St. Margaret's Priory and then as the bell for vespers was being rung she was noted by the reeve's men who were following her, staring from an upstairs window, at her house."

"So she couldn't have been in the forest killing her lover," said Gabriel with finality.

"And that means she must have had an accomplice."

"And that is why you went to speak to Master Bux?"

Mabel shrugged. "There are few men with whom she might have formed a liaison."

"You sure Bux is one of them? Come on Mabel... He and his wife have not long been married!"

Mabel shrugged again. "His wife is a very sweet woman, Gabriel, who dotes on him. I really don't think she would be able to see what was going on—if there is anything going on. Of course there may be another man in a different place."

"How are we going to prove it?"

Mabel ladled her cooking out into two bowls.

"Pottage?" she said.

*****

Gabriel and Mabel sat over the fire.

"Where do you think, Mistress Honfleur has her other businesses? Exactly?"

"And what are they?" said Mabel.

"The bird lady said they were on the London Road. But I'm not so sure."

"The houses there are nearly all residential."

Gabriel prodded the ashes with a stick. "You don't think we're making a storm from a rain droplet?"

Mabel laughed at his image.

"You mean that the man was a felon. What are we doing caring about who killed him?"

"Well... sooner or later the law would have caught up with him and no doubt hanged him. Whoever killed him has saved the law a job," said Gabriel.

"You don't think that whoever killed him is a greater felon than he was?"

"And I suppose there is someone running around out there, who wants to kill you."

"AH, yes. That makes it important," said Mabel with a wide grin.

She rubbed the sore patch on her head. "I'd like to pay him back."

Gabriel chuckled. "I'm sure you would. I've seen you in action, remember... paying someone back."

"And I was..."

"Magnificent... if deadly."

"I had no choice. I'll try not to be so... magnificent again. But if someone is going to try to kill you... then I may have to..."

"Leave it all to me."

Mabel made a strange face and went to look out of the door. "It gets dark earlier this time of year. What say you that I..."

"Not tonight."

"But Gabriel..."

Suddenly someone came into Mabel's view and she drew back into the shadows of the house.

"Mistress Mabel?"

"Master Sweetcheeks?"

The undercook came into a sliver of yellow light thrown on the cottage wall by the dying sun.

"I need to have a word with you."

"I am very busy, Alban."

"Please. I don't want to speak to that awful knight, Warrener. He scares me."

Mabel smirked in the semi darkness.

"It's important I speak to you," he whispered.

"Why me?"

"Well you are the one who is interested in my cousin's death, aren't you? Heaven knows why you are but... you want to know the truth. And I can't live with not telling the truth. And I'm sorry if you got hurt."

"Then let's sit outside here and you can tell me what you want me to know," said Mabel, gesturing to a log which she had placed close to the door a while ago. She loved to sit there of an evening and watch her cousins, the bats, hunting for insects.

Alban Sweetcheeks, although a little nervous, seemed happy to offload his information.

"I told you my cousin was a wicked man. But he was very wealthy. And he hid it all away."

"Do you know why he disappeared into Savernake?"

"To throw the authorities off the scent. At least that's what he told me... but..."

"But what?"

"I don't really believe it. He was waiting for something to happen... something special."

"You don't know what?"

"No. I don't. But he said it would be the crowning glory of his career. And he laughed—as if that was a special joke."

"Oh..."

"And then he was killed."

"Do you know who did it?"

"No but..." he took a deep breath. It was with great delight he suddenly said, "There's something you ought to know about Mistress Honfleur."

"I thought you told me that you didn't know her very well."

"I don't. Not really. But I did lie to you. I do know one of her servants well."

"I didn't know she had servants," said Mabel in surprise.

"Oh yes. She has women who look after her properties."

"You mean like a housekeeper?"

"Ah, no nothing so grand." Again the man was perspiring. "They are cleaners and general maids and they live in the house on St. Martin's Lane."

"But they can't. There's no room for them. I have seen all those rooms."

"Oh yes there is. In the attic."

"There's an attic in that big house?"

"You get to it from the outside. There's no inside stair but round the back there's a series of rickety old steps."

"How many maids... servants?"

"Last count there were three."

"And you know... which one?"

"I know Aimée."

"And what might she tell us?"

"She cleans at all the woman's houses. And... other things..." He looked away, almost in embarrassment.

Mabel almost wanted to jump up and cry out in joy. She even contemplated kissing Alban. "Do you know where they are?"

"No."

"Would she tell us where they are?"

"She would... for a small fee, I feel sure."

Mabel got up and wandered about in the gloom. "Would she come here?"

"I doubt it. But I could go and see her and she would tell me... for a..."

"Small fee... yes."

Mabel swore she could hear Gabriel chuckling inside the house but Alban didn't flinch, so maybe it was her imagination.

"When might you do this Alban?"

"Well... if I can get off and if I can get a lift with a cart, I could do it tomorrow."

"Very well."

Mabel left him and then immediately came back. "Stay here. I will get you some money."

She disappeared through the dark doorhole.

"Psst. Did you hear that?"

"I did. We have a chance to find her other properties."

"Then we might be able to explore them and search for the profits of her business dealings."

"It's obvious they are places not known about by the town reeve, or he would have searched them long ago," hissed Gabriel.

"If Scarepath has put all his business dealings in her name, it's likely no one knows about it."

"Except the notary. And they'll be sworn to secrecy."

"So I need some money," whispered Mabel. "Enough to make the servant talk."

"How much might that be?"

"How do I know?"

Gabriel tipped out his purse. "That's all I have."

"It's more than I have."

"Let's hope it proves worth it."

Mabel came out into the growing darkness. "You had better be telling the truth, Sweetcheeks," she said as she gave the money over to him. "If you fail me. I'll be looking for this amount back with interest. "

"I'll not fail. I'll have the information for you by this time tomorrow."

He nodded and faded into the evening.

Mabel wanted to hug Gabriel. "We might be getting somewhere now."

"We better had."

"Oh don't be such a grump! What do you need money for anyway?"

Gabriel sighed. "You have no idea how much it costs to be a knight without land, Mabel."

"Then you need to get yourself some land."

"Ah... yes. That is just what my father says."

"Well, for once I think your father is right."

Gabriel looked at her face in the gloom of the cottage. "Marry you mean?"

"Er... what?"

72

"Marry land and money."

"Oh."

"You once asked me why I spend so much time with the Lord Stokke."

"Above the forty days you owe him?"

"Yes. It's because my father and I don't exactly see eye to eye." He had told her this before but had never elaborated upon it.

Mabel sat down. She wasn't sure she wanted to hear this.

"He wishes me to marry a particular lady, an heiress who would bring a substantial estate into the family and coffers of coins."

"And you won't…"

"I have said I will think about it."

"How long have you been thinking about it?"

"Three years."

"Is the woman still… available?"

"Oh yes. She won't be of marriageable age until next year."

"What? Twelve?

"No, her father insists on sixteen."

"Oh."

"Yes, I could marry for money and land. But I am not sure if I want to. Oh it's been expected of me all along, but somehow when it comes to it… I can't seem to say yes."

"What is her name?"

"You don't want to know that."

She was silent in the dark.

"Avice, her name is Avice de Gers."

"Oh… Is she pretty?"

"I really don't know. The last time I saw her she was about ten."

"Oh." Mabel really didn't know what to say next. "You had better go to the manor. They'll be locking the door soon."

Gabriel rubbed his hands over his wrecked face.

"Right." He stood and made for the door.

"Lock and bar the door after me."

"I will."
"Goodnight."

*****

Mabel didn't sleep well that night and it was tormenting to wait for Master Sweetcheeks to contact them the next day, which was a Sunday. Mabel was all for flying out to look at the attics of the servant girls. Gabriel wanted to talk to the other people in the building owned by Honfleur, those they had not yet met, but in the end they didn't go.

Mabel busied herself at church and at her house all day. Gabriel went in search of some hawking equipment from the mews on the manor estate.

They met in front of Mabel's cottage as the light was leaching from the sky.

And waited. Sitting on the log, they waited for Alban Sweetcheeks to come and they watched the bats dipping to and fro over the river and under the trees.

"He isn't coming."

"If he's run off with that money I'll... I'll... kill him," said Mabel with gritted teeth.

"And then I'll kill you for trusting him with it."

They waited a little longer.

"He really isn't coming."

They looked at each other over the distance of a foot or so.

"Are you thinking what I am thinking? said Gabriel.

"Sadly... I am."

"Come on."

They threaded their way to the kitchen building in the now almost complete black of night. Gabriel reached back to catch hold of Mabel's hand. "Stay close to me."

They entered the kitchen yard, always situated away from the main halls owing to the risk of fire. There were three of these buildings at Bedwyn.

Sweetcheeks rarely slept in his kitchen, for he thought himself better than that and bedded down in the hall most nights. But he did have a space where he kept some of his things. Gabriel snatched up a candle and shone it over the rows of sleeping bodies on the kitchen floor. There were some complaints but mostly people just moaned in their sleep.

"Where's his place?" he whispered.

"There and it's empty. He's hardly ever there anyway."

"Perhaps he's sleeping in his kitchen tonight."

Only the scullions slept in the main kitchen and they didn't go into Sweetcheeks' domain; the room where desserts, pastries and flummeries were made.

Gabriel held Mabel's arm and pushed open the door. "Alban?" he whispered.

There was no answer.

The candle flame only gave them a very small circle of light and Gabriel looked around for another candle or a lamp.

Mabel bumped into a stack of turves.

"Shhh."

"Well if you weren't holding on to me so hard, I wouldn't have to follow you so closely and I wouldn't...."

"Shhh."

They listened.

A little wind had grown up and there was a tapping which sounded like a plant hitting a horn window pane.

"He isn't here," said Gabriel finally.

"Maybe he never got back from the house."

"You think he was waylaid there?"

"He was snooping... someone might have... what's that?"

Suddenly into their ears came a creaking. Gabriel would have said it sounded like ships' ropes cracking. Mabel would have likened it to the crackling of barley ears in bright sun when ripening.

"What's that?"

"I just asked you that?"

Mabel came closer to Gabriel. "I don't... like it."

Suddenly Gabriel had put himself in front of her and said, "Don't look up!"

Of course, she looked up.

"I said, don't look up! Why do you always do what I tell you not to do?"

"Anyone who says not to... Oh my God!"

"Exactly."

Suspended from a hemp rope which creaked in the slight breeze coming from the door, was a body.

Master Sweetcheeks was no longer so sweet cheeked.

CHAPTER SIX ~ THE HOUSES

"Why would he kill himself?"

"He didn't," answered Mabel.

Gabriel paused with his cup to his lips.

"When they cut him down, didn't you see the marks on his neck?" she asked.

"I didn't see anything. I was too busy keeping order amongst those who'd come to gawp."

"I saw fingermarks. It was strangulation. Strangulation made to look like a suicide by hanging."

"Let's hope the coroner comes to that conclusion. We are the first finders. We'll have to give evidence," said Gabriel. "I hope they don't blame us for the murder."

"Aw... come on Gabriel, they'd never blame you."

"Why not me? It's a well-known fact that they always blame the person who finds the body."

Mabel scoffed. "The coroner is a knight. He'll not find another knight guilty. Now a humble housekeeper... she'll be fair game."

"You have been with me. You can't have killed him. Besides what's the chances that the coroner works out it's murder?"

"He probably won't. But the constable will. He's extremely thorough. And I haven't been with you all the time."

"I'll lie."

"You know it won't do your reputation any good."

"My reputation...what does... that...?"

"A knight associating with a common girl... if it gets out you spend the night in the cottage of a commoner woman...what then your chance of marrying land and money?"

"You're not a common girl. Anyway... knights do it all the time. It's almost expected. No one cares nowadays."

"I'm a free woman, yes but I'm not of your class, am I?"

"Nothing has happened!"

"Well people won't believe that will they?" said Mabel.

"Aw... well... we shall push that boat out should we need to."

Mabel instantly imagined them pushing out a boat onto a serene silver lake into a glorious sunset, as arm in arm they kissed...

"What?"

"I said, does anyone know we've been talking to Sweetcheeks?" said Gabriel.

"Hmmm I don't think so. Only this girl, Aimée. Alban might not have told her too much about us. You realise we now have to go and search out this girl, Aimée?"

"It was all going too easily. We might have known something like this would jump out to bite us!"

"Poor Sweetcheeks. He was a little person caught up in a huge problem. I feel so sorry for him."

"Two people dead now and one attempted murder," said Gabriel. "You might not feel so good about him if it was him who told on you."

"I'll go to the house and find Aimée's attic. Identify her. Then I'll talk to her," said Mabel.

"Not on your own you won't!"

"What will you do? You can't change yourself into a cat."

"Do you know what...?" he said, "I've never tried."

Mabel laughed so hard her jaw cracked!

*****

A sleek tabby cat prowled along the alleyway at the side of the triple gabled house. Her ears were pricked up, her nose was twitching and her whiskers knew something was up.

Almost at once a large dog blocked the end of the lane. It was bulky and bullish.

'Oh fiddle faddle,' said Mabel scanning the sides of the place for somewhere to jump.

The dog growled and advanced. There was no escape but to run back the way she'd come.

"Nice doggy... kind doggy. I'm sure you like cats don't you?"

"He doesn't like cats, Mabel," said a voice.

"Prrrp, purrr. Meeeeeow," was meant to mean, 'what are you doing here and if you are here... why can't you do something?'

Gabriel was supposed to be keeping watch on the lane to the front. He had left his horse Bertran, at the front door. They had ridden, Mabel riding pillion for a change, from Bedwyn, to save time and too much effort on Mabel's part.

He picked up a pebble and threw it near to the dog.

The dog watched it and then turned back, its lips drawn over its wicked yellow teeth.

'That's done it.'

The dog dribbled spittle and howled in a high pitch which sent shivers through Mabel's fur. Never before, when she'd been a cat, had she actually felt the hair stand up on her back. It wasn't a pleasant experience.

"Raaaagh!" roared the dog.

Mabel stood on her hind legs, trying to make herself as tall as possible. "Psssssss," she said, showing her teeth.

"Felix... Felix...where are you? Dinner!" came a cry.

'God... yes. I'm dinner,' said poor Mabel.

Gabriel was waving his arms and growling back at the dog.

"Felix! Good boy. Come for your dinner." There was the sound of someone knocking a metal dish.

The dog licked its lips. At the thought of a proper dinner the spittle started to flow even more copiously.

"Dinner, Felix!" said the female voice from somewhere in front of them.

The dog turned reluctantly and slunk off.

"Phew." Mabel looked back at Gabriel and, in a very feline way, gave him a nasty stare.

"Well at least you could have changed into something more frightening. He'd have got me for sure," said Gabriel.

'And sunk his teeth into your mailled arm,' thought Mabel. She pictured the dog's teeth dropping out with a chink, one by one.

She moved on and came to a set of wooden steps.

At the top, she looked back. Gabriel must be watching the front of the house again, for he wasn't visible now.

'I hope this dog doesn't live anywhere too near,' said Mabel in her cat voice. 'I don't want to be his dessert.'

She leapt up onto a window sill and jumped down into a dark cramped space. How could anyone live in such a place? It was damp, dusty and cold and only just enough light came from the window and through the ill-fitting tiles of the roof to be able to see what sort of a place it was.

Mabel's cat eyes adjusted to the gloom.

No one was home. If you could call it a home.

There were three pallets laid out, one against each wall. Mabel noticed there was a chamber pot in the corner, thankfully empty and a small table which was piled with crockery. A cloak hung on a peg knocked into the wall by one bed and another bed had untidily piled up blankets in the middle. Stubs of tallow candles were stacked up in a box under the table.

Someone had been sewing, for there was a small basket of thread and a pair of well patched hose stuffed into it.

One of the beds had a small chest underneath it. Mabel pawed it until it was out in the middle of the bare wooden floor. No matter how she tried, her cat paws and teeth could not open it.

She looked round for a key. Nothing.

It's no good I shall have to become me and see if I can get into it.

She was just about to turn deosil when the small door in the far end opened and a girl stepped through.

"Prrrap!" said Mabel in surprise. Her feline senses had let her down!

"Aw. Hello pussy, puss," said a childish voice. "How did you get in here?"

Before she knew what was happening, Mabel was lifted from the floor and set down onto a lap. The girl started to pull her careworn hands through Mabel's soft, grey, striped fur.

"Aw, you must have come from one of the neighbours. Aren't you lovely?"

It wasn't in Mabel's nature, either as a cat or as a human being, to be horrible or unkind but she did feel a little irritated when the girl started to fondle her ears.

'God! Is this what cats have to put up with?' said Mabel to herself. She wanted to claw the girl's hand.

Another girl came in after her. This one was older and skinnier. "What've you found there?"

"A tabby cat. It was here when I got home."

"Aw, Aimée, it'll be full of fleas, throw it out."

'FLEAS!' Mabel stiffened.

"Oh now look at what you've done. She doesn't like you."

'You're right there,' said Mabel but it came out as 'Meeeeeaaow.'

"Perhaps we could keep it to catch the mice."

'Pah!' said Mabel, 'I'm not catching any mice. I don't do that sort of thing.'

"That means if it wasn't an efficient mouser we'd have to feed it and we have enough trying to feed ourselves!" said the second girl.

Mabel struggled in the girl's arms.

"Oh, she doesn't like you being unkind to her."

"You had our chest out from under my bed?" said the skinny one, eyeing the displaced box.

"No, Estrild. Maybe the cat did."

"What would a cat want with our money box?" said the skinny one with malice.

Aimée hugged Mabel to her body. Mabel's face and whiskers were all screwed up. That was the most unpleasant feeling.

"You better not have taken anything."

"Why would I do that? The money is for all of us. Anyway I haven't got the key. It's your turn this month."

The skinny girl had gone down onto her knees and was unlocking the chest with a small key which she kept on a piece of string around her neck.

She tumbled the few coins through her fingers. "Looks to be all here."

Aimée tittered, "You can't count it. You don't know how to count."

"What you sayin'?"

"Nothing, Estrild."

The girl Estrild, took out two coins and shoved them into her tight sleeve.

"I'm going food shopping. Get rid of the cat."

She exited and they heard her clomping down the steps in her heavy pattens.

They also heard her say, "Good afternoon sir," rather sweetly.

And Mabel recognised the answering voice.

"Good day, mistress."

Ah, so Gabriel was close by.

Mabel struggled some more and managed to free herself. She sat on the floor and straightened and washed her whiskers keeping a wary eye on the girl, Aimée.

Suddenly there was a scratching on the door. Mabel lost concentration and stopped her toilette.

"Is there anyone home?"

Aimée had picked up Mabel again and opened the door. "Oh hello. You are a bit early."

"Am I...?"

"We haven't had our dinner yet."

"Well..." Gabriel's eyes strayed to the cat. "Perhaps I can just be a moment. That is a lovely cat you have there."

"I want to keep her."

"Er... she doesn't look as if she wants to be kept."

"Parragh!" cried Mabel as she jumped from the girl's arms.

Gabriel looked as if he was going to be deflected from his purpose and so Mabel started to curl around his legs.

She then went to Aimée and did the same.

"You wouldn't be Aimée by any chance?"

"Yes, yes I am..." The girl took a lock of her unbound light brown hair and twirled it around her fingers.

"Who would like to know?"

"Well I would..."

Mabel stopped her curling and spat. "Psst."

"Erm." Gabriel had got the message. "I am a friend of Master Sweetcheeks."

"Oh Alban. Dear kind Alban. I like him."

"And he likes you."

"Oh, I know."

"He said that you'd tell me where the other houses were situated which Mistress Wymark Honfleur owns. The ones you clean."

The girl threw back her head and laughed. "Clean?"

"Er yes... you see I have a friend... who... needs a job and... I wondered if..."

Aimée's brown eyes changed colour. They deepened and became suspicious.

"You have a friend who needs a job? You do? A knight?"

"Well it's a friend of a friend and Master Alban knows her too."

Aimée came close to Sir Gabriel. She was no longer watching the cat.

Slowly so as not to cause a stir in the air, Mabel turned deosil behind the girl's back.

"Really? Well if that was true... you'd know that... there isn't a lot of cleaning done."

"Oh well..."

"Dear Master Sweetcheeks knows how much 'cleaning' we do."

"You have taken our money, Aimée," said Mabel.

The girl spun round. "Lord save me! Where did you come from?"

"Master Sweetcheeks gave you our money and he was supposed to..."

"What's going on?" The girl backed to the wall.

"There's nothing to be frightened of," said Gabriel. "We aren't here to hurt you."

"Where's the cat?"

"Alban gave you the money in exchange for information. Only we couldn't meet with him, because... because he's dead," said Mabel sadly.

The girl's eyes narrowed. "Dead? Why... why... should he be dead?"

"We don't know. Someone doesn't like us looking into the death of Master Scarepath and..." began Mabel. "Did you kill him? Scarepath or Sweetcheeks?"

The girl started to shake.

Mabel came forward.

"My friend is quite right. We aren't here to frighten you. We'd just like to know what it was you told Master Alban?"

"Why?"

"Then we can perhaps have enough information to find his killer."

"Why should you care?"

Mabel and Gabriel looked at each other.

"We do care. We... are..." Mabel halted. What were they? "We are seekers after justice, Aimée. Strange though that may seem. We... sort out... problems. Find the truth."

"Usually murders," said Gabriel with a sweet smile, though it didn't quite work because of his healing scar.

"We are very sorry about Master Sweetcheeks. We feel responsible because if we hadn't asked him to come to you, he might still be alive."

Aimée's hand had convulsively gone to her neck.

"Are you keeping back the money he gave you, Aimée?" said Mabel. "Keeping it back from the... communal chest?"

"It's mine."

"Indeed it is," said Gabriel, "but the goods were never delivered. We never got to know what we asked him to find out. Master Sweetcheeks was killed before..."

"How?"

"How what?"

"How was he killed?"

Again a look passed between Mabel and Gabriel.

"He was strangled," said the knight.

Aimée fell onto her bed. "Oh that's awful."

"And so... all we'd like to know is, where these houses are and we shall leave you to spend our... your money. If not..."

A tearful face looked up. "If not?"

"We shall be forced to tell the lovely Estrild that you have some money tucked into your bosom which is not going into the communal pot."

"She'd kill me..."

"Ah, well." Mabel shrugged.

Gabriel crouched on his haunches.

"Come on, mistress. Save yourself a lot of... aggravation. We promise we are not the authorities we are just..."

"Two people interested in the truth," said Mabel.

Aimée wiped her eyes. "If I tell you... it won't come back on me will it?"

"No, of course not…" said Gabriel.

"We cannot be absolutely certain… no," said Mabel. "But we can protect you. We promise."

"And you will bring Alban's killer to the gallows?"

"We shall do our best."

Aimée sniffed and swallowed.

She looked around the scruffy little room.

"Where's that cat gone?"

*****

"The house of the dairy maids in Avebury Lane? Where's that?"

Mabel shrugged. "I'm not quite sure. I've heard something like it but can't remember."

They were hurrying down the track at the side of the double gabled house.

"And the house at… what was it?"

"Savernake Turn."

"Where in Heaven's name is that?"

"Well, that's possibly the house on the London Road which Mme. Birdwoman was talking about. The only one we certainly know of is the tall house on Figgins Lane."

"You know it. I don't."

"It's right by the river. Rather a scruffy place. Another lodging house. Not quite so nice as the one up on St. Martin's Lane."

"Do we visit?"

"I do."

"And get picked up and hugged again?" said Gabriel with a crooked smirk.

"A cat's a good disguise."

"Unless there's a nasty dog about."

"I can look after myself."

"Well then let's go. Let's find the one you know first."

They didn't walk together. Mabel walked behind Gabriel, so that it might look as if she was his servant. They didn't want too much gossip.

Mabel gestured that they turn into Figgins Lane, a narrow road between the High Street and the little ford where the river Kennet spread out and became shallow.

They stood looking up at the house.

"Seen better days."

"All the properties here have seen better days. Many of them simply fall down," said Mabel.

"Looks as if this one ought to."

Mabel pushed the daub wall with her forefinger. "Nah. Good for a few more hundred years!"

Gabriel stepped forward and called out. "Hello...open up. Sir Gabriel Warrener for... for the town reeve."

"Inspired," said Mabel under her breath. "Now they know your name."

He gave her a sidelong look as if to say, "Does it matter?"

"You might have used an assumed name."

"Like you do...? Cat."

"Whadaya want?" A head could be seen at a first floor window. The face was squashed up against the bars, looking down at them.

"Inquiring about lodgings," said Gabriel.

"Piss off," said the man.

"You have no rooms?"

"Rooms. Ah yeah. We have rooms. But we ain't open."

"Well then..."

"You can't bring your own doxies."

"I beg your pardon?"

"Piss off."

Gabriel was not used to being spoken to in this way. "I think you'd be wise, my man, to open the door."

The speaker was obviously drunk. He paraphrased Gabriel's speech with as many expletives between the words as he could manage.

Gabriel felt a tug on his sleeve. "We've seen enough, sir. I don't like it anyway."

Gabriel looked up. The man had gone and the shutters were now across the window.

"Come on. I think we are getting the idea." Mabel towed him up the lane. "I think the house of the dairymaids might be up here. Come on."

They followed the road around the end of St. Peter's churchyard and past the castle mount. Up a slight incline and almost to the common, they found a wattle-fenced lane which looked very little used. Grass grew over the mud of the surface. Nettles spilled out, tall and profuse, from the edge.

"There doesn't look to be a house up here!" said Gabriel.

Eventually they came out onto a fenced yard. This place was in much better repair than the last.

"I'm going to become a cat and see what I can find."

The house was behind some trees, very secret with a screen of bushes on all sides.

Mabel looked round quickly.

"Here I go."

Gabriel walked into the garth, followed by a tabby cat.

"Not such a large house, just one floor," he said. "But newer I think."

He scouted around the side. "Not overlooked at all."

"Prrrp," said Mabel as she jumped in through the window.

There was no one there and Mabel turned back into herself and opened the door to Gabriel.

She loosened a shutter to let in more light.

"Well that's interesting."

Gabriel walked into the middle of the room.

"A lot of servants live here," he said.

"Hmmm." She was busy moving the coverlets of many beds, all of which were contained within small partitioned rooms with curtains.

She found a box. "Ah… I know who made this."

There was no money in the box but a few meagre possessions. A tawdry brooch. A lock of hair wrapped in parchment. A small horn cup. And finally the stub of a beeswax candle.

"But nothing to tell us who owns any of this."

"And nothing to do with Mistress Honfleur."

"She's such a secretive woman," said Mabel.

They left the house as they'd found it, Mabel locking the door and jumping back out and down the nettley lane.

"But you know what's going on, don't you?" she asked.

"She must be giving lodging to people who are out at work during the day. People who can't afford much."

She stopped dead in the track. "Gabriel…"

He bumped into her. "What?"

"The work that goes on there is done at night, mostly. Secretly."

"What…you mean?"

"I mean that it's a brothel. One which isn't licensed by the town. One which doesn't pay a fee to operate."

"You mean… the town knows that places are being used for…" His face went a puce colour and the scar stood out across his cheek.

"Are you really so naive, Gabriel?"

"Wha…wha…wha…"

"There's only one licensed brothel as far as I know in town. But clever Mistress Honfleur and her lover Scarepath, have had quite a business going. No wonder there was so much money to be made."

"Why does no one know?"

"The girls are probably scared to death and the clients don't want to be identified."

"The house on St. Martin's is where she lives but this house and the one on Figgins Lane are the places where the business is done. It's all about sex."

"And this house at Savernake Turn?"

"Well, we won't know until we get there, but it might be that it's the heart of it all. And that is where we'll find the money," said Mabel.

"Good Lord!" said Gabriel. "I had no idea."

Mabel's eyes went up to Heaven.

CHAPTER SEVEN ~ THE HOUSE ON TURNABOUT LANE

"And where is it then?"

"Master Farmer says it's known locally as Turnabout Lane."

"Ah..."

"But it's somewhere on the edge, the very edge of the forest."

"That's why they called it Savernake?"

"Apparently, it's town land and not the King's forest."

That morning they'd managed to be up really early. Mabel had completed chores which she had neglected at the manor for a few days. And they now sat over an early dinner or a late breaking of fast, at Mabel's large table.

"I have an idea."

"Oh Lord!" said Mabel facetiously.

"Don't be like that! It gets us where we want to be, both of us and with an excuse to be there. And no one will suspect anything."

"Oh?"

Gabriel fished out some pieces of leather from his pannier.

"What on earth are those?"

"Jesses."

"What?"

"For flying falcons."

"Ah no, Gabriel... no..."

"You change yourself into a peregrine. I'm allowed to fly a peregrine as a noble..."

"Where did you get them?"

"They belong to the lord."

"Well, you can put them back."

"Aw no, Mabel, listen."

"Not listening. You are not going to... to...truss me up in those..."

"Mab..."

"NO!"

*****

Mabel sat on the large table and, as much as a bird could pout, she pouted. She sulked. She glowered. It was easy to glower with the eyes of a peregrine. They already looked evil and glowery. Mabel managed to take that evil to new depths.

Gabriel was crooning to her as if she was a real bird.

"Now then my lovely."

Mabel pecked at his hand.

"Ouch."

"Mabel. This goes on your foot... don't struggle now. It's difficult enough without a bow, or somewhere for you to perch."

"ARRRRWK!"

"Yes, I know. So help me."

"QWAAARK!"

"I need to get this onto your ankle."

"PRAAARRK!"

"I know... you won't like being tethered but if we meet anyone, it's maybe something they'll know about. This leather strap is free falling. It allows me to..."

"GRRRARK!"

"Mabel, it has to look convincing."

"CARK!"

"Look… climb onto my glove and I'll do my best to make it look right without you actually being tied."

Mabel glowered some more.

"Right. Here we go."

They walked out of the cottage together. Bertran, Gabriel's beautiful pale horse, was standing patiently outside.

"Now, you'll have to learn to balance…"

'Don't be so foolish. Falcons have an immensely good sense of balance,' said Mabel in falcon.

"Oops!" Gabriel mounted the horse and Mabel righted herself.

She pecked his glove twice in annoyance.

"Now, now," said Gabriel.

"Right, let's practice. I'll toss you up, you fly about a bit and return to my glove."

He held out his left hand.

Mabel sat hunched and did not move. She stared at him with evil in her eyes.

"Mabel for goodness sake. Stop pouting like a three year old."

"Good day, Sir Gabriel, my lord."

"Good day, Miller."

This was one of Mabel's neighbours looking up at him from the lane on the other side of the fence.

"I see you're off with a bird."

"If I can get it to behave, I am."

"Got permission to fly in the forest, have you?"

"From the warden himself."

"Aw that's good. Doesn't do to flout the laws."

"No. Certainly not."

"You… call your bird Mabel… sir?"

"Ah no, you misheard, I called her…erm…'Grable', Miller."

"Ah…"

"It's an old word for digger. On account of her propensity to dig

93

in her claws when she's in a bad mood."

Miller laughed and with a further chuckle asked, "Have you seen Mistress Wetherspring this morning, sir?"

"I believe she is at the manor today."

"Aw, right."

"Good day, Miller."

"CARK!"

"Well you do, Grable, dig in your claws," said Gabriel.

Mabel moved her claws about on the leather of the glove just for spite.

"Now off you go and show me what a good girl you can be."

Mabel lifted off and went to sit on one of the middle branches of the oak tree in her garden.

"Grable you come back here."

Gabriel trotted Bertran over to the tree and lifted his hand with its protective leather glove.

"Come on. We are wasting time."

Mabel settled, Gabriel took out the hood and moved it to his teeth.

"CARRRRRUK!"

"Mabel, you have to wear it. It prevents you from being distracted. You'll fly off at the least…"

"QWAAAAARK"

Gabriel sighed.

"Alright. You're a woman, not a bird. You won't fly off or get distracted. Just behave—please."

Mabel fluffed up her brown feathers and settled herself more firmly on his fist.

"Off we go."

*****

They trotted to the main road and after a few miles Mabel was allowed to fly freely, though she never stooped or went for any bird or animal.

She came back to Gabriel's fist as they stood on the hill which led down into the outer area of the town.

"Now Mabel... search around. We know Turnabout Lane is somewhere here. And there must be a road to it, even if it's quite hidden. You'll find it, my girl."

Mabel flew off, her bells ringing and Gabriel watched until she was merely a speck in the sky.

He dismounted, took a drink from his water flask and looked around. Here were rough grasslands with a few outlying trees. He could see the town below; a number of houses clustered at the base of the hill where the London Road began.

He sat on the soft grass and leaned back on his elbows.

This was such a lovely spot.

The downs rose above the town to the north, almost treeless and alive with shifting shadows. The green forest to his back; miles of trees with glades and meadows and little villages like Bedwyn.

He saw the river Kennet, a silver band winding its way on to the county of Berkshire.

It was a lovely spot to live.

Could he ever put down roots here?

He pushed that thought to the back of his mind. It was never going to be possible.

After a while of filling his head with nothing but clouds and grass, he heard at last the tinny rattle of Mabel returning.

He jumped up and held out his hand.

She missed and landed on the grass.

Then turned three times to deosil.

"Mabel, are you alright?"

"Perfectly."

She tidied her hair back into the crespinette that she wore to contain her hair at the base of her neck. "There is a house about half a mile up there. We must have passed the road. There's nothing else at all, that I can see. It has outbuildings and quite a bit of land. Even stabling for horses. It's much grander than anything else we've seen."

"Then it must be that. Hop on. And I'll take us there."

With Mabel as a falcon again, they travelled up the hill and searched for the lane.

"CARK!"

"Here somewhere?"

The falcon floated up on the air currents and spotted the lane.

She dived and then when she knew that Gabriel had seen her, she led the way through the trees until they came out into a green space before a large house.

"Is there anyone here?" said Gabriel from the corner of his mouth.

Mabel flew round the building.

She saw movement; a maid out in the backyard who looked like she was churning butter. Mabel's keen eyes caught sight of a man in what looked like a stable block but she could see only one horse.

She settled onto Gabriel's fist again and stared out to the house.

"Anyone home?"

Mabel bobbed her head up and down.

"Let's see if we can engage them."

"Helloooo!" yelled Gabriel. "Anyone home?"

The man came from the back of the house. "Hello, sir."

Gabriel left Bertran and put on his most kindly demeanour. "I seem to be a little lost. Erm... might you tell me where I am."

The man looked oddly at him. "Do you want a room, for the night or just for the few hours, sir?"

"Oh no... I don't want a room."

"Well... in that case... you've come to the wrong place. Space is all we have."

"I told you. I'm lost. What is this place?" Gabriel absently stroked Mabel's neck feathers.

"No one gets lost here. You have to make a special effort to get here."

"Well... I can assure you I didn't make an effort. I lost my bird. She flew up and landed in a tree just over there and then... I followed her."

The man folded his arms.

"What is this place?"

There was no answer.

"Who owns it?"

Gabriel fished in his purse. "Might this loosen your tongue?"

"It depends who's asking."

"Sir Gabriel Warrener."

"Oh, that's a fancy name."

The knight lifted his arm and Mabel flew off a few feet, landing in the top of a bush.

"Seems you lost your bird again, sir. Very careless."

Gabriel brandished the coin in front of this man's eyes. "Who owns this place?"

The man snatched at the coin but failed to snaffle it.

"Ah... my question first."

"I think you probably already know. Mistress Honfleur owns it. It's an inn."

"Ah. It's a bit out of the way for an inn." Gabriel gave him the coin.

'So much for being penniless,' said Mabel to herself. 'Flashing around his coins like...'

"Does Mistress Honfleur have a room here?"

"Yes. Why? Why do you want to know?"

"I might like to... engage the woman. I hear she's very beautiful."

The man scoffed. "Good luck with that then."

"Is there a key?"

"A key?"

"To her room"

"Only one key and she's got it."

"Hmmm. I can't pay her a surprise visit then?"

The man laughed. "It would be a brave man who did that."

"Alright, so how do I get to see her?"

"Your best bet is to find her at her home in the town. The house of the three gables on St. Martin's Lane."

"How often does she come here?" asked Gabriel looking round nosily.

"Not every week. Maybe once every so often."

"Does she bring any money here?"

"I..."

"Where does she keep her money?"

The man's face drained of blood. "Ah no... that's not something I can tell you."

Gabriel stepped forward and grabbed the man by the neck of his tunic.

"Where?" He pushed him up against the fence.

"In... in a safe chest."

"And where's that?"

"In her room."

Gabriel let go and smoothed out the fabric of the man's clothes. "Hmmm. Is she always alone when she comes here?"

"No, not always."

"A man?"

"Erm... I think that's enough information for the money you gave me."

"You do realise that to be successful in business, you need to keep on the right side of the law," said Gabriel, stepping forward again. "It can make running a business very difficult. The law."

"Ah... you the law then?"

Gabriel didn't answer but just glared at the man.

Eventually he asked, "I'll ask again, did she come here with a man?"

"Sometimes... yes. Sometimes he comes after her."

"Always the same man is it?"

"Erm... I am going to get into trouble for this."

"Well then, we won't tell anyone will we?"

"Erm... yes, it was always the same man."

"Ah." Gabriel stepped back. "Can you describe him to me?"

"Oh, I...."

"Of course, I could always take you back to town, roped to my saddle and lose you in the town lockup for a while."

The man licked his lips.

"Was it Scarepath?"

The man rubbed his face. "Nah. He's dead meat."

"Ah... so he's dead is he?"

"Where you bin? Everyone in the town knows Scarepath's been murdered."

"Does Mistress Honfleur miss her erstwhile lover, do you think?"

The man gave Gabriel a sidelong look. "How would I know?"

"So, back to my question. Describe this man."

"I... I... can't."

"You're afraid to tell me?"

The man put up two hands. "I can't. I just can't."

"Who are you more afraid of... this man..." Gabriel slowly took out his knife. "Or me?"

"You wouldn't, sir." The man tried to back away. "You wouldn't. You're a knight... with..."

"Oh... I wouldn't pay too much attention to all that... er... what's your name?"

"Hugo, sir. Hugo of Chisbury."

"Hugo. All that chivalry. It's nonsense." Gabriel brought the point of his knife up to the man's neck.

"There are knights... and then there are knights..."

Mabel giggled in a birdlike way on her perch a few feet away.

"Some knights would kill you straight away. Where you stood... no quarter. Dead. Others would just carve a little bit off you... just to have a bit of fun. A bit at a time."

The man was perspiring and trembling.

"I leave it to your imagination to work out which kind I am."

"No sir, please."

"What does he look like? How old is he?"

"Thirtyish. Tallish, light haired, clean shaven."

"Fat, thin..."

"Ordinary. Thinks himself a bit above the rest of us..."

"Ah... like a knight..."

"Er, no sir. Begging your pardon, sir."

"Superior bugger is he?"

"He's nobody. But he likes to lord it."

"Ah."

"We just have to do as we're told. And he doesn't even own the place."

"Mistress Honfleur does. And she likes this man so you have to do what he says?"

Hugo nodded, very carefully, his eyes crossing as he eyed the knife point.

"He's a flash bastard."

"Ah, is he? In what way?"

"Always has the best clothes. Jewellery..."

"Now... jewellery is interesting."

"He likes it."

"Ah, that's definitely something I like about him." He shoved his knife back into its scabbard with a thunk.

Gabriel walked away and whistled, lifting his arm.

Mabel soared up and landed on his glove.

"If anyone asks you... we haven't been here. You haven't seen me."

"Pah... that's the same for everyone who ever comes here!"

Gabriel mounted Bertran. "Thank you Hugo."

He turned his horse.

"Oh Hugo... do you stay here overnight?"

"I do, sir. And my wife Enid. In a small cott at the back."

"Good. God keep you." And they rode away.

*****

"Well! I'm seeing a different side to you now!" said Mabel as she smoothed down her kirtle.

"Really?"

"Sir Gabriel Warrener, defender of women, children and old ladies and the scourge of…"

"Got the information, didn't I?"

"You could have just let me get in there to look around and saved yourself a penny!"

"It might have been dangerous."

"An old woman and a cowardly servant?"

"We weren't to know that."

Gabriel plodded on and Mabel walked beside his horse. "What was all that about them staying there at night?"

"I wanted to know if the place was guarded at night."

"It doesn't need guarding. It's an inn with a brothel. There will be plenty of men and women there at night. All night."

"I just wanted to know."

They walked on in silence.

"Gabriel, why are we doing this?"

"What?"

"Why are we bothered? We know that Scarepath was a villain. We know that Honfleur probably is. We know that she's got a lover and that he's probably a murderer. Why are we bothered?"

Gabriel stopped, threw his leg over Bertran's ears, dismounted and walked beside him.

"They killed Scarepath. They killed Sweetcheeks, whom I thought you liked…"

"I did."

"They tried to kill you."

"Well… yes."

"And for that I want to bring them to justice. I'll not have you in danger, Mabel."

She looked over at him. His face was very serious.

"I will have to return to our lord soon and I am not leaving you alone with a possible murderer."

"Oh."

"You know... how I feel about you... I would never forgive myself ... if..."

Mabel looked away, tears welling up at the back of her eyes and there was a tightening of her throat.

Gabriel stopped.

"Tonight, we are going to get into the house and search for the money. And probably jewels. You heard that man. He said the lover likes jewels. What's the betting there are jewels too hidden in that house and if we can find them we can identify them as stolen, tie them to the thief and murderer."

"And let the town reeve know?"

"And let the town reeve know."

"Then if we are going back to get into the house, why are we walking away?"

"You want to spend the rest of the day sitting around here, waiting?"

"We could go down into the town and I could get into the house with three gables and search the room of Master Bux. If you ask me, that description fits him perfectly - I bet he's the lover of Mistress Honfleur."

"You think that he is going to keep anything in his room which will incriminate him?"

"Well no... perhaps..."

"He has a wife. He can't possibly keep anything there which will make her suspicious."

"That is good thinking, Gabriel."

"I know."

They walked on a few paces.

"Is it really why you want to know the truth? Because my life might be in danger?" said Mabel at last.

He took her arm in his hand.

"What do you think?"

She looked up at him. He wasn't a really tall man but Mabel was so small she had to look up.

Gradually as her eyes searched his face, examined the scar and all the little dents and lines made by the wolf-man just over a month ago, his face got closer. She saw his lips close. He placed them softly on hers.

"Oh."

He moved his lips gently on her own for a heartbeat and then pulled away.

"Now what do you think?"

Mabel was suddenly embarrassed.

"I er... I think that we shall go home and have some supper and come back when it gets dark."

He smiled. "A good plan, Mabel."

*****

Mabel crept along an inner corridor on four silent cat feet. She had never seen a house like it. The floors were all made of stone. The walls were made of daub and wattle but here and there they were faced with wood panels and some were solid stone. There were separate rooms along the corridor all of them with doors... not a curtain in sight. This was even more luxurious than Bedwyn Manor.

She had jumped into the building through a small unlatched hatch which seemed to be for loading something into the building. Perhaps firewood?

Once inside, doors were no problem for her. If she could not get through as a cat then she'd simply be herself and open them.

She made her way to what seemed to her to be a central hall. There were only three people there. And they were drunk and laughing, making a lot of noise. One woman, two men.

But, damn they would see her as she opened the door for Gabriel. None of them were the servant or his wife. She didn't know these people. They didn't know her. Three turns to deosil, she became herself and bolstering her courage she marched to the front door and opened it.

No one took any notice of her.

"Ah, sir. I have been waiting for you. Come. I have a room prepared."

"Ah yes... Cecilie. I have been looking forward to this."

They scurried through the hall and disappeared into the darkness of the long corridor.

"Who's Cecilie?"

"One of my aunts."

"Ah…"

They crept on.

"There's hardly anyone here," said Mabel at last at a whisper. There are about ten rooms but only one door is locked."

"That is likely to be hers."

"I can get in under the door and open it for you."

"Right. Let's look."

They reached the door and Mabel looked carefully at it.

"Too well fitting for a mouse."

"So what can you do?"

Mabel turned withershynnes and her body shrunk and flattened before Gabriel's gaze. Her eyes popped out of her head and grew on the side of her face. Her nose split and grew long and segmented. Whilst she shrunk she also elongated and her body became wriggly with joints at every segment. She had fourteen legs and she became a soft rust colour.

'Oh fiddle faddle,' she said to herself. 'How do I get all these legs to coordinate?' She moved forward.

'Right left left right… right left. Oooh. She tripped. Concentrate

Mabel!'

Gabriel could no longer see her in the gloom. "Mabel!" he said in a loud whisper. There was no answer. He doubled over. He could just see the back end of some insect, crawling under the door.

"Mabel?"

Surely not? He answered his own question when a while later there came a soft sliding sound and a click. Then after a short while the door opened very slowly.

Mabel stood there breathing heavily.

"That was one of the hardest things I have ever done," she whispered.

"What?"

"Crawled into the damned lock and turned it without a key."

"How?"

"I don't think that centipedes are designed to curl up into a ball around a keyhole."

"Why a centipede?"

"The door was locked and we didn't have a key. I had to get into the lock, of course. "

"Quick, let's get in, out of sight."

They closed the door quietly. Mabel looked completely exhausted.

"You sit there for a moment, I'll do the looking," said Gabriel.

He'd brought a candle and a strike-a-light with tinder and after a few false starts, he lit it. "Here, take this and light another. There must be one here."

The room came into view.

It was sumptuous. Even more beautifully furnished than the private rooms at the manor of Bedwyn.

Painted cloths were displayed on the walls. The floor around the bed was laid with rush matting. The furniture was high quality and there was a lot of it. Silver goblets stood on the table with a jug. Mabel looked into it. Red wine.

"I have a feeling someone is coming tonight or why would they fill the jug with wine?" she said.

"Then we must hurry."

"How many chests are there?"

"Four. You take those two, Mabel."

"They'll be locked Gabriel, you know they will."

"Can't we force them?"

"And let them know we are onto them?"

"Do we have a choice?"

Mabel set her eye to one of the chests and peered into the keyhole. "I might be able to turn it."

"Have we time?"

Gabriel was just about to take his dagger hilt to the hasp of the chest when there were voices outside the door.

"Thank you Hugo. That will be all for tonight."

"Mistress."

Mabel and Gabriel both mouthed, "Honfleur," blew out the candles and dived for cover.

Mabel quickly turned withershynnes again and became the tabby cat.

Gabriel squeezed himself behind a hanging and pulled in his feet tight to the wall.

A key turned in the lock.

Honfleur called Hugo back again.

"Hugo! The door was open!"

"Oh no, ma'am, it can't be."

"It IS!"

"Only you have the key, ma'am."

"Oh, go away, will you?"

The door opened.

Mabel saw the woman enter and close the door behind her.

'Oh fiddle faddle!' said Mabel to herself in a cat whisper. 'That's done it!'

CHAPTER EIGHT
~ THE CAT AND A MOUSE ~

In the light of the small lamp which she held, the woman's eyes ranged over the room. She immediately went to the chest by the bed to see if it had been tampered with.

Taking out a small key on a chain around her neck, she unlocked it. Mabel could briefly see the glint of gold and the shine of silver.

Wymark sniffed. "I know you're here. I can smell the candle you extinguished."

It took only a heartbeat for Gabriel to step out from the painted cloth.

"Good evening Mistress Honfleur."

"You!"

He bowed.

"Forgive me for letting myself into your private room."

"How did you... know I was here? How did you get in?"

"I have a secret weapon."

She watched him for a moment and, with a sigh, reached up and took off her veil, wimple and crespinette. Ringlets of coppery fair hair cascaded to her shoulders and beyond.

She lifted the jug and poured wine into the two goblets.

"Will you take some wine with me and tell me exactly who you are and why you are here?"

"I will gratefully accept the wine and tell you who I am. As I told you before, I am Sir Gabriel Warrener and, madam, I simply cannot lie, I am here because I am totally enamoured of you."

Mabel could not help but make a scoffing noise. It came out like a cat sneeze.

"What was that?"

"Nothing... I heard nothing."

"I distinctly heard..."

"Madam." Gabriel took the distance between them at a leap. Clasping hold of her hand he brought it up to his lips.

"Ever since I saw you in the town I have been captivated by your beauty."

The woman laughed.

Now, Gabriel could see into the money chest. Bags of coins and small wooden boxes were stacked up inside it.

Wymark pushed the lid and let it fall and as it fell it made a sharp crack.

"A good try Sir...G..."

"Gabriel."

"But I do not believe you."

She held out the wine for him. "Come and sit with me here."

Mabel was a little too close for comfort and so she stepped back into the shadows. Gabriel could see the tip of her tail swishing in the gloom.

"Of what are you not convinced, dear lady? That my name is Gabriel, that I am grateful for the wine? Or that I am deeply in love with you?"

"The wine is the best that Gascony can provide. You may be giving me your real name, it's true. But as to you being in love with me... ah no."

"Oh, Mistress Wymark, you are simply the most captivating woman I have seen in a very long time."

"Are you so shallow, Sir Gabriel that you love at a mere look?

Grow weak at the knees at nothing but beauty?"

Mabel realised Gabriel was going to have a hard time convincing the woman and gaining her trust.

"On the contrary, I feel I know you. Your reputation goes before you. Clever, astute, cultured, tough, a woman not to be trifled with..."

"Ah you have heard the talk in the town. Not to be trifled with. They think I killed my lover, Scarepath."

"Did you?"

She lifted her goblet to him.

"I suspect that you were growing tired of him," said Gabriel. "I suppose you had had enough of the old man. You disposed of him to take on a ..." Here Gabriel came closer to her. "Younger man."

"A younger man? My, my!"

"You need look no further, mistress, may I call you Wymark?" He went down on one knee. "Here is one who would do your every bidding."

She laughed again and leaving him on the floor went round the room lighting more candles and lamps.

Everything came into focus including a grey tabby cat.

Gabriel bounced up and stood in front of Mabel to conceal her. "Tell me, why do you hide yourself away here?"

"I do not hide, Sir Gabriel. "I keep a room here to get away from... things and I have a horse here too, in the stable so that I might ride here and there. When dear Simon was in the forest, this was convenient for him. He did not like to be seen in the town."

"Now it all makes sense."

"Good."

"And the 'rooms'?"

"This is an inn, sir. You would expect an inn to have rooms."

She sat down and arranged her skirts around her.

"Come and sit so that I can see you more clearly."

Gabriel perched on the end of the bed.

"You are not afraid to think that I killed my lover, sir? Not afraid of me?"

"No mistress, that makes you even more interesting to me." He leaned forward. His ravaged face came into the light of a candle.

"Oh... my! How disfigured you are. You must tell me the story about that."

"No matter how many times I were to tell you, you would never believe me."

"Oh, I am sure I would," she simpered.

Gabriel sighed. "Alright. I received these wounds when I fought with a man-wolf in the Forest of Savernake. I was defending the life of a maiden of great beauty... but not as beautiful as you, I must say."

Mabel growled low in her throat. 'Cheek!'

Wymark's shoulders were shaking with mirth.

"I told you that you would not believe me."

"A man-wolf?"

"A shapeshifting man. Oh yes... it's not just legend. These creatures really do exist. I know it. I have met one."

"I hope you vanquished this man-wolf."

"But of course."

Mabel let out a small squeak. "Prrp."

'Cheek! Vanquished him indeed.'

"I am amused by you, Sir Gabriel. You tell a good tale."

"No word of a lie, ma'am."

"I will probably find that the truth is much more dull and that you obtained your scar in a drunken brawl somewhere."

"Madam! I do not engage in brawls."

Gabriel leaned into the bed on his elbow. "However, I have found that since I obtained this disfigurement, I have proved very 'popular' with the ladies. It seems to give me some... special quality. A certain dangerous piquancy!"

"Pah!" said Mabel.

"Is that so?" said Wymark, coquettishly.

"They all wish to hear about my duel with a shapeshifting man.

In detail."

Gabriel was swishing his hand from side to side behind him to indicate to Mabel that she should try to get out of the room.

"What are you doing, Sir Gabriel?"

"What? Oh, do you not find that it is a little warm in here?" He began to fan his face with his hand.

"Then take off some of your clothes, do," said Wymark.

Gabriel leapt up. "Is there no window to open?"

"No, not in this room. It is in the centre of the house. There are no outside walls."

"Oh."

'Damn,' thought Mabel, 'then he cannot get out.'

Suddenly there seemed to be a fracas out in the corridor.

"Wymark!" Someone was calling the woman's name.

"Jesus!" Wymark Honfleur jumped up.

"Ah... you must hide. There behind the hanging... there is a small door to another room next to this. He must not find you here."

Gabriel did not need another invitation. But how was he to rescue Mabel? Ah no. She could fend for herself. She could be anything she wanted and get out of the room.

"Wymark!" came the voice, closer now.

"The door is open!" she shouted.

Gabriel disappeared just as the man entered the room and the draught from the opening door disguised the swishing movement of the hanging.

"Did I hear voices?"

"I was talking to myself."

Mabel scooted under the table at the same time as trying to get a good look at the man. Not paying full attention to where she was going, she knocked the leg of the trestle and one of the goblets fell onto the polished wood.

"What?"

A small silver mug then fell to the floor with a clank and running away, Mabel managed to jam her back right foot into it.

She ran across the space before the door. Trip, trip, trip, clank. Trip, trip, trip clank.

"Yeeowll!"

"A cat... a bloody cat!" said the man.

"Get rid of it!" said the woman. Then she seemed to recognise it as the cat she'd seen in town.

"It's the same cat! I'm sure!"

"What?"

"After it!"

The two of them then began to chase Mabel around the room.

Trip, trip, trip, clank, went Mabel's metal shoe.

She stopped to shake it off. Wymark made a leap for her and managed to get hold of her tail. Mabel turned and struck her with sharp claws.

"Ahhh!" The woman let go.

"Yooowwwll!" Mabel screeched as the man stopped her with his foot. She changed tack and ran behind a hanging.

The man started to beat the hanging with his hands to try to flush Mabel out, but she wasn't so easily scared.

The dust from the hanging came out in clouds and the man coughed and sneezed.

And as the man laboured, unable to see, Mabel came out of the bottom and jumped onto the nearest piece of furniture which happened to be a pot board.

She made sure she pushed everything from the shelves, breaking pottery, denting silver and scratching the wood. The pair flailed around trying to stop her.

Wymark tried to grab her again. This time she'd learned her lesson and had a blanket wrapped around her hands.

Mabel bit down with her lovely large fangs.

'Take that!' What the other people in the room and Gabriel heard was 'Praowwwwhiss'.

"Argh...!" Wymark shook her fingers free of the cloth.

"It bit me!"

"We have to corner it. You go that side, I'll go this," said the man. Mabel did not recognise the voice at all.

They walked slowly towards Mabel, forcing her into a corner of the room.

She dashed between their legs.

'Ha!' she was too fast for them.

She jumped onto the bed and clawing her way up, leapt onto the fabric half-tester. The feature was none too stable and her weight made the old and flimsy material dip. Slowly it folded and tore.

"YEEoowl!" Mabel was tipped onto the bed and folded into the fabric.

"Get it... get it...!" shouted Wymark.

"What with?"

"Kill it... quickly."

The man took out his knife and made for Mabel wrapped up in the material on the bed.

He stabbed down twice.

The cat lay still.

*****

"No!" cried Gabriel from his hiding place behind the little door in the next room. No one heard him, for there was too much superfluous noise. He peeked through a gap in the hanging. Should he go to Mabel's rescue now or just flee because she was surely dead? Wasn't she?

He took a heartbeat to decide and just as he was about to move from the protection of the hanging, his knife in his hand, he heard Wymark yelp.

"Nooooo! It's a mouse!"

The mouse in question had jumped from the bed and was now running for the wall behind the pot board.

'Good old Mabel.'

"Argh! A mouse," the woman screamed.

"Pull yourself together woman. It's only a mouse," said the man.

"I... I... hate mice. They frighten me!" Wymark had clambered up on the bed and was clinging for dear life to the upright post.

The man was searching the bed for a dead or dying cat.

"Where the Hell has it gone?"

"What?"

The man picked up the blanket and shook it. He lifted it to the light and saw the two holes in it made by his knife blade. But no blood.

"It can't have escaped."

"Nooo.... Get that mouse... get it... Please!"

"Come on down, Wymark. Don't be foolish. It can't hurt you. Not like the ruddy cat."

The woman sucked her injured fingers.

"I... I'm afraid of mice."

"Now that is just plain foolish."

"I know but..."

"You are never more than a few feet away from a mouse. Anywhere"

"I know but still."

"The cat was probably in here chasing the mouse."

The woman was helped down from the bed. "Probably. But..."

Wymark sat on the edge and sniffled.

"Better?"

"Yes. As long as you think the mouse has gone."

"Look, the mouse has probably gone into the wall. It's miles away by now." The man searched the room with practised eyes.

"It's that damned cat I can't understand."

Wymark was shaking. "It's a shapeshifter, that's what!"

The man roared with laughter, "A what?"

"A shapeshifter. You hear about it, don't you?"

"It's a children's story."

"No... no... I'm sure they exist. Someone I know had a scar from a man who changed into a wolf and attacked him."

"Wymark that is nonsense." But he sounded just a little worried.

"No... it's true. They can change into whatever they want."

"A wolf?"

"Or a cat or a mouse."

"That is the most ridiculous thing I have heard."

'Yes,' said Gabriel to himself as he tried to get a good look at the man but, sadly he had his back to him and the light was poor. 'I would probably have said that once.' He fingered the scar on his cheek.

He backed off and looked at the little room in which he stood. How to get out? There were no windows and the door was locked. No sign of a key.

Mabel had vanished to the other side of the large room belonging to Wymark. Was she going to be able to find her way to him, as a mouse and let him out?

His brain was jumbled. He sat down on a stool to think.

Fishing in his purse, he brought out the tinder and strike-a-light he'd brought with him to light a candle.

There was nothing for it.

He struck and fed the resultant tiny spark to the tinder. Then he laid it onto the floor by the door to Wymark's room hoping that the draught would fan it. He fed it more fuel—an end of a blanket he'd found on the floor. He blew on it gently. The flame lifted up and licked the bottom of the wall hanging.

There was a restrained hum from the next room. Wymark and her lover were crooning to each other.

Give it a bit longer and they were bound to notice the smoke as it wound its tendrils up and through the doorhole in the wall.

Gabriel picked up the blanket and threw it onto the bed. It needed something more to get hold of. This room was not as well appointed as the one in which Wymark lived.

Whoosh! The bedclothes went up as if they had been made of

straw. Well, the pillow was made of straw. Smoke was now everywhere; more smoke than flame and as Gabriel searched for a place to hide, he brought his cotte up over his mouth and nose. The last thing he wanted to do was cough and betray himself.

He held his breath.

Hadn't they noticed the smoke yet? Were they so engrossed in each other that they would allow the fire to consume them?

"Do you smell smoke?" It was the man's voice.

She sniffed. "It will be Hugo cooking his evening meal."

"No... this is... like... burning."

"Maybe he's burning his evening meal," Wymark giggled.

"Where's it coming from?"

"How do I know?"

The man was now up and using his nose to locate the source of the smell. He pulled back the hanging and a gout of flame licked out at him.

"Jesus' wounds!"

"What?"

"Fire!"

Wymark leapt up from the bed. "Where?"

"The room next to this one."

In the time it takes to spit, Wymark was out of her door and sorting the jumbled keys she kept on a large ring; she unlocked the door to the small room.

"Ah no!"

"Fire!" shouted the man running into the space and taking up a blanket, he began to beat the bed with it.

At this time of night the inn was more populous. People came out of rooms in various states of undress.

"Fire!"

Wymark ran down the corridor calling, in search of Hugo.

As everyone was panicking or helping to put out the fire, Gabriel made his escape through the small door, jumping over the flames at the base of the door and pulling down the hanging. One look behind him and he was out and running for the exit.

'Oh God Mabel! I hope you've managed to get out,' he said to himself.

*****

Twenty two yards, two feet and two inches away, Mabel, was running for all she was worth on her little mouse legs. She had no idea where she was. She was sure she'd already been round in circles in this room.

She stopped to listen, and heard the call of 'fire' behind her.

Her mouse whiskers twitched as she caught the whiff of smoke behind and the smell of fresh air before her.

Fresh air meant a window or an open door.

She scurried at the base of the wall and turned a corner. A man was just coming in to the front door and he shut it fast. Hugo. But there in front of her was a stone based platform to a wall. If the construction of her own house was anything to go by, this would lead her to the outside. She searched for a hole and found one. Wriggling her way in, she found a passage through the ill-fitting stones and was quickly outside.

Now to locate Gabriel.

*****

He came racing out of the front door a little while later.

Mabel had turned herself into a pigeon and was circling the inn. Oh how she would have liked to have been a swallow but sadly, they were all gone from the locality now. Gone wherever it was they went for winter.

Gabriel stopped, looked round and then fled into the trees of the forest where he'd left Bertran.

He called as he ran, "Mabel!"

A wood pigeon came streaming down from the tiled roof of the Inn. "Hoo, hooo, hoo. Hoohoo."

"Mabel?"

She ducked over him and almost landed on his head, rising up again and making off in the direction of home.

"Then let's go."

They'd put almost a mile between the inn and themselves before they stopped.

Gabriel dismounted and sat with his back to a tree. "Whew!"

A pigeon landed close by and waddled closer. "Mabel?"

"Of course it's Mabel."

She turned deosil and dropped to the grass by him, then she too leaned herself on the trunk of the tree.

"That... was..."

"Too close," said Mabel.

He turned his head. She looked grey and incredibly tired.

"Come on, get up on Bertran. You can't do any more. You're completely exhausted. We'll talk when we get home."

Mabel accepted the lift up onto the horse's back. Gabriel launched himself behind her and she snuggled into him.

"Well at least we know what's going on now. And we know where the money is."

"Umm."

"But we still don't have any actual evidence of their wrongdoing."

"Umm."

"No confession. And we don't know who the man is."

"No."

"It's not that Bux fellow is it?"

"Dunno."

"We thought it was him but now... I'm not so sure."

"No."

"I wish we could have got a glimpse of his face."

"Too dark and…"

"Too much going on."

There was a little silence as Bertran trotted on.

Gabriel took a firmer hold of Mabel.

"I was so worried when… when the man…tried to stab you on the bed."

Silence.

"Oh Mabel I thought he'd got you."

Silence.

"I didn't know what to do."

Silence

"My heart was in my mouth when he…" Gabriel swallowed. "When he took the knife to you. I really thought he'd got you," he repeated. "God, I was scared."

Silence.

"Oh Mabel! I do care for you. I couldn't have anything happen to you."

Silence.

"You must have been the mouse, I suppose?"

Still there was no answer.

He looked down.

Mabel was fast asleep, her cheek squashed against his breast.

He squeezed her lovingly and hurried Bertran into a quicker step.

CHAPTER NINE

~ MAGPIES AND JACKDAWS ~

"**S**he knows who you are and she can find out where you are now," said Mabel the next day when they got together over the opening of the hen house.

The geese ran out first.

"Brownwenge, come on... I don't have all day!" The hen rushed out clucking angrily and flicking her tail feathers.

Mabel pulled back the door to the hen house and peered in.

"Elesia...? Shoo, shoo."

Elesia made a strained clucking sound and Mabel bent double to peer into the small building.

"Ah... you're broody, eh? Alright. I'll leave you."

She ruffled the white head of her brown and white hen. Anyone would think that she was able to speak chicken!

"Gabriel, are you listening to me?"

"What...? Ah... yes..."

"She knows where you are. She must know that you and I are... friends... Those who wanted to get rid of me must surely know now that you and I are investigating them."

Gabriel had been leaning on the hen house gate staring into space.

"We need to find out who this mystery man is," he said.

"That would be good, but save following every man of thirty-something in the town, I fail to see how we can do that," said Mabel. "We can only hope that the man, whoever he is, did not see you or know you exist. If he does, then you are in as much danger as I am."

"How can he know?" Gabriel straightened up. "He couldn't see me. I didn't see him. He didn't even know I was there."

"Let's hope that Wymark Honfleur still wishes to keep your presence in her room a secret."

"You saw her. She seemed frightened of him. She got rid of me as quickly as a ferret runs down a hole."

"He's obviously a jealous lover."

Mabel came out from the hen enclosure, leaving the gate open so her hens could peck around her garth. "I need to get back into that inn and see what I can find. If the man visits, follow him and find out who he is."

"You can't go on your own," said Gabriel, his hands on his hips.

"Oh? And what use can you be? No one will know that I'm even there. You can't go back, Honfleur will recognise you and she won't be happy that you set fire to her building, I can tell you. She's already suspicious of you."

Gabriel squirmed. "I can't let you go alone."

"You would be more usefully employed going into town and speaking to the town reeve."

"Oh?"

"To let him know about the brothels. He needs to shut them down. Or make them pay. Or something. And recover the money and anything that's been stolen."

Gabriel felt annoyed. "And how am I to explain to Master Barbflet that I know all this about the brothels without arousing the suspicion that I have been there. He's going to think I've been a patron!"

"And that's terrible, is it?"

"I can't say what we were actually doing or how we found out what we did. That would land you right in the mud!"

"Harumph."

"There's no point in following the woman, I suppose? She might lead us to the mystery man."

Mabel picked up a few eggs and put them into her kirtle. "Master Barbflet's men failed to find Scarepath and couldn't connect the woman Honfleur to him once he'd been punished and had gone into Savernake. Every time she went into the forest, they lost her. You think you'll do any better?"

Gabriel sighed. "Well I know where she is now, don't I?"

Mabel gave him a look which said, 'Don't you dare.'

"I'm going to the manor to write to Lord Stokke. I'm overdue with a report for him."

"I'm going off to think, " said Mabel."

*****

Mabel did not go off to think. She had done her thinking.

She turned three times withershynnes and said, "I wish to be a magpie."

She grew a very long feathered tail which upon first sight seemed black. A closer examination would have revealed it to be a lovely glossy dark green. She grew wings which were iridescent blue tinged with purple. No, magpies were not simply black and white birds.

Her eyes filled out, dark and piercing, and her beak grew sharp and dangerous.

Mabel flew up into her oak tree and cackled like an old crone ending with a rattle which sounded like someone was rolling pebbles in a box.

Everyone knew the 'maggotty-pie' but no one wanted to particularly engage with it. It was a bird of ill omen. It was known by everyone that you had to salute a single magpie if you saw one, or something bad would happen to you. Therefore people would give Mabel-magpie a wide berth. And if you could not, you had to be very, very nice to a magpie. Folk wouldn't risk being horrible.

Just to illustrate this, Little Johnny Chatterwell was passing close to Mabel's house when she swooped down to rise again over her perimeter wattle fence.

"Hello Master Magpie. How is Mistress Magpie and all the little magpies?" he called out as he ran along. Mabel noticed he'd now got a pair of shoes, but they were really far too big for him.

Mabel rose up over Barr Field Coppice and on over Faggotty Copse. A few deep flaps of her wings allowed her to glide serenely for quite a way until it was time to flap the beautiful shimmering wings again.

It wasn't long before she'd reached the edge of the forest and dipped down to look at the town.

She landed on the roof of the house on St. Martin's Lane. Magpies are one of the few birds that can both walk and hop and Mabel walked and hopped on strong feet along the ridge of the house. Just to reassure everyone she was actually a magpie, Mabel dragged a few pieces of moss from the roof as if looking for food and spat it out.

Her keen eyes roved all over the lane and the properties around and about. The pesky dog which she'd encountered last time was nowhere to be seen.

Time to move indoors.

Mabel hopped and flapped down to the ground.

Looking round carefully she flew up into the window on the first floor—the scribe's room.

The room was just as it had been when she'd last been there. The inkpot and pen were sitting on the sloping wooden desk. Mabel pulled out the quill with her strong beak. No ink in the pot.

The parchments which they'd noticed before were in exactly the same place. None had been moved. There were no new ones. Nothing had been added or taken away. And they were all dated quite a while ago. Everything was covered in dust.

Mabel flew up and pulled at the black gown hanging on the peg behind the door.

No one had worn this for a while, for a puff of dust came off it as she tugged at it and it was obviously rather moth eaten.

The bed was tidily made and didn't look as if it had ever been slept in. There were no personal possessions, no further clothes. Most men that Mabel had known had at least some toiletry items for keeping the beard or tonsure tidy. This scribe had nothing. The man who inhabited this room had no pack. It was odd, but Mabel couldn't see at that moment why it was odd.

What was the man's name? Scrivens that was it.

He worked at the castle.

Mabel went off to find him.

*****

She landed on one of the crenellations of the castle walls and took a good look round. She'd never been here before. My! How busy it was. People coming and going. Carts leaving and entering. Folk scurrying from one part of the building to another. Soldiers patrolling the walls; deliveries going into the kitchens. The smoke from dozens of fires hung like a fog over the buildings.

Mabel managed to identify the kitchen with its large louvre above the huge fires which cooked food for the dozens of people who worked and lived here. She saw the chapel with its coloured glass windows and the King's Hall close by, also with large glazed windows.

She hopped along the wall. Where did the scribes who recorded the daily life of the castle and town ply their trade? She needed to have a closer look.

She found the royal mint where coins were made and managed to follow the moneyer with his two guards as he deposited some of his daily manufacture of silver pennies in the strong room. Here was a scribe who noted down the amount on a large page. He was a young man of a mere twenty summers and somehow Mabel did not think that this was Scrivens.

She hopped from window ledge to window ledge following the man as he made his way back to the office where the records were kept. Mabel didn't realise that would be in the castle keep.

Eventually the man puffed up the steep steps and ducked into the white painted edifice. One more internal stone staircase and he came out in a room full of scribes.

Mabel followed carefully, half flying half hopping up behind him; luckily no one else was around on the stairs and there was no one to wonder what a magpie was doing in the castle keep.

Mabel ducked into the stone surround of a window and peeped around the corner.

"Ah John, you're back."

The young scribe threw down his parchment, and dropped his bag to a desk. "All recorded and entered. My! Master Striker's been busy today. He's taken just a third home with him."

A man came up to him. "Good. We need to have you record the wages today, John. Get moving."

"Yes, sir."

Was this master Scrivens? He seemed a man with authority and presence, just as Mabel had imagined him in her head. The main man here.

He took up a large ledger type book, tucked it under his arm and wandered to the back of the room.

"Ashelford."

"Yessir."

"Your next task."

"Yessir."

He dropped the book on the man's desk with a thud and a puff of dust. The man Ashelford settled his inkwell straight again and mopped the spill of ink.

The older man once again took a turn of the room with an eagle eye for the work being carried out by the scribes. He looked over the shoulder of a nervous man who was writing in a mixture of black and red inks.

The scribe master screwed up his eyes. "Oh... oh..." He leaned over and his expression became one of disgust.

"For Heaven's sake, Scrivens. How many more mistakes are you going to make? Start again on that line!" He cuffed the man over the top of his head. "Don't you know that the King likes his spelling to be uniform? Here we do not spell expedite, expediate."

Mabel Magpie blinked. So the older man was not Master Scrivens.

"Yes, Master Stoneford." The man Scrivens ducked his head and reached for his pumice.

"Concentrate man or we'll have to flog it into you."

"Yes, Master Stoneford." Scrivens wriggled his bottom upon his wooden seat. "I'm sorry."

"You're always sorry."

The master of the scribes moved on. "I am just stepping out for a moment. There is no need for any of you to take this as an opportunity to shirk your duties. Carry on as normal."

Mabel watched him disappear behind a hanging woven cloth. His footsteps receded down the corridor.

One man with profuse dark hair looked up and grinned. "Honestly Scrivens, you are the most unholy idiot."

Scrivens carried on with his head down.

Suddenly there was a sharp 'thonk' and a piece of pumice bounced from the forehead of the unfortunate scribe.

"Knobhead Scrivens!" yelled another scribe. "If you make him cross, we'll beat your non-existent brain out through your ear!"

"He's already cross," said a blond headed scribe from the back row of the desks. "His girlfriend dumped him last night."

"Aw, that right?"

"He won't be getting his oats then," said another. 'You know what that means?"

They all laughed.

"Yeah!" said John, the only one here referred to by his first name, "he'll need to get them somewhere else."

"What... the brothel?"

Mabel's ears fluffed up. She stepped closer. Aha! Was she about to learn something?

"Nah... you remember last time?"

"Ah... you mean meek and mild Martin?"

"The very same."

They laughed again. "He couldn't sit down for a week."

"Aw... and who do we have here that's meek and mild ?" asked Ashelford. "I'd watch it, Scrivens, he'll have you ... he will. Watch yer arse!"

The man called Scrivens shivered but kept his head down.

One more missile was launched his way, this time a piece of charcoal and it hit his cheek making a small back mark.

Mabel hopped into the middle of the stone shelf which acted as a sill for the window.

"CARK!"

"Jesus' Bones!" shouted the dark haired scribe, jumping from his desk.

"CARK!" Mabel yelled louder and fixed them all with a nasty eye.

"Get it out before it shits on the work."

"You do it. You know how bad it is to interfere with a magpie."

Suddenly Scrivens jumped up from his bench, and waving his arms he leapt in front of Mabel. She rose up and flew outside the window landing on a drip ledge above.

Scrivens yelled up at her, "Be gone, you devil!"

Ashelford muttered, "Hello Master Magpie. How are you today?"

Scrivens turned and gave him a wicked stare. "It's a bird... that's all."

"Best wishes to you and your family," said John, climbing back onto his seat.

Mabel heard Scrivens mutter under his breath. "You idiots!"

*****

Mabel came back into the scriptorium just as Master Stoneford returned. All was silent except for the scratching of pen on parchment.

Mabel scrutinised the hunched figure of Master Scrivens. He was a smooth faced man of about thirty something with thin mousy hair combed over a balding pate. His eyes were a pale blue, a very pale blue and this made it difficult to see where they were focussed.

Now though, his eyes were definitely focussed on his work but Mabel got the impression that every so often he gave a surreptitious glance at his boss and co-scribes. It was obvious he felt unsure.

She was just about to move off when the master scribe said, "That's it for the while. Go and get dinner. Be back here by the time I ring the bell. Or else." There was a large bell sitting on his table.

The scribes shuffled out and Mabel heard them dashing down the stairs.

All except Master Scrivens. He was a little tardy wiping his pen nib and cleaning his fingers.

"Scrivens... don't you want to eat?"

"I do Master Stoneford... but..."

"Then go..."

Scrivens got up and arranged his black gown around him, pulled down his belt and reached for his scrip. He was just about to follow his fellow scribes when Stoneford stepped in front of him.

"You're an annoying little prick, Scrivens, do you know that?"

"I probably am, sir."

"I'm warning you... one more foot put wrong and..."

"Sir, I am sorry..." Scrivens half bowed as if he was trying to make himself small. "I will try to be..."

"Pah! Try? I don't think you have it in you to try..."

"Please, sir."

Stoneford came within an inch of Scrivens' face and whispered to him. "I can make your life very difficult, Scrivens. Very difficult."

"I'm sure you can, sir."

The pale blue eyes shifted their gaze at once and Mabel suddenly saw an absolute loathing in them.

But Scrivens did nothing. He did not retaliate.

"Look at me, you apology for a man."

Scrivens dragged his eyes back to the man an inch away.

"You know what they say about me, don't you?"

"Oh... I'm sure it's just gossip and nasty rumour..." Scrivens' expression was one of horror but there was something else which Mabel wasn't able to fathom.

"It's all true."

"No, sir. Surely..."

Out of the blue, a hand came up and Stoneford slapped his scribe across the face hard. Scrivens staggered back.

Mabel saw the look of absolute loathing on Scrivens' face escalate to murderous hatred, an indescribable anger and then it was gone, to be replaced by a look of fear and panic.

The man then doubled up and cowered with his arms over his head.

"You are despicable, do you know that? You have no backbone. No... nothing. You are a non-man..." The master raised his fist and threatened Scrivens again but this time made no contact. The scribe flinched and backed into a corner.

"No... I..."

Mabel had seen enough. She flew into the room and attacked the master, flying over and over at him with outstretched claws. He fell to his knees and crawled on all fours under a table. Who was the coward now?

Mabel laughed but all the two men in the room heard was, 'cackle cackle cackle', over and over.

Scrivens made for the door and disappeared.

Mabel then escaped out of the window with a loud 'Kwark!'

Feeling pleased with herself, she flew across the bailey of the castle and out to the forest trees before she turned three times deosil and became Mabel Wetherspring again.

"Haha. That'll teach him! Foul man."

She sat down with her back to a tree and stared up at the scudding clouds.

What had she learned?"

It didn't seem as if the scribe used the room he paid for at Mistress Honfleur's. If he did, he made no impression on it whatsoever. But there was one thing she'd definitely learned. Master Scrivens could not be Mistress Honfleur's lover. He was far too weak and cowardly. He was not the man they'd seen in that room the night that Gabriel had set fire to the bed. His voice was not one of confidence like the man they'd heard.

So who was he?

Aw no... she might have been right when he said that they'd have to interview every man over the age of thirty in Marlborough. It was an impossible task.

A little later a fast pigeon flew rapidly over the forest trees towards Bedwyn and landed in the old oak tree in Mabel's garden.

*****

"Where have you been?"

"Gathering information!"

"Mabel, I told you, you weren't to go on your own. You didn't tell me that... you..."

She gave him an 'I'm disappointed in you,' stare.

"You lied to me."

"No. I... I... Just avoided a complete explanation."

"What?"

"Because I knew you'd be... upset if I went on my own."

"I am upset... yes. I am really upset."

"There you are, you see."

"I told you not to go on your own..."

"That's why I don't tell you because you're too... too dominating."

"What?"

"I can manage on my own. I don't need you."

"So... shall I just leave then? I'm obviously no use to you."

Mabel looked a bit nonplussed. "If that's what you want to do."

"I definitely have no wish to control you."

"Well that's good to know."

"I... erm..."

Mabel rounded on him. "Gabriel. You are not my lord. No man owns me. This means that I do not follow orders like some footsoldier you might like to boss about!"

"It's dangerous."

"I'll be the judge of that."

"If they realise that you are spying on them..."

"And how are they going to do that?"

"They nearly had you last time."

"But they didn't!"

"I care about you, that's all."

They were face to face in Mabel's cottage, inches apart and both were angry. The stares they were giving each other would have frozen stone.

But suddenly Gabriel leant forward and kissed her on the lips.

She stood, her arms to her side and let him and then, "Do you want to know what I found out or not?" she asked as she pushed past him to poke the fire.

He came to the other side and sat on a stool. "And that is...?"

The man who rents the room from Mistress Honfleur at the house on St. Martin's does not live there... I think...There's no evidence of anyone using the room at all."

"So why rent it?"

"I don't know. He's a lowly scribe at the castle. I've seen him at his place of work."

"You went to the castle?" Gabriel stood up so quickly his sword slapped on his thigh.

"That is where he works. And I saw him. He didn't know I had

by his workmates. He's not wyn...

Gabriel reseated himself. "Is it that objection... fellow, Savary?"

Mabel thought for a moment. "If he's playing a game and he has no intention of moving out, yes it might be him. But somehow I got the impression from what you told me that he really meant what he said. That he felt that his reputation was being damaged by living in the house formerly owned by a felon."

"Oh, there's no doubt he values his reputation very highly. He's the worst kind of King's man. A castle worker who, just because he does work at the castle, thinks he's someone special."

"Do we know what he does?"

"No..." Gabriel furrowed his brow. "We never got the chance to find out."

"Then perhaps we should go and find out."

It was not lost upon Gabriel that she'd said, 'we.'

"If we go... what will you be this time?"

"I was a magpie when I was spying on Scrivens. I suppose a jackdaw might be a good idea. There are quite a few at the castle. No one is going to notice one more."

*****

Mabel soared over the castle bailey and came to rest on the apex of the roof of the King's house. She saw Gabriel at the gate making inquiries about Master Savary and she watched as a tubby guard gesticulated over to the corner of the castle wall to the north.

She flew directly there and landed on the roof tiles.

Gabriel, leaving his horse tied to a post at the gate, sauntered over the bailey, negotiating unloading carters and the soldiers doing pike drill in the dusty square of the middle.

"Master Savary?"

"Who wants me?"

Today the man was dressed in yellow and was wearing the flashy belt which Gabriel had seen on their last acquaintance.

"Sir Gabriel Warrener of the mesnie of the Lord Stokke."

"Ah yes... I remember you."

The man looked down his long nose at Gabriel and Gabriel tried to get a good look at him. Was this the voice he heard that night at the house on Turnabout Lane? Everything had been muffled by the painted hanging lying before the door between them. He couldn't be sure. He'd try to get a look at him from the back to see if he could identify him.

"What do you want? I'm very busy." The man had a parchment in his hand and was, it seemed, ticking off entries on it.

"Yes, I know you are an important man here and I'm sorry to interrupt your duties."

Gabriel looked up. A jaunty jackdaw had worked its way down the roof. Perhaps Mabel might be able to recognise him.

Gabriel drew the man out of the building which seemed to be a sort of office attached to the stables.

"You are marshal here, are you not?"

"I am. I am responsible for all the horses, rounceys, pack ponies and mules." The man puffed out his chest, "Their feed, their quarters, their care in general..." He was obviously very proud of his role.

"That is a very responsible job and a role of authority. I can see why you decided you could no longer stay in the house of the felon, Scarepath or his doxy."

The man looked into the distance and screwed up his eyes, as if he was imagining the house with the triple gable on St Martin's Lane.

"It was a comfortable place with a reasonable rent but I am settled elsewhere now."

"Oh... where have you managed to find lodgings? I'd be interested only, I need somewhere for my servant."

"Longstretch Lane. Halfway up. But the rooms are all taken now."

"Ah... shame."

"If there is nothing important you need to ask, I must get the feed in for the night."

"Ah... I was just wondering..."

"Yes?"

"If you might be able to tell me anything about the woman who owns the house you lived in."

"You asked me before."

"I know but I felt that you were reluctant to speak about her when you lived under her roof. Perhaps now...?"

A terrible kerfuffle started up above them. Both men looked up.

Four jackdaws had appeared on the apex of the stable building and were clacking a nasal 'ark, arkark.'

They hopped down the roof to the edge.

Master Savary gave them hardly another glance.

"Only that she was a loud woman with the morals of an alley cat. She tried to proposition me the second night I lived there... disgusting!"

"Loud? Immoral?"

"Foul mouthed when roused. I hear that Scarepath and she were well matched. They argued a lot."

Gabriel saw the jackdaw at the edge of the roof move closer to him as if for safety. Or maybe to listen in. "Is that so?"

"Not that I ever met him, of course. But I could hear. We all could."

"No, of course."

The four jackdaws were now flapping their wings and making for Mabel on the thatch above Gabriel and Savary. "Nuhnuhnuhnuh" they yelled with a nasal tone to the cry.

Savary began to walk back into the stable.

"Master Savary, can you believe that Mistress Honfleur would kill her lover Scarepath?"

He walked back out into the light. "My dear young man, that is precisely why I couldn't stay another moment in that house."

"Oh?"

"Anyone who crosses her seems to end up... damaged... or dead. I was not taking that risk."

"Oh!" said Gabriel, quite nonplussed.

The jackdaws rolled over Mabel like a wave and she gave a terrible squawk.

Four onto one.

Gabriel tried to scare them off by shouting and shaking his arms at them but they were determined to do harm.

Mabel fell off the roof in a flutter of black feathers and the four followed, rolling over her pinning her to the ground and pecking for all they were worth.

The noise was ear splitting.

Mabel was right, no one did notice one more jackdaw... except the resident jackdaws!

"Off, off!" shouted Gabriel as he made for the squirming black pile.

The four eventually flew up and after a couple of passes where they thought to return, they drew off up to the keep roof. One of them stayed on the stable roof ridge to keep watch.

"Mabel," said Gabriel with concern. He picked up the jackdaw from the earth. Folk were looking at him strangely, including Master Savary. He stared haughtily back, popped the jackdaw into the neck of his cotte and made off back to his horse, his nose in the air.

CHAPTER TEN ~ THE CASTLE

Out of the town and a little way into the trees, Gabriel halted Bertran and with a thumping heart he reached gently into the front of his shirt.

With a kindly grip he closed his hands around the little body and fetched it out. The jackdaw's head fell back loosely and he cradled it rubbing the black feathered breast with his thumb.

It was still breathing and he tried to wake it by calling softly to it.

"Oh, Mabel. I told you it was dangerous. Now look at you. You can manage on your own, eh?"

Its beak opened once or twice as if it was taking in more air.

He reached for his flask of water always hanging at his saddle and poured a little amount into its mouth.

The bird snuffled and shook its head and the white eye snapped open. He felt the muscle tone come back into the limp body.

"Oh Mabel... thank Heavens." He began to look her over for damage. It squawked and wriggled in his grip.

"Alright, I'll put you down on the grass."

He tried to set it down on its claws but it fell dizzily to its side.

"Oh please tell me they haven't done any permanent damage."

"Nyaaaa!"

At last the jackdaw managed a wavering stand and kneeling in front of it, he steadied its body carefully.

"Can you manage on your own?"

"Kwaaark."

"You'll need to be more steady to turn deosil."

The bird shook its head as if it was a dog fallen into a pool, trying to rid its hair of water.

"Look, I'll carry you home in my saddlebag…"

"Kwark!"

"I'll leave the flap open. You've no need to be contained."

"Kwark!"

He reached for it and it pecked his hand.

"Mabel, don't be so foolish."

Suddenly he was aware of someone behind him.

"Well that's gratitude for you," said a voice.

"Mabel!"

She stepped forward from a grassy bank.

"I think in the tangle of bodies, you picked up the wrong jackdaw," she laughed.

"Oh, Mabel!"

She leaned over the little bird. "I think I did this one damage… poor thing, but it was really going for me. I had to fight back."

"Do you think it will be alright?"

"I expect it's just stunned. It will be able to fly away to its friends in a while."

Gabriel sat back on his haunches. "I was really worried."

"I have told you many times, I can take care of myself."

"Well this time…" he pointed to some scratches on her hands and a round gouge on her neck. "This time you have sustained damage. We need to get you home and bathe those wounds."

Mabel rubbed a sore patch on her head. "I think I've lost a patch or two of hair too."

They both looked down at the jackdaw now sitting upright staring at them both.

"Let's see if he'll go."

"He?" asked Gabriel.

"Oh yes… this is a he," she chuckled. "Believe me, I know."

"I wouldn't dream of arguing with you."

"Well, that'd be a first."

Then she smiled sweetly and picked up the bird. "Come on Jack, let's see if you can fly."

She lifted him up and threw him into the air. At first he dipped but then found his wings and was off into the trees like an arrow from a bow.

"That's that, then."

"I am so glad you're alright."

"Thank you for intervening. I was losing when you frightened them off and picked up Jack there."

He couldn't believe she'd just admitted she'd needed him.

"Why did they go for you so nastily?"

"Territory. I was a lone jackdaw with no friends or family…"

"They recognised that?"

"Oh yes. They are very, very bright birds. They know all their family and where they patrol. That roof obviously belonged to one clattering of daws."

"A what?"

"That's what they're called, a number of jackdaws is a clattering."

"Well, I never," said Gabriel chuckling. "A clattering! Just what they sound like."

He gave Mabel a hitch up to his saddle.

"I don't suppose you'll try a jackdaw again now you know they are so… aggressive."

"Oh, I might. But I'll keep my wits about me next time."

Gabriel sighed and they clopped gently home to Bedwyn.

*****

On the way Gabriel turned over a picture of the face of Master Savary in his memory. Was this the man in that room at Turnabout Lane?

"Mabel, did you get a good look at Master Savary?"

"The man you were talking to?"

"Yes. He's marshal at the castle."

"No, not really. That's a job which requires him to spend a lot of time at his place of work, isn't it?"

"Yes, it is, I know."

"I doubt he has time to indulge in love affairs with dubious women."

"He's too stuffy, anyway."

Mabel thought hard as they swayed along with Bertran's easy gait. "Nah... it's not him is it?"

"No. I doubt it."

"So out of the three men who live or lived at the house with the triple gable, none of them could have been Wymark's accomplice."

"Do you really think she could have murdered Scarepath and Sweetcheeks herself?" asked Gabriel, picturing Wymark as a vengeful harpy of a woman with an evil grin wielding a knife to cut the throat of a seasoned villain.

"She's scared of mice, for Heaven's sake!" said Mabel with a laugh.

"Does that mean she couldn't do it?"

"Oooh..." said Mabel, in frustration, "I don't know!"

"Where do we go next for Heaven's sake?"

"I don't know. I have to think."

Gabriel scoffed. "Last time you said you'd think... you didn't think at all and went off by yourself. Does this mean that you'll lie to me again about where you're going and fly off on your own once more?"

"I need a rest," she said, snuggling into him, as much as she could snuggle into a hard, spiky coat of maille, and didn't answer his question.

*****

Mabel woke the next day to the sound of her chickens clucking and screeching. In haste she threw off the bedclothes and thrust her arms into a clean shift.

Unbolting the door, she pushed her feet into her shoes and without tying them, made off down the path at a shuffle.

"I thought I'd let them out. They were making such a rumpus," said Gabriel.

"Ah... yes, I'm late letting them out today," she yawned.

"You're shivering, go and get dressed properly," said Gabriel, casting an appreciative eye over her figure, visible through her thin linen shift which was shown up by the sun behind her. "It's nearly autumn, it's chilly."

She looked up, almost expecting to see the swallows which were usually diving over her garden. They had all gone. And the swifts. All she could see now were flocks of starlings and a flutter of sparrows. Very few birds were singing at this time of year.

She wrapped her arms around herself and slopped back to the cottage in her loose shoes.

Gabriel secured the gate of the henhouse, picked up the eggs and followed. By the time he entered the cottage, Mabel had dressed herself in her red kirtle and was buckling on her belt.

Gabriel folded his arms and grinned. "Ah. Is this the best kirtle? I hope it's in my honour?"

"It's Sunday. It's my church kirtle."

"Ah, yes."

"Help yourself to milk. It was fresh last evening."

Mabel pulled her bone comb through her ringlets and tied them up in a loose cloth which acted like a cap.

Gabriel came closer. "I've had a letter from Lord Stokke."

"Oh?"

"He asked me if I had any idea if the person who attacked you might do so again."

"Well, since we don't know exactly who that was…"

"Obviously I had to tell him we didn't know who it was, but that we could make some intelligent guesses…" said Gabriel.

"We can't really truthfully say, can we?"

Mabel came closer to him. An uncomfortable feeling was welling up under her breastbone. "Does this mean he wants you back at Rutishall?"

"If I can convince him we aren't close to solving the mystery or that you're still in danger…"

"If we do solve the mystery, he will want you back."

She sat down on the edge of her bed. "Part of me wants to know and part of me doesn't."

Oh, damn the fact that Gabriel was a soldier beholden to his lord, who owned many properties around Wiltshire and who visited them all in turn taking his household with him. If Gabriel had been a miller or a humble farmer or…

He was looking at her oddly.

"What are you thinking?"

"I was thinking that if you were not a soldier you would not have to go to be with Lord Robert. And things would be much less complicated."

Gabriel looked despondently down at the beaten earth floor. "And if you were not who you are… what you are… then you and I would never have met and you would have gone on to marry some farmer or poultry keeper or some… Oh I don't know… apothecary… somewhere."

"But perhaps I would not have loved them, Gabriel."

"No… you might not. And I would probably be saying yes to my father and marrying Avice de Gers, whom I do not love."

"But you would not have been scarred for life by a shape-shifting wolf and you would have been handsome to the end of your days."

He smiled with a slight shrug.

"It's all my fault," she said.

"It's not your fault. It was just... an unavoidable series of events," said Gabriel softly.

They looked at each other in the low light of the morning, filtering in through the door.

Mabel got up and opened the shutters; more light flooded in. Suddenly she thought of the escapade in the House on Turnabout Lane.

"I do wish we could have seen who Wymark's lover was. But the light was too poor at that house."

This made Gabriel think about the light and shade of the stable buildings and what Master Savary had told him the day before.

He sauntered to the door and looked up at the sky. "Looks like it might rain."

He turned back to her. "Savary told me that... and these were his own words... 'Anyone who crosses her seems to end up... damaged... or dead. I was not taking that risk.' "

Mabel suddenly stopped what she was doing. An egg went rolling over the table and she just managed to save it. "Other people have been hurt? Have others ended up dead?"

"Perhaps he was talking about Master Sweetcheeks?"

"How would he connect Sweetcheeks with the house in which he once lived?" asked Mabel.

"They didn't know each other, did they?"

"Not as far as I know."

"But Sweetcheeks did visit that girl in the attic."

"Hmm."

"This has to be a fatality in the town. Master Barbflet would know about that."

"We can hardly go to the town reeve, Gabriel, and ask him who has been murdered this past year or so. What excuse could we give?"

"And another thing. The only person connected with that house we haven't spoken to is Master Scrivens. What might he have to say?"

"Gabriel, you really think that man will speak to you about murder? He is frightened of his own shadow. He'd be terrified of a knight."

"Then he won't mind a girl speaking to him, will he? I'm sure you can be really gentle with him."

"It's Sunday today. He won't be at work."

"Then maybe we'll catch him at home."

But they did not find him at home in the house of three gables that Sunday. And they got caught in a really bad thunderstorm on the way back from Marlborough and were soaked. Gabriel had been right. It had looked like rain.

*****

Everything was fresh and clean after the rainstorm which lasted most of the day and returned at night to plague them with claps of thunder.

Gabriel tossed on his pallet in the hall of the manor and Mabel, also unable to sleep, walked about her house, wrapped in a blanket, thinking. Why hadn't Gabriel asked Master Savary what he'd meant about others ending up dead? She certainly would have done. She wouldn't have let that utterance go by without a probing.

Ah yes. He'd given up his questioning when Mabel had been attacked by the jackdaws. He was worried about her and had let Master Savary go.

Her fault again.

She needed to make amends.

As soon as it got light she'd go back to Marlborough, get into the castle and find Master Scrivens. Then she'd change into herself and see what the man had to say, if anything.

And then, she'd find Master Savary and ask him about what he knew.

It was a plan.

She felt a tiny bit sorry for not telling Gabriel where she was going, but he would only want to come and interfere and she was best at this sort of thing on her own.

Then she thought… 'Oh no… he will worry. I can't do that to him.'

So she took out her carefully rationed parchment, (a small piece she'd saved and scrubbed many times with pumice,) and charcoal and scribbled him a note.

By the time he found it and perhaps acted upon it, she would be at the castle and in possession of new information.

She needed to get into town quickly. Three turns to withershynnes and her nose lengthened and hardened. Her body shrank and grey feathers sprouted all over her. She lifted her arms and they'd become a powerfully muscled grey feathered flying apparatus. Patient as the transformation was taking place, she looked down at her feet; always the last part of her to change. They too were powerful, strong clawed, pink digits, three facing forwards and one backwards. She lifted off, jumping with them and soared up into her oak tree. Settling her feathers and making sure she was content with the transformation, she turned her pigeon beak towards the north and with one or two slapping flaps, she was briskly off over the village.

*****

Gabriel too had had a terrible night. His eyes felt like they were full of grit and his limbs ached. He slipped from his pallet and from a dream, no, a nightmare-filled sleep and stood to stretch, his sinews cracking with the effort of it.

He often dreamed if he did not sleep early in the night and they were seldom good dreams. He'd fallen asleep about the hour of matins, long into the night, when the thunder had eventually rolled away. Often, it was said, folk were awakened during this time with dreams God has given to them. God used dreams and visions to bring instruction and counsel to us as we sleep. But Gabriel could see no benefit or counsel in the dream he'd just had.

He rubbed his face.

He'd go and relate to Mabel what his dream had been, while he could still remember it. Maybe she'd have an explanation?

He passed her water trough, now filled to the brim with rainwater and washed his face. His fingers brushed over the scars on his cheek. They no longer hurt. That was thanks to Mabel.

He called out to her as he approached the door. Maybe she'd slept late again because she too had been up half the night with the thunder and torrential rain?

Ah no. She was up; the chickens were scratching about the yard and the geese were hissing at him from a safe distance.

He smiled. They made a great deal of noise but they were harmless really.

"Mabel! It's me. I have something to tell you."

There was no answering call, no noise from the interior of the house.

Gabriel pushed open the door.

As he did so a shaft of light fell on the central table and picked out a pale patch of something lying there.

A note.

"Gabriel. I have gone to the castle. I'll travel quickly as a pigeon and I'll be a cat, so don't worry. Back as soon as I have spoken to Masters Savary and Scrivens."

"Oh Mabel!" said Gabriel loudly. "Why do you do these things? She'll be way ahead of me." He also thought how awkward it might be if any of her neighbours were to have seen what she'd written until he remembered none of them could read.

He ran back to the stables and quickly got the groom to saddle Bertran.

Throwing himself into the saddle he rushed after her.

*****

Mabel cat was slinking along the roof of the stable block looking for a safe place to jump down and enter.

The castle was busy as usual. Bustling. There seemed to be soldiers everywhere and since Mabel had last visited, the stable was much busier with horses. It seemed as if there were more visitors than usual.

She'd seen where Master Savary had an office and, keeping to the edge of the building, she sidled into a doorway which she thought led to the place where he worked.

No one bothered her. She sat for a moment taking in her surroundings and pretending to wash her ears. Her green eyes missed nothing; the grooms with the entering and exiting horses, the heralds on their rounceys and the King's messengers dressed in green, who took the documents here and there across the land.

Master Savary was seated at a table rubbing his temples in a distracted way as if he had pain there.

"Ralph. You will just have to tell him that it will be a little late. There's nothing for it. The King is expected shortly. Surely he understands what difficulties that throws up for us?"

"Yessir."

A young man nodded and pushed past Mabel. She was in no hurry to change into herself. She wanted to watch this officious little man.

He scratched something onto a parchment, sanded it, folded it and sealed it.

"John!"

"Yessir."

The young man who Mabel had last seen in the scriptorium of the castle keep, came into view.

"This is for the Grange Barn immediately. We need more bedding."

"Yessir. I'll get Peter to take it."

"Good man."

Savary stood and bent his back rubbing the small of it with his knuckles.

147

'Ah,' thought Mabel. 'A man who spends most of his time seated and bending over. Poor posture.'

He closed his eyes and Mabel took the opportunity to spin deosil and become herself.

"Master Savary?"

The man spun round.

"Ah... yes... thank you for coming," he said, unperturbed.

"What?" Mabel was a little confused.

"I suppose that your father, Doctor James, is very busy. I'm not surprised. This royal visit has us all at sixes and sevens," he said.

"I think..."

"I'd heard that his daughter has been helping him out. It's very commendable of you, my dear. And helpful."

Well, this was a different side to Master Savary. He was almost human.

"Er... yes. His... erm...e yes aren't what they were and it's good I have the time and the knowledge to help." Mabel was thinking on her feet.

"Well that's good for me," he smiled.

"What can I do for you?" Mabel hoped that Master Savary's problem was an easy and not too embarrassing one.

"My neck. Too much looking down at my work. Have you a little something to relieve the tension and pain?"

"Oh yes indeed." It was a good thing Mabel had a firm grounding in herbs and healing. And it was fortunate that she had the small pot of unguent she used upon dear Gabriel's face, in her purse.

"I happen to have just the thing here."

"Well, I did tell your father about my problem, he must have prepared you."

"Oh yes, he... erm... did."

He moved further into the room where Mabel noticed there was a sort of bed with one side against the wall.

"I sometimes stay here of a night when things are busy as they are today. Might you manage to treat me here? It will save me time. I'd rather not come to the infirmary."

"Of course."

The man undid his belt, pulled off his yellow cotte and sat sideways on the bed.

Hesitantly Mabel pulled down the back of his shirt and began to massage his neck and shoulder.

He took in a sharp breath as she swiftly managed to find the knotted muscle.

"It was some storm we had last night wasn't it, sir?"

"Indeed it was," said Savary. "I didn't go home because it was so wet."

"My father tells me that you used to live in the house owned by that villain Scarepath."

"Yes, my dear, I did. But not for long. It was an experience I'll never forget though."

She kneaded the muscles in his shoulder and he almost purred with delight.

"Oh... you must have a few tales to tell, sir. He was such a terrible man, I hear."

"No more terrible than the woman he took up with and who..."

"Oh... do you think the gossip is correct and she killed him, then?"

The unguent was sliding nicely into his skin and she reached for another blob with her finger.

Master Savary was enjoying being the centre of attention of this nice young lady.

"Ooh... that's very good. My, you are very accomplished at this, aren't you?"

"I've had a lot of practice."

"She could certainly have done so. I can tell you, living there was a nightmare. People coming and going at all times and people going missing..."

"MISSING?" Mabel was a little too insistent and he gave her a strange look over his massaged shoulder.

"I mean, missing? Oh really?"

"Well there was a servant girl who disappeared into thin air. One of our scribes who lived there too. And Master Scriven's wife. That was a terrible thing I can tell you."

"The scribe who lives there?"

"Ah yes. Do you know him?"

"He comes to my father for an eyebright concoction for his eyes," lied Mabel.

"Ah yes, I expect that too is an occupational hazard. We are both martyrs to our jobs."

"Was she ever found?" asked Mabel but Master Savary was off telling her about his illnesses and how, as much as he loved his job and what an important job it was, his body was suffering because although he had a delicate constitution he was so dedicated to his role and pushed himself to the limit.

All she could do was listen and rub.

Then a female voice called from the light filled doorway.

"Master Savary, it's Isabel James."

"Damn!" thought Mabel. Quickly she ceased her rubbing, put her pot on the bed and backed into a dark corner.

"Master Savary called back. "Ah, how many daughters does dear Doctor James have?"

"Erm… can I come in, sir? My father sent me."

Savary pulled up his shirt and looked behind him in perturbation. There was no one there.

A tabby cat with a long grey and white striped tail, jumped up onto the table mewling and made for the open door.

"Well! Where did that come from?" said Master Savary in surprise.

*****

The cat sped along the wall by the moat. There were people

carrying supplies up into the keep and other people coming down with empty boxes and sacks. Mabel wound her way between their legs across the bridge and up the steps and entered the whitewashed keep.

Up the steps to the floor where the scribes plied their trade; she hopped from one window ledge to another until she was half way around the keep. She peered in the window.

There was no one there. The scribes' room was empty.

Damn...! She thought that they'd all be there busily scratching away and she might draw Master Scrivens out with some ruse or other.

Then from the inner corridor came the master of the scriptorium, the objectionable Master Stoneford. In his wake came Master Scrivens, towed along by his scapular.

Mabel froze and peered around the window embrasure.

The mild mouthed scribe looked round quickly to see if they were alone.

Stoneford rounded on him. "You... you think you can speak to me like that? I'll have you flogged," he said at a loud whisper.

"You're very brave aren't you when you think there's no one around to hear or stop you," whispered Scrivens.

"Stop me? I'd like to see them try!"

Suddenly Scrivens came very close to the master, pulling the stuff of his scapular from his fingers. Mabel was suddenly taken aback.

"You tell and I'll break you. Remember that." The whispering voice was sinister.

Stoneford faltered.

"You! You are frightened of your own farts, you..."

"That's what you think."

"I can call..."

"Call then. Everyone is busy. No one will hear you, Stoneford." The scribe's face was an inch from the master's and it was giving him a look of pure hatred.

Scrivens backed him up against a wall.

"From now on, you do as I say... is that understood? And you keep quiet."

"Why should I...?"

"Because if you don't... I'll kill you."

Mabel craned her neck. Beads of sweat now stood out on Master Stoneford's brow, she noticed.

His face suddenly wore a very scared expression. He tried to wriggle away.

"Can't we come to an arrangement?"

"No. We can't. You can't frighten me like you did Martin Johnson. Or blackmail me."

Stoneford had had enough and pushed his assailant away with a strong arm and then he ran for the corridor and towards the inner stairs. Scrivens ran after him.

Mabel cat followed.

Stoneford made it to the first step before Scrivens caught him and spun him around to face him.

"I won't. I won't stay silent," babbled the scribe master. "I won't be afraid of you."

Scrivens, with a look of complete disdain, gave a slight sigh.

"Ah that's a pity."

"Get your hands off me."

Scrivens dusted down the man's robe as if, where he'd held onto him, his hands had made a mess.

"Oh I'm so sorry, I'd no idea that I was crumpling your robe."

Stoneford was momentarily off guard. He let go of the wall, straightened his robe and jutted his chin.

Scrivens' hands left the clothes of the master scribe and in the next instant, with a deliberate two handed push and an horrendous gritted teeth grin, he propelled the master down the stone steps.

Master Stoneford fell from the top step with a surprised yell and tumbled head over heels. Mabel felt sure she heard a 'snap' sound. The body bounced from the stones of the steps and from the sides like a tossed rag.

Master Scrivens followed the falling body and kicked it down a few more steps until it lay at the bottom, broken and bloodied and in a very unnatural shape. There was no doubt to Mabel that the man was dead.

She made a small shocked 'prrrpp' sound as she followed Master Scrivens down five steps.

He looked up. She stopped dead. She looked down at him from a few steps from the top. Her green eyes narrowed.

The face. The face of the man she thought she knew, was instantly one of pure evil. He was no longer the mild and mouse-like man she'd seen before. He smiled nastily.

"Hello pussy," he said and pushed past her.

"Meeeoooow!" said Mabel

WITHERSHYNNES 2: CAT'S CRADLE

CHAPTER ELEVEN
~ MURDER IN THE CASTLE KEEP ~

Mabel was welded to the spot. What had she just seen?

Scrivens ran up the steps and back into the chamber where the scribes worked. It was obvious he was trying to make his escape at the other end of the corridor where there was a second staircase.

Pulling herself together she bounded up the steps behind him; she had to stop him from making his exit at another stairwell. Mabel felt sure she could head him off.

Leaping over the scribes' desks like a pursued hare she was suddenly at the second stairwell before him.

"What do you want?" he yelled "Get out of my way. You mangy..." He didn't have the chance to complete the insult as Mabel scratched him and hissed nastily.

He backed away and, with an oath, went the way he'd come. Mabel followed.

Staggering down the steps where Master Stoneford lay, Scrivens jumped over the body and bumped straight into Master Savary coming into the base of the keep and was steadied by his two hands reaching out to grab him and prevent him falling.

"Ah Scrivens. I was looking for a scribe to write a..."

Savary noticed the cat first and then the crumpled body of Master

Stoneford.

"What the...?"

"I was just coming for help," said Scrivens, his face once more reflecting the mild and timid man he'd pretended to be. "I found him just at this moment." He managed to seem terrified.

Mabel hissed again.

She rubbed herself against Master Savary's legs.

"Get off! Go on... get off!" Savary lifted his foot. "I can't stand cats!"

He kicked her in the side and Mabel went flying. Luckily she landed softly on the grassy bank of the keep and regained all four paws.

"Oh! Master Savary... what shall we do? It's poor Master Stoneford. I fear he's missed his step and fallen over that cat and come down the stairs," said Scrivens, pointing to Mabel. He was once more the subservient, fearful and lowly scribe.

How the man could change!

Mabel yowled.

"Get that cat away!" shouted Master Savary as he bent to see if Stoneford was still alive.

It was obvious he could not be, for no man could be alive and have a head so strangely dislocated from his neck.

"We need to find the captain of the guard. I think it's Master Andrew...Master Merriman today," said Savary. "He'll be at the gate I expect. Oh and the doctor."

"I'll go and find them." Scrivens ran off speedily down the steps of the mound of the keep and over the moat bridge.

Mabel yowled again. 'For goodness sake, he's a murderer; you just let him go... you idiot!" All Savary heard was 'Meeeeeooowpsssstgrrowlpssstmeeeeyowl!'

The marshal stood up and shouted at Mabel.

"Off, shoo... you aren't helping. Go away!"

He tried to get hold of Mabel bodily to move her but she was having none of it.

She spat and scratched and made contact with his hands.

"You vicious creature!"

Savary backed away and with a gigantic arc of his leg, he fetched Mabel a huge buffet to her underbody. His boot made contact and knocked the breath from her cat lungs.

She lifted into the air, and without even as much as a breathless screech, tumbled down the grassy bank of the keep and into the water of the moat.

*****

At that very moment Gabriel was racing across the centre of the bailey.

His eyes searched the buildings for a tabby cat; for Master Savary or for someone who he thought might be Master Scrivens.

His gaze was caught by a strange grey shape flying through the air up by the keep steps and by a scribe haring down those steps at breakneck speed.

"What... What's going on?"

The man was pink faced and out of breath. "I think Master Stoneford has tripped over a damned cat and has fallen down the stairs. I fear he's hurt."

"Hurt?"

"Master Savary is with him." He pointed up to the door partially visible through the arch of the bailey wall.

Gabriel looked up. He could see nothing. But he did hear the most almighty wailing cry accompanied by a lot of splashing.

People were looking at him strangely as he ran around trying to locate the noise. He bolted for the archway and turned left to the moat path under the bridge where he spotted Mabel cat struggling in the water.

"Jesus, Mabel!" He knew she couldn't swim as a human and she was floundering in the water as a cat.

Most people just laughed and watched as the poor cat struggled. There was no doubt they were going to let it drown.

Gabriel slid down the bank and waded into the water. It wasn't too deep at the edge but he needed to be careful, for he was wearing maille and that was not something he wanted to be sporting in the deeper waters of the castle moat. He had no intention of falling in.

"Mabel... here... come..." He stretched out his hand.

Mabel spluttered and went under again.

"Paddle, Mabel. For God's sake."

Now she could see Gabriel, Mabel stopped panicking and allowed her animal instincts to take over. Despite the pain in her side, she moved her paws with short fast strokes and found that she could be quite an efficient swimmer.

Gabriel leaned over as far as was safe and grabbed her by the neck fur.

Hauling her up, her eyes tightly shut, dripping and still paddling her feet, he threw her gently onto the grass.

He then dragged himself to safety on all fours.

Some of the onlookers clapped; some laughed, others grimaced in disappointment and all of them went back to work.

Kneeling on all fours, he took in some deep breaths.

"Mabel Wetherspring, you had better have a really good explanation for all this," he said.

*****

Mabel dried her fur on Gabriel's cotte as they rode through the town. She hadn't the energy, at that precise moment, to change back into herself. After a while and once they were out in the forest, Mabel jumped down from Gabriel's arms and turned three times deosil.

She was bursting to tell him what she'd found out; what she'd witnessed.

But he was angry with her.

He had muttered the whole way from the castle moat to the outlying forest trees.

"Why you must go and... It's not as if... You are the most infuriating cat there has ever been... You frighten me Mabel... you really do... trouble follows you around! Why can't you be like everyone else?"

"Because I'm not like everyone else!" she said on the last and tenth repetition of this phrase.

He did not stop his horse but went on walking him.

"I am angry with you, Mabel and I daren't speak to you for fear of..."

Bertran clopped on until he was a few feet ahead of her.

She ran to catch up. "Don't you want to know what I saw?"

"No. I don't."

"Oh, don't be so childish, Gabriel!"

He turned in the saddle. "If I hadn't arrived when I did, you'd be a drowned cat now!"

"Someone would have fished me out."

"You didn't see the looks on their faces," he said. "It was great entertainment for them. I would not have put it past any one of them to have pushed you under for the sheer fun of it."

"Nonsense!"

Gabriel looked up to the Heavens. "Give me strength, my Lord. There was some kind of an emergency going on and people were engaged with that. THAT is why you managed to escape. If I hadn't been there..." he reiterated.

"Don't you want to know what that emergency was?"

"Don't you ever go off like that again!"

"I left you a message."

"And what if I hadn't seen the message?"

"Do you want to know or not?"

"I can't go on being worried about you every..."

"There'd been a death and I witnessed it. Or rather Mabel cat did."

"It's fraying my nerves… and what's more…"

Suddenly he realised what she'd said. "What? You what?"

"It was murder, Gabriel."

"Who?"

"The man who is in charge of the scriptorium. His name was Stoneford."

"What's he got to do with Scarepath and Honfleur? Or Savary for that matter?"

"Only that Master Scrivens pushed him down the stairs and he's dead."

"What? Scrivens is dead?"

"Oh, Gabriel, please keep up. Scrivens pushed Stoneford down the stairs. He killed him. Right in front of me!"

"And you were a cat when this happened?"

"Yes."

"Thank God for that!

"No. He doesn't know I saw it."

"What happened?"

"Oh, you want to know now?"

"Of course I want to know."

And so she told him. Rapidly.

*****

They sat by the hearth in Mabel's cott and stared at the little flames licking the collection of twigs which served as an apology for a fire.

Gabriel stood his boots in front of the meagre warmth.

"Wish I'd brought my servant."

"You have a servant?"

"Of course. I left him in Rutishall. He would know what to do with my boots and he'd clean my maille so it doesn't rust."

"Oh, I'm sure I could do that," said Mabel trying to get back into his favour.

"Hmmm. I am able to do it myself, you know. I have been a squire."

He then sat in silence and stared at the ruinous state of his boots. "Whatever possessed you to go off and confront the two men?"

Mabel sighed. "We needed to know what Master Savary was on about and Scrivens had told us nothing about the house in St. Martin's Lane either. I thought it would be easier if I went alone and spoke to them."

Gabriel pressed his fingers into his thumping temples.

"Tell me again what happened." He rubbed his forehead. "Slowly this time."

"Have you a headache?"

"I have. It's called Mabel Wetherspring."

She took his ale pot and shook some finely pulverised white powder into it, which she'd taken from a small chest on a shelf at the back of the cott.

"Here, this will take the edge off the pain but sadly, it will do nothing about Mabel Wetherspring."

Despite his pain and the growing worry for Mabel, he smiled. "You are the most…"

"I've heard it before… thank you."

He glared at her under his eyebrows.

She chuckled. "You really do not have the face for glaring. You just look… comical. Your eyebrows are too light in colour to be effective at glowering. Even with your scar."

Mabel glowered and showed him how it was done.

"Hmmm," he said in an irritated tone.

She poked the fire.

"Well. Master Savary said that living in that house in St. Martins was… and I quote, 'a nightmare. People coming and going at all times and people going missing.'"

"Like whom?"

"A scribe from the scriptorium who used to live there and Master

Scrivens' wife."

"He had a wife?"

"Apparently. Oh... and a servant girl went missing too."

"Well, well."

"And so I thought I'd go and speak to Scrivens about his wife but then..."She shivered. "You should have seen his face. It was pure evil. It seems the man can make himself into anything he wishes."

"Like you then?" said Gabriel sarcastically.

"No. NOT like me."

He wiggled his eyebrows and Mabel laughed.

"When I saw him, he was being accosted by that man, Stoneford. Then suddenly, he turned on him. Told him he had to keep quiet, say nothing and do as he was told. It was all at a menacing whisper."

"And Stoneford fought back?"

"No. He fled and when they got to the steps..."

"Now, this is important Mabel. You have to be absolutely sure of what you saw. You say he pushed him... he didn't fall or trip? He didn't trip over you, as this Scrivens man said he did?"

"No. I was behind them both. Standing on the upper steps. I saw Scrivens put both hands onto Stoneford's breast and push. Then, for good measure he gave him a couple of kicks to help him down to the bottom. He was already dead by then."

"You are sure it wasn't an accident and that Scrivens meant to kill him?"

"Listen to me Gabriel. I saw it. Besides, the man had just threatened to kill him."

"You didn't tell me that," said Gabriel.

"Ah well... in the heat of the moment I forgot."

Gabriel stared at her and shook his head. "Why would he wish to kill Stoneford?"

"Because he was bullying him. Because he knew something about him that... that he was going to tell."

"Whom was he going to tell?"

"I don't know. He never got the chance to say. Or I didn't hear him say."

Gabriel got up and walked about in his bare feet. "It will be put down to an accident. I know it will."

"It will. And it's not the truth."

"How can we make Scrivens pay for that? How can we bring it out into the open?"

"I don't know," said Mabel "but one thing I'm sure about is that Master Scrivens is not the mild man he appears to be. Not long ago we thought he couldn't be Mistress Honfleur's lover but actually... it could be him. It really could. I didn't hear his proper voice as he was whispering most of the time and it was echoey in the stairwell, but...I'd swear it was him. He is just such a superb dissembler."

Gabriel put his hands to his head and tugged at his hair in frustration.

"We need to confront him somehow. Both Honfleur and Scrivens."

"But before we do that we need to find out what happened to his wife and the other two missing persons. It seems to me that Stoneford knew that Scrivens had something to do with their disappearance."

"And another thing..."

"Yes?"

"We still don't know who hit you over the head and why," said Gabriel.

"It wasn't Sweetcheeks."

"No. It must have been Honfleur or her lover."

"But why?"

Gabriel sat down again and picked up the netting which Mabel had been working on when she'd had a spare moment. He ran the hemp-spun threads through his fingers.

"Because I'd been asking questions and they didn't like it." He looked straight at her with his bright blue eyes. "How did they know where you were?"

"Honfleur was listening to me talking to Scarepath in the forest before he was killed. I am sure I never mentioned where I was from. And she couldn't have followed me."

"That means it was likely that it was Sweetcheeks who betrayed you. I know you liked the man but it must have been him."

"He was very frightened of Wymark, I think."

"He was very frightened of someone," said Gabriel, idly winding the thread round his fingers. "And that someone strangled him."

"To prevent him letting us know anything…"

"Ah no," he sighed as thoughts crossed his mind, tied a knot in the thread, took it in both hands and began to wind it into patterns.

"I really can't see anyone killing him purely over the fact that he was about to tell us about the brothels which Honfleur and her lover were running. He must have known something more."

"Like what involvement Scrivens had in it all?" Mabel watched Gabriel's fingers twirling and picking at the thread. "One thing puzzles me."

"Oh?" Gabriel twisted the threads over on themselves.

"Why do Honfleur and Scrivens, if he is her lover, hang about here? Why don't they take their ill-gotten gains and fly?"

"Because they're greedy. They'll never have enough. And I have an idea that they enjoy the danger of it."

"Scrivens doesn't need to be a lowly scribe being bullied by his fellows. He could just take off."

"Something is going to happen and they need to be around for it, is my guess."

"Erm… Gabriel… what are you doing with my netting?"

"Here… take this bit here and push it up under there."

"What?"

"A finger and a thumb…"

Mabel screwed up her forehead.

"What for?"

"It helps thinking."

"Does it? As far as I can see, all it does is make a mess of my threads."

He held out his hands. "Go on."

She carefully took the thread from him and he stretched out his fingers and made yet another pattern and pulled it tight.

"There now take this one and pull it over this one."

"I see your finger is healed nicely."

"Yes. Not bad now. I've had to exercise it a bit and there's a little loss of sensation but… it's alright…"

Their fingers brushed each other.

Gabriel's eyebrows went up in a questioning manner. "You have really never played cat's cradle with anyone?"

"No."

"This one over here. And take it from me."

"I had no one to play with."

"Ah yes. Whereas I had… have three sisters. Now I fold this over there and that over there…"

"What a pretty pattern."

Their hands and faces were getting closer and closer and the winding of the threads was getting slower and slower. Their foreheads touched as they pulled the threads of the cat's cradle.

"I hope this will undo when we have finished," said Mabel, spoiling the moment.

Gabriel took the threads from her hands, performed some magic and there was the thread back again as a single strand but with a knot in it.

He picked the knot undone.

"There!"

"You must teach me to do it properly."

"I will."

Again his hand brushed hers as he gave back the thread.

"Now you can go on weaving your…what is it?"

"I'm making a net upon which to trail a flower up the wall of the house."

"Ah… Erm Why?"

"Because I can and I want to and I want to have a sweet smelling flower growing by the door in the summer. And if I plant a woodbine it will be a charm against evil."

"As good a reason as any," he said with a blank expression.

He stood. "Right then…"

"Are you going back to the manor?"

"I want to write to the lord."

"You can't tell him I saw a murder!"

"No, but I'll think of something."

He jammed on his boots. They were still a bit squelchy. "Good evening, Mistress Wetherspring."

"Good evening, Sir Gabriel."

*****

"I've been thinking, Mabel," said Gabriel as he opened her door the next morning.

He was prepared for her usual quip of, 'Oh no…' or, 'well there's a thing' or some such utterance.

All he could hear was a high pitched squeal from above him.

He looked up.

A beautiful russet kite was circling on the air currents, its forked tail splaying out as it rode the concentrated area of wind high up in a cloudless sky.

'Squee-wee-wee-wee-weeoop.'

Two or three beats of the wings and it sped off over the forest trees, circled and called again.

'Squee-wee-wee-wee-weeoop.'

Gabriel yelled up into the air. "Mabel"

He looked around quickly. No one was about. No one had heard him call her.

That was a good thing. She'd be very cross with him if he'd given her away.

The kite looked down and fixed him with a pale yellow eye.

"Weeeee weeee, oooop!" it screamed and circled the garth.

Gabriel watched as it disappeared from view into the back garden where he knew Mabel could not be overlooked.

She came round the corner of the house tidying her hair into a head cloth wound around her pale golden brown locks.

"What did 'Squee-wee-wee-wee-weeoop,' mean then, Mabel?" said Gabriel with a lopsided grin.

"It meant… 'This is lovely and I'm enjoying myself,' and, 'What do you want?'"

"Sorry to put an end to your fun."

"I have to go to work in a moment anyway."

"Well, before you do. I have an idea." He waited for her to say something.

She tightened her belt. "Yes?"

"How about we try to draw Scrivens out—make him confess?"

"How? He's not going to do that easily. And apart from me seeing him kill Stoneford, we have no evidence that he killed anyone else. Or has done anything else for that matter."

"So, we must get it."

"And this is to be achieved… exactly… how?"

"Follow him. Watch him… and Honfleur."

"And find out what happened to his wife and the other missing persons?"

"If we can."

Mabel chewed her lip. "Alright. Let me just do a few jobs and then I'll go off to the town."

"Ah no. We'll go off to town."

"Have it your own way."

She reached into her house and pulled on a red shawl. Closing the door she said, "And what will you be doing when you get to town?"

"I am going to make inquiries about those people who went missing."

Her heart skipped a beat. "Be careful. If anyone involved with this gets to know you are in possession of knowledge about them, things could get dangerous. I saw Scrivens' face, remember."

"And I could say the same for you."

Gabriel turned to walk to the manor house and Mabel followed him after closing her cottage door.

"I don't want to have to rescue you again as a drowning cat, Mabel."

She gave him a sidelong look. "I'd better be a fish then," she said.

CHAPTER TWELVE ~ THE KING

The King had come to Marlborough Castle.

If the place had been busy before, then it was absolutely heaving now. There wasn't a spot of space in the bailey which wasn't taken up with carts or knight's equipment; chests, boxes, folded tents and racks of weapons. The stables were full. There were tents all around; in the meadows and along the sides of the roads.

Mabel flew in on to the castle wall and took stock.

Goodness me! There was hardly an inch to spare.

She relocated to the roof of the King's House, the hall where he stayed when he came to Marlborough.

She wasn't the only sparrow toing and froing. There were several sitting on the roof making cheepy noises and a few flying back and forth between the mound of the keep and the roof of the stables.

Mabel hopped down onto a ledge. She just had to see if she could see the King. She'd never seen him before. The most elevated person she'd ever met was a friend of the Lord Stokke's, some sort of clerical person; a bishop she seemed to remember. He'd come to dinner and had complimented her on her beautifully turned out napery.

She stood still on the ledge and looked around. Ah, no. The windows were glazed; she couldn't see in from here. Everything was just a blur of coloured images; blue, yellow and green. Little pictures of a King upon a horse with his servants crowded around him and the biggest hunting horn one could ever be able to blow. This particular king seemed to be having difficulty holding it.

But there was one window which was just slightly open. Mabel squeezed herself into the gap.

All was bustle in the place. There were some green liveried servants fixing together a bed... a large bed. Others were taking bed linen and napery from chests and one man, who looked very important, was undoing a small box and peering in.

Was he the King? She'd heard he wasn't a big or tall man but she had absolutely no idea what he looked like. If his coins were to be believed, he had a round head, a bob of messy curls, large stary eyes and a beard which looked like the pelt of a goat!

A trestle table had been erected and a red cloth of great sumptuousness was being laid upon it by more green-clothed servants.

Then a rather scruffy bearded man came up and looked at the bits and pieces which had been laid on it.

He wore a dirty saffron coloured cotte with a border of green embroidery and a shorter supertunic of green. His blondish chin length hair was greasy and dirty and he kept scratching it. Then he yelled, "Petit! You ready with that bath yet?"

"Yes, my lord. Any time you'd like to bathe now."

An old grey headed man with a slight stoop came into her view.

"Nice and hot I hope?"

"As you like it, sire."

Mabel nearly fell off her perch. This scruffy, unkempt person was the King? She found herself very disappointed.

In her mind the King had to be tall, handsome, elegant, well dressed, suave and sophisticated, not this shabby, mucky individual with a slight paunch. She was sorry the minute she thought this, for she knew that the King had probably been on the road for a long time. Of course he was scruffy and a bit grubby... like anyone else would be.

She watched as he strode over to a curtained area, unbuckling his belt and letting it fall, throwing off his outer green robe. He then wriggled out of his saffron cotte and threw that at a servant. His shirt was of mucky white linen and that too went over his head. He waggled the arms around for a moment like a flailing crayfish and the old grey-headed servant came forward to help him take it off. Now he was just in his braies.

Then he went behind the curtain and Mabel heard a splash and...

"Ahhhh. That's perfect, Petit."

"Good, my lord," the elderly servant replied. "Take your ease. I shall return in a moment."

'Oh,' thought Mabel. 'I really must see the King in his bath.' Her little heart was beating fast. What would Gabriel say when he knew that she'd seen their monarch in his bath?

She lifted off flying high into the roof rafters and dipped over the curtained area.

There was John, watched over by a servant with his nose in the air and a large towel over his arm. He didn't dare look at the royal body, she supposed.

The steam from the bath drifted upwards; the King's bony knees came up out of the water like two pink eggs and he scrutinised some apparent blemish there and picked at it.

Mabel perched on the screen which surrounded him and stared.

He was just like... well... anyone else, really.

He was slightly overweight, his skin was as white as a swan apart from his face, neck and lower arms. He wasn't made of gold or anything special, he was just a man with blue eyes.

He lifted a foot from the water and fiddled with his toes.

Mabel giggled.

The servant looked round.

"Roundarse?"

"Yes, my King?"

"You making strange noises?"

"No, my lord."

"Good."

John slipped down further into the water and it splashed over the side soaking the towels which were laid there.

Mabel couldn't believe her ears. Was this fellow actually called Roundarse?

Suddenly John took a deep breath and falling backwards, plunged his head into the water.

Mabel could not but fail to see the royal genitals bouncing up and down in the waves made by the action. She closed her eyes.

When she opened them, the King was still submerged.

'He's drowning... oh my God... he's drowning.'

She hopped from foot to foot.

"Cheep... cheep... CHEEP!"

Her cheeps were covered by the noise of John surfacing, splashing and yelling for soap.

But Roundarse had heard and seen her. He lunged for her, yelled and flapped the towel at her.

"Oi... get out!"

"Wassup, Roundhouse?" shouted John.

Mabel flew up onto a purlin.

"Sparrow my lord king, got into the room."

"That all...? SOAP... PETIT!"

"Coming right away, my lord!"

The grey haired man, Petit, scurried behind the screen. "I wanted to find your favourite."

"You're a good man."

The old retainer smiled and handed over the soap with a flourish.

Petit lifted a jug and..."May I, my lord?"

"Aye, off you go," said the King.

The jug was poured over the King's hair and Petit began to soap it vigorously.

"Oh that IS so good," said John, jiggling about in the water.

'Well, well,' said Mabel to herself, 'he likes to keep clean.'

She smiled a sparrow smile.

"What shall we wear this morning, my lord?" asked Petit, rinsing his King's hair with another jug of hot water.

"Shall we have the red with the grey silk, Petit? Then I can wear my rubies."

"A good choice, sire."

Mabel was enjoying this domestic scene. Her view was excellent from here. She could not only see the King but all his servants, his bed and clothes, all his possessions and my goodness, laid out on the trestle on the red damask cloth, all his lovely jewels.

Her interest was piqued by a large ruby on a gold chain which sat centrally amongst sapphire pendants and beautiful emerald and ruby rings.

She left the purlin and drifted down to a lower beam.

Servants were wheeling in unlit braziers and lamps were being positioned here and there about the room, ready to be lit in the evening, thought Mabel.

One man entered the room, swept the goings on with narrowed eyes and carried his lantern to the table of jewels where he took some time deciding where to seat it.

Mabel heard the splashing of the King as he rose from his bath. She could just see him and Petit as he wrapped a towel around the royal loins.

He then stooped and took up a strange garment which was made of patterned silk of several colours. He laid it over his arm and walked beside his King as John stepped out from his bath.

Petit helped him into the sleeved garment and tied a fabric belt around the royal waist.

Mabel could not take her eye from the amazing—well she did not know what to call it—open cotte perhaps, which fell free at the front and folded over in many gathers. It was beautiful; silk of patterns like flowers and in many colours.

"Wine, my lord?"

"Why not, Petit?"

Mabel fluttered up again and changed her vantage point as the King came out into the room, goblet in hand, to watch his servants finish constructing his bed.

He seemed genuinely interested in how it went together for, now and again, he'd make some comment to his faithful retainer and they'd smile at a shared joke.

The original people were now exiting the room. Other servants came in to make up the bed with linens and Mabel was impressed at their level of fastidiousness. She could not have taught them better herself.

Clothes were now being laid out upon the coverlet and the King made his way to the bed to look at them.

"Ah... yes... PETIT!"

"Yes, John?"

These two must be good friends for the old man to be allowed to call the King by his first name.

"Did you get that mark from my grey silk?"

"I did... completely. It's as good as new."

"You are a miracle worker, old friend."

Mabel smiled. This was not how she imagined her King would behave.

The old man laughed. "No miracle... fullers earth... that's all."

Mabel thought about her own pot of fullers earth at home in her office.

She was then treated to John towelling his hair, throwing off his robe of silk and standing stark naked on a rug of woollen cloth with his arms out to his sides. She stared at the rug. It was easier than staring at her King's private parts.

Two men approached. One took up the King's clean shirt and carefully slid it over his head. The other went down to his knees and gently teased the braies over the man's warmed pink knees and tied them. John then released his arms.

God! The man doesn't even dress himself. I bet he has no idea how to tie a knot.

Mabel flew in a short burst to the rafter above the table of jewels. No one saw her.

Oh my they were so beautiful. How much must they all have cost?

What a tale she'd have to tell Sir Gabriel Warrener when she returned home.

Her eye roved over the aquamarines, (though Mabel did not know what they were really called,) the emeralds and the sapphires.

Something was odd. She could not put her claw on it.

John was now dressed in his red cotte. Petit was fussing with the pleats at his waist. John sipped his wine and did not seem to mind.

The grey silk was lifted up and John put down his cup to accept the sleeve hole.

"Red and grey is so pleasing to the eye," said John suddenly. "Don't you think, Petit?"

"It's perfect for a man of culture and authority. A green youngster could not carry it off but a man, such as you, my lord, a man of maturity and..."

John laughed and his voice rang up to the rafters. Folk turned in their chores, to look at him.

"Ah Petit... No flattery now."

"Me... flattery...? How long have we been together, my King?"

"Too long."

They both laughed.

Mabel was fascinated by the ordinariness of this master and servant's relationship.

She had thought John would be unapproachable, haughty, noble, priggish but he was... very much like one of her kind uncles. The one who always made her laugh. God rest him; he was dead now.

Mabel began to wonder about what John had said. Red and grey. Were they really colours which complement each other well?

Mabel realised this ritual, the bath, the dressing, the whole setting out of the King's possessions was one which must have happened every time John stayed at one of his castles.

Suddenly, with a jolt to her middle, she saw what had bothered her. She stared.

The jewel table.

The aquamarines, the emeralds and the bright sapphires. Pendants, rings and chains.

The ruby pendant was not there and neither was the large ruby ring. She also thought she'd seen two ruby brooches.

'Oh. My. God,' said Mabel, the sparrow, as she thought back a few moments. 'I know what has happened and I know who has taken them. And I also now know why our culprits have not been in such a hurry to leave the town.'

But all the King and his menials heard was 'CHEEP, CHEEP, CHEEEEEP!'

*****

Mabel left the hall as an enormous roar went up.

John must have realised that his rubies were missing. It would take him a while to realise that they had not been mislaid, but had been stolen. The thief had achieved it so easily. Why was security so lax? Mabel suddenly knew without doubt that the King had believed it unthinkable that anyone would dare to steal his possessions from under his nose. He trusted his staff implicitly. And, after all, the thief had looked like a member of his staff.

She flew rapidly over the bailey trying to locate the figure of the man she'd seen placing the lantern on the jewel table.

Where would he go?

Up to the scribe's room? No… she didn't think he'd go there again. She had to find Gabriel and tell him what she'd seen. And what she suspected.

But where was he? He'd said that he was going to speak to the girls at the house with the three gables on St. Martin's.

176

She flew rapidly to the outer wall and stared down the road to the marketplace. Was that Scrivens hurrying along in his black robe? He'd not worn that in the King's House. She recalled that he must have got hold of some livery. And shed it again.

He would blend into the press of people in the town and she'd never find him.

Looking around to make sure no one could see her, she turned three times withershynnes. "I wish to be a pigeon." She could now fly faster and catch up to the felon. If she had to confront him herself alone, somehow she would. She followed him.

*****

Gabriel was standing in front of the house with three gables. He felt uneasy, though he couldn't tell why.

This time he'd left Bertran at the livery stable on the Marsh. Secrecy was important, he thought. Best to leave a knight's conspicuous horse elsewhere.

He gave a cursory look round. No one seemed to be about.

He squared his shoulders. He could deal with Mistress Honfleur should he need to. Even if she was angry with him. Surely she knew it had been him who had set fire to her house.

He recalled her glorious mane of spun red gold hair and her angelic heart shaped face.

How lovely she was.

And he also recalled that she was probably involved in a murder. Or two. Mabel's little face came into his mind and a warm glow invaded the area of his heart.

Mabel wasn't beautiful, or seductive, elegant or overly refined but she made ten of this woman Wymark. Of that he was sure.

He took a deep breath and called out.

"Mistress Wymark!

After a while he laid his ear to the wood of the door. He could hear nothing. Good!

Looking round and making a quick glance around the corner into the alleyway, (no dog), he scurried along the wall to the back of the house.

Up the stairs in three bounds and he stood before the attic door.

"Aimée, it's Sir Gabriel Warrener. Let me in."

The door opened slowly and only a crack.

"Oh... it's you," said Aimée nervously. "Have you brought your cat with you?"

"Er... no... and it's not my cat."

He tried to push the door. "Are you alone? I want to speak to you."

"I haven't got anything to say," said Aimée

He managed to get a foot in the door. "C'mon Aimée, you know I won't hurt you."

"Have you got that scary lady with you?"

Gabriel smiled to himself. Wait till he told Mabel she was scary. "No, she's busy."

The door opened. "Alright then. What do you want?"

"Like I said, to speak to you. I need some answers to some questions."

"What for?"

He ignored her. "Have you lived here a while?"

"Two years, why?" said Aimée.

"Do you remember another girl... living here?"

"Felicia you mean?"

"There's you and Estrild..."

"And there's Joan."

"I haven't met her have I?"

"No... she's at Angel House."

"Where's that?"

"The house on Figgins Lane. She'll be finished soon and home if you want to..."

"Ah. That's what you call it." Never was a place so misnamed he thought. "And there was Felicia too?"

Aimée twisted her hair around her finger. Gabriel considered that she thought it made her look more coquettish. It didn't.

"Where did she go?"

"Who?"

"Felicia."

"I don't know. She disappeared."

Gabriel sat on the low bed. His sword scabbard scraped on the ground. "What happened?"

"I... I... don't know."

"Did she move away? Go to another house, like the one on Turnabout Lane? Did she leave the town? What?

"We just never saw her again. She lived here with us and..."

"Did she take anything with her when she disappeared?"

"What do you mean?" Aimée clutched at her neck.

"No... not money but her things. Did she take clothes and suchlike?"

"No, she didn't have many things but she left them all. I don't know why. Mistress Honfleur said we could have her things as she didn't want them any longer."

"Didn't want them?" Gabriel looked perplexed. "Why not."

"Where she had gone she wouldn't need them," she said.

In a very childlike way the girl tried to imitate Wymark Honfleur. "And if you ever breathe a silly bull of her name to anyone..."

"A silly bull?"

"Yes, that's what she said."

"Oh yes. I see."

"Then you too will not be needing any of your things ever again."

Gabriel leaned forward and rested his elbows on his knees. "Aimée. Did you ever think about what happened to her?"

"That night I did but then... after that. No."

"That night?"

"The night she went downstairs."

"Into the main house?"

179

"I was asleep and woke up but I could see her. She was spying."

"Spying? How? Where?"

"Here." Aimée dropped to her knees and pulled one of the beds a little way from the wall with a woody squeal.

Gabriel followed her and realised that the floor of the attic was directly laid upon the roof beams of the ceiling below. It was easy to see what was going on underneath them through the cracks. And through one wide gap in particular there was a good view of the bed in Wymark's room.

"Who was she spying on?"

Aimée gave an embarrassed giggle. "Mistress Honfleur of course. And her lover."

"Aimée, do you ever spy on them?"

"Oh no. I daren't do that."

"Aw come on... I won't tell." Gabriel nudged her suggestively with his elbow. "I'd love to know what you see."

"You know... them... doing things."

"Ah... that?"

He got up and dusted his cotte. "So, Felicia saw them and what did she do?"

"She went down to see if she could see better and hear what they were saying."

"Why?"

"She never told me."

"Did she tell anyone else?"

Aimée shrugged. "I never saw her again."

"Tell me... do you think they killed her?"

"Why would they do that just because she saw them with no clothes on?"

"Ah..."

"Well, that is against the rules. The priest says we must keep our clothes on."

"Does he now?"

"She could have told the priest and then Mistress Honfleur would be in trouble and have to perform a penance." Aimée was perfectly serious.

"Yes. I suppose she would."

Suddenly from somewhere below, there was the bang of a door.

"Has someone come home?" asked Gabriel.

"There's no one in. Mistress Honfleur is out at the big house and everyone else is out at their marketing. They always go out in the morning. Maybe it's Mistress Bux returning from her shopping."

"Master Savary has moved out hasn't he?"

"The ugly one? Yes."

"And Master Bux is at his work?"

"I suppose so."

"The only one still in is the old bird lady?"

Aimée shrugged again.

'So', thought Gabriel. 'Who has just come through the front door?'

"Felicia isn't the only one to disappear is she?"

"The silly clerk. He had a wife. She left him."

"Do you know her name?"

"Margery, I think."

"Did she disappear too?"

"No. She left him."

"Who said that?"

"Mistress Honfleur."

"Did you believe her?"

"Why not? She knew them both. And that silly clerk was a stupid man. I'd leave him too."

"Master Scrivens? Is that his name?"

"He was called Geoffrey. I know that. I heard her shouting 'Geoffrey... oh Geoffrey!'"

There was the sound of clomping on the stairs in the main house and another door banged.

"Master Scriven's wife, Margery, was it? She just disappeared too didn't she? Do you think they might have killed her too?"

Aimée shrugged. There was no point in labouring it, Gabriel thought.

"Aimée, did you ever hear of anyone called Martin living here?"

"Oh, Martin was nice."

"Who was he?"

"Another scribe at the castle. I haven't seen him for weeks but his room is still there for him. For when he comes back."

"The room on the first floor at the front? I thought that was Master Scrivens' room?"

"Aw no. That one is under here." She pointed to the floor.

Suddenly Gabriel had worked it out. Pieced it all together.

He was about to turn to say thank you and leave when a small door at the end of the attic opened, one which had been hidden in the darkness. Gabriel had had no idea it was there.

"What the Hell?" said a voice.

Gabriel froze.

A man came forward and stood in the light from the unshuttered window.

He was a smooth faced man of about thirty-something with thin mousy hair combed in strands over a balding pate and he wore a long, dark robe.

Gabriel affected not to have seen him but thought quickly. Was this the scribe, Scrivens?

"Thank you Aimée. I will see you again next week." He fished in his purse for some money. "I'm very pleased with you." He was trying to make it seem as if he'd been one of her clients.

He pressed a coin into the woman's hand. "Take care," he said with great feeling.

As he turned for the outer door, the man leapt for him and brought a knife hilt down on the back of his head.

He heard Aimée screech as he fell senseless onto the dusty boards.

CHAPTER THIRTEEN ~ THE JEWELS

Mabel flew along the High Street behind Master Scrivens. He had to be the one who had lifted the King's jewels.

He was hurrying along looking neither right nor left and pushing his way past people, rudely. He jogged up the incline of Kingsbury Street, along Silver Street and across The Green disappearing into the alleyway where the old houses leaned into each other and blotted the light. Mabel had heard this was the oldest part of town, first settled when the Saxons rampaged across the country. At the end lay the house with three gables.

He barged in the front door and slammed it behind him.

Mabel alighted on the roof.

Now what? She had to stay with him to find out what he did with the jewels. Once she knew where he'd hidden them, she could go down to Master Barbflet and tell him.

She suddenly had a vision of herself standing in front of the King trying to explain how she'd seen Scrivens steal his jewels.

No. That wouldn't work. How could she explain that she'd been sitting in the roof beams of the King's House? She should not have been in the building at all! Woman or sparrow. Somehow she had to lead Master Barbflet and the town council to their own conclusion.

She heard another door bang and footsteps ascending a stair.

If Gabriel was here, he might be in trouble.

Then she heard an almighty screech and a heavy thud.

As quickly as she'd ever moved, Mabel descended to the lane and turned withershynnes. "I wish to be a large dog." Mabel grew tall and muscled like one of the powerful and large hunting hounds which Lord Stokke possessed. Her teeth lengthened and her jaw became powerfully large and wide. Short brown hair grew all over her and a long balancing tail grew out of the bottom of her spine.

As her body was changing she thought to herself, 'Why not a cat again?'

And an answer came immediately into her canine head. A large dog could be dangerous. And she somehow had the idea she needed to be very dangerous.

She reared up on her hind legs and peered into a ground floor window. They were all shuttered and barred.

'Damn.'

The front door was similarly thick and impenetrable. But then she had a thought. She remembered how the man Scrivens had just barged through it. He hadn't locked or barred it. However, she'd become a large and heavy dog. That should count for something.

Mabel took a deep breath and ran at the door. It banged back on its hinges and she had to dance out of the way in order not to be walloped by its return.

Her claws skittered on the stone floors as she ran around searching for the man. Scrivens was not on the ground floor.

Then came another cry. A woman's.

Mabel looked up. She was sure it had come from above her.

But where exactly?

She spent a moment of indecision and anxiety trying to work out how she could know where Scrivens had gone.

Then she smelled him. 'Of course!' She was a hunting dog. And they had incredible noses.

She also smelled someone else.

'Oh my God! Gabriel!' she cried.

But all the world heard was "HOOOOWUL!"

*****

Gabriel was not quite out cold but he was unable to defend himself. He felt hands remove his sword belt and pat him over for concealed weapons.

Then those same hands lifted him and pulled him to the stairs.

His eyes shot open. 'Ah no. You're not going to throw me down the stairs like you did Master Stoneford,' his brain said.

He couldn't however keep his eyes open and although he knew what was happening, he was powerless to prevent it.

But he was not thrown down the stairs. They were wooden and thankfully wouldn't have done the same amount of damage that had been done to Master Stoneford but even so, it could be nasty. Gabriel tried to struggle.

Then he realised he was being dragged by the feet one step at a time. His head banged on the steps. His spine was bruised under his maille but his gambeson saved him too much pain.

"Ahhh."

When he'd reached the bottom, he was well and truly befuddled.

He couldn't tell what was happening but Scrivens had dragged him to the room which he and Mabel had thought belonged to Mistress Honfleur. Now he knew that Scrivens and she shared the room.

Scrivens took the thin belt which circled his own waist and tied Gabriel to one of the posts which held up the ceiling, his hands behind him. Then he searched around for a piece of cloth with which to gag him. He stuffed it into Gabriel's mouth.

Gabriel's head lolled forward. Everything swam before his eyes.

Even though he couldn't see clearly, he watched the fuzzy movements in the room as Scrivens took off his fusty old black robe and dressed himself in a clean white shirt and a cotte of blue with bands of green and white embroidery at the hem.

To Gabriel the man looked like his head was floating above a green sward in a blue sky.

Gradually Gabriel regained his wits and his first thought was, what had happened to Aimée? Had she too been struck and incapacitated?

'Why had the man kept hold of him? Why had he not just put a knife into his throat?'

Well, he was glad he hadn't but by the expression on the man's face, his future didn't look certain. He was keeping him alive for some reason. But why and for how long?

*****

Mabel tried not to panic. She lifted her nose and sniffed. Gabriel was surely here somewhere, but he had not, it seemed, walked through the hall.

No, he'd been upstairs to the attic. That's where he'd said he was going but her dog nose told her that he was closer than that.

She put her nose to the ground and tracked.

No, not here. Not in the gallery where the woman with the birds lived. She scooted down to the clerk's room. Not there, but the smell of Gabriel was closer.

She looked round. There was a curtained alcove in the wall which she'd missed before and now she made for it. Narrow wooden slats went up steeply to, what Mabel thought, was the far end of the attic.

Half way up those steps, Mabel turned. No. He had been here but she was sure he was no longer there.

She snuffled hard. 'Ah... found him!'

Mistress Honfleur's room.

Without a real thought for her safety, Mabel jumped at the door. It held fast. She howled in anguish. And beetled towards it again. It rattled but did not open.

She knew Gabriel was in that room and he needed her help. She could tell.

Now she could hear a voice. It was laughing.

And it wasn't Gabriel.

*****

"Our brave knight?"

"Mmmmouhmmmhnnndiiiou" said Gabriel through the gag.

"How did I know?" The man poured a goblet of wine and swilled it through his teeth.

There was a mighty bang on the door and a terrible howl.

"I have informants. Just as you do... did." Scrivens no more than glanced at the door.

"Whaumoouniaeee?"

"Was that, 'what have I done with Aimée? Oh poor girl. She fell and hit her head and you took that opportunity to plunge your knife into her heart, didn't you?"

Gabriel groaned.

"They'll find your knife in her ribs."

Gabriel chewed on his gag and managed to get it to the front of his mouth. There came another bang at the door.

He spat out the gag. "Mabel... he has a knife. Be careful."

All he could hear was a snuffling at the base of the wooden panel.

Then there was silence and the creature who had been banging on the door was silent.

"Who are you talking to? There's no way in. Is Mabel your girlfriend? The nosy bitch from Bedwyn?"

Little did both men know but the dog had been replaced by a tiny beetle, as small as a beetle was possible to be.

Mabel the beetle scurried under the door and into the room.

She quickly took in the situation.

Gabriel, seated on the floor tied to a central post and Scrivens, no longer the dowdy scribe, standing over him holding a knife.

"You have no idea, brave knight, what has been happening…"

"I have a fair idea."

Scrivens laughed again.

Mabel quickly became a mouse.

"The first one was Martin, wasn't it?" Gabriel wanted to keep him talking until Mabel could decide what to do. "Martin the timid scribe who Master Stoneford assaulted whenever he had the need."

"Poor Martin. Couldn't stand the treatment meted out by our nasty Master Stoneford. Sadly, he'd found out what we were planning and he had to go. Everyone thought it was because of Stoneford. Alas no." He drained the goblet of wine and poured more.

"He heard you plotting with Wymark?"

"His is… was… the next room. These walls are rather thin.'

"So you kept the lie that he was still alive by retaining the room as he left it. What did you do with his body?"

"Most knights I have known have been quite dense creatures. You on the other hand… are…"

"And you have been leading a double life ever since."

The man bowed. "One moment the lowly shy and retiring scribe, the next a confident, wealthy businessman."

"Why?"

Mabel almost wanted to leap up and explain to Gabriel why this abominable creature had stayed in Marlborough under a disguise but she thought better of it.

She scuttled under the bed and poked her tiny pink nose from the foot.

"You'll find out why. But we'll be long gone."

"You and Honfleur?"

"Wymark… the beautiful Wymark and Geoffrey Scrivens. Who would have thought it eh?"

"She likes ugly men," said Gabriel with a grin. "First the elderly, bald headed, paunchy Scarepath and then you."

That earned Gabriel a punch around the head with a fist.

Gabriel spat out blood. He'd bitten his cheek. "You killed Scarepath, I suppose? Once Wymark had got him to give her all his property."

Scrivens laughed.

"You have no idea!"

"And poor Sweetcheeks had to go, too?"

"Sweetcheeks killed Sweetcheeks. He was useful. But then he got too scared. It was his own fault."

"And Master Stoneford?"

"You can't possibly know about Stoneford."

"Oh, but I do. I'll give you a blow by blow account if you like."

That earned him a second buffet around the head.

"You have no idea what's waiting for you; what is your name by the way?"

Gabriel smirked. "I don't think you need to know."

"You damned...!" Scrivens went for him again but was brought up by a low growl behind him. However, even though he looked perplexed, he didn't look round.

"But I do think you need to know that the large dog which is behind you and ready to spring is called Mabel," said Gabriel.

Scrivens laughed, "I'm not falling for that one."

Mabel growled loudly deep in her throat, baring her teeth.

Scrivens tossed a quick look over his shoulder. "How the Hell?"

"Magic isn't it?" said Gabriel with a light giggle. "How did she get in here?"

The scribe backed to the wall. "The minute that dog leaps, I'll plunge my knife into its breast."

"No leaping Mabel," said Gabriel. "I'd go for the ankles if I were you, or the fingers."

Scrivens looked from one to the other.

"Or possibly the cods."

To add to the tension, at that moment the main door rattled as the key went into the lock and it opened and Wymark Honfleur entered.

She stood stock still.

"What on earth is going on here?"

"I was followed by this... man, my love. I've no idea why... except that he's something to do with that woman from Bedwyn."

"Her lover, I suspect," said Wymark, completely calm. "Well...Sir Gabriel!" she said.

Gabriel saw Mabel pull a strange face. A strange face for a dog anyway. She'd stopped growling and was listening intently.

"What does he know?"

"Nothing."

"We have to get going."

Wymark eyed up the dog. "Is it his dog?"

"He seems to be able to control it."

Mabel made a high pitched yelp. Wymark jumped. 'Control?' said Mabel to herself. 'Not a scrap of it. No chance!'

"Get rid of it."

Mabel growled again and made a feint towards Scrivens, baring her teeth once more.

"Get rid of them both."

Honfleur turned to leave.

"Wymark. He's a knight. He's worth money. Someone will pay to have him back."

Wymark did not turn to look at him. "All your own idea, is it? This ransom thing?"

"Well... I know knights can be ransomed. Someone will pay good money for him. That's why I kept him."

"Oh, I really doubt it, you see I'm an impoverished knight with no land and very little to call my own. No one will care much for me," said Gabriel.

Wymark leaned over him. "Then you have just signed your death warrant, Sir Gabriel."

"Let me take his finger off and we can send it to..."

"To whom?" said the woman.

"Now hang on a moment," said Gabriel.

"Grrrrooowll," said Mabel.

"To his lord. He's bound to have one. They all do."

"Ah... You're wrong there, my good fellow," said Gabriel jovially. "I'm a landless and masterless knight. Worth nothing."

"Well, if that's the case you're no use to us," said Honfleur. "At all."

Mabel sprang for the post where Gabriel was tied and paced back and forth in front of him.

Scrivens didn't know what to do.

"He has left a sword upstairs, I'll go and get it. It'd be a better weapon with a longer reach against that beast."

Slowly he made for the small staircase but Mabel was there at its base, before him.

"Does the bloody thing understand everything we say?" said Scrivens hovering.

Mabel was really snarling and growling now and looked as if she meant business.

"Oh come on... Just leave them here. We'll lock the door behind us. No one will find them for a long while," said Honfleur.

Scrivens circled the dog. Mabel went with him. "Jesus! It's not going to let me get out."

"Where are they?"

"On the bed."

"You keep the dog busy, I'll get them."

"Get what?" asked Gabriel.

Mabel wasn't going to let anyone get the King's jewels which she'd seen were in a black bag lying on the bed.

She flew in one gigantic leap onto the bed and straddled the bag.

"Oh, Holy Mother of God, it understands everything," said the scribe.

"It really is the most amazing dog," said Gabriel, smiling. "Yes you're right. It does understand everything. Everything you say."

"What?" said Wymark, suddenly rather wary.

"It's not really a dog you see…"

"What do ya mean… it's not a dog? We can see it's a bloody dog," said Scrivens.

"Mabel, can you perhaps raise your right front paw?"

With a canine sigh, Mabel raised her paw.

"And might you perhaps pick up that bag in your teeth and GO BACK THE SAME WAY YOU CAME?" said Gabriel with great emphasis. He'd no idea what was in the bag but he knew it was important.

Mabel stared at him. She hated to think about leaving him but she understood what he'd meant. What Gabriel didn't understand was, as a tiny mouse, Mabel wouldn't be able to carry the bag, certainly not under the door.

She picked up the jewels in her teeth and growled.

Wymark came closer to Gabriel. "You told me a tale once. About a shapeshifter."

"Ah yes. I did. About the wolf which gave me this scar."

"Are you telling us now, that this… this creature is something of the same sort?"

"I most certainly am. And it is invincible. You'll never best it."

"You managed to, you told me."

"Ah, well no," said Gabriel a little shamefacedly. "I told a teeny weeny lie there. I didn't beat that wolf." He pointed with his head, "She did."

Scrivens was completely lost. "She's a wolf?"

"Well she can be if she wishes… yes."

The two felons looked at each other. Was this an elaborate ruse or was this knight telling the truth? Of sorts.

"Get the bag Geoffrey. If she's really a woman, she won't hurt you."

"And if it's really a dog?"

Wymark shrugged and took out a long wicked-looking knife which hung from her belt. "Then when it sinks its teeth into you, I'll kill it."

"Why do I have to do it?"

"Because I tell you to."

"Suddenly you're the boss are you?" The man's face was going puce with anger.

"Do it... or I'll kill you now." Honfleur moved quickly and stood before Scrivens.

"Aw, come on sweetheart..."

Honfleur made a swipe at Scrivens meaning to wound him on the forearm but he stepped back quickly. "Do it!"

"Jesus... you mean it, don't you?"

Gabriel could not fail to see the funny side of this. He gave a short chuckle. "Oh I have always wanted to see a falling out of thieves."

"Then if you want to see anything, keep your mouth shut. It's easy to put out your eyes." Honfleur's face was a picture of evil.

Gabriel raised his knees and shuffled nearer to the post.

Honfleur moved slowly to Mabel's right and Scrivens to her left.

The dog backed away, snarling.

There was nothing for it. She didn't want to confirm their suspicions but she had no choice.

As quickly as a cook dices turnips, Mabel turned withershynnes three times. "I wish to be a large wolf," she said in her head.

A dog to a wolf was not a major transformation and it was accomplished quite quickly before the very eyes of two terrified thieves and murderers. They had no idea what she was doing.

Once they realised they were faced with a large snarling wolf, they both backed to the door.

"Jesus' Bones!" said Scrivens.

"Hellfire!" yelled Honfleur. "It's true!"

"He's right... it is a shapeshifter," yelled Scrivens, his face a mask of horror.

Both turned at the same moment to make for the main door which was still closed. Honfleur opened it and Mabel wolf followed her slowly, snarling menacingly.

The performance was making Gabriel just a little bit uncomfortable as he remembered his own encounter with a wolf.

Scrivens made a dash for the door hole. "We have to get out!"

"The jewels!"

"Leave the jewels, woman!"

Both felons exited at once and were suddenly stuck in the doorway. They struggled together, pushing and yelling. Honfleur, with gritted teeth and without any hesitation, plunged the knife still held in her hand, up into the torso of her erstwhile lover. Scrivens fell to his knees in the door gap with a sigh as the breath left his punctured lung. In that breath, Honfleur was gone.

Scrivens looked round with a surprised expression on his face, blood dribbling from the corner of his mouth. Mabel had stopped and stood looking at him with her yellow wolf eyes.

The scribe sought out Gabriel's face. "She killed them... it was her... she killed them." And he fell on his face as dead as a desert.

CHAPTER FOURTEEN
~ THE PALE HORSE ~

Once she had become herself again, it didn't take long for Mabel to undo Gabriel's bonds.

"God, Mabel... you even scared me."

"You were quite safe."

"What's in the bag?"

"Ah, yes." Mabel undid the drawstring.

Gabriel whistled.

"We wondered why Scrivens and Honfleur stayed in Marlborough and didn't simply run off with their takings? This is why. They were waiting for the King," said Mabel.

"These are the King's jewels?" Gabriel bounded up from the floor and shook the dust from his cotte. Mabel explained to him how she'd seen Scrivens steal them.

"Jesus. We have to get rid of them!"

"Don't worry..."

"But Mabel!"

"I'll put them back where they belong."

"Do I want to know how you are so certain that you can do that?"

"Probably not."

"Oh... and erm... there's a dead body upstairs... with my knife in it." He hovered at the bottom of the steps. "I'll just go and retrieve it.

No need for you to...erm...come and see..." He vanished.

She called after him. "Gabriel... who's dead?"

"Poor Aimée," came the reply. "Scrivens killed her."

"No..." Mabel felt a lump rise to the back of her throat. She looked over at Scrivens' body slumped in the doorway. He deserved to die, she thought. That poor girl; that poor child-like girl; another victim of his greed. She and Gabriel had promised to keep her safe. And they'd failed. Miserably.

She crossed herself and said a prayer for the soul of poor Aimée, who'd had a short and unhappy life.

Gabriel clomped down the narrow stairs. She noticed his knife was back in its scabbard and his sword once more hung at his hip.

He rubbed the back of his head and stretched his bruised back. "Wouldn't mind a pint of ale and a drop of your headache powders."

"We must follow Honfleur, see where she's gone."

"What do we do with the King's jewels? We can't keep them on us. They'll be searching the town."

"Leave that to me."

"Should I tell the town reeve about Aimée?"

"No, I don't think so. Her friends will find her... sadly... It's best we aren't found here."

No sooner had the words left her mouth, than there was an appalling scream from upstairs.

"Ah... she's found. Quick... we mustn't be seen. I'll be off to Turnabout Lane. You collect Bertran and meet me there."

As he left, Gabriel glanced back to see Mabel, half woman, half pigeon, pick up the bag of jewels in her beak. It was the strangest thing he thought he'd ever seen.

*****

Mabel flew fast across The Green, her powerful pigeon wings briefly sweeping the air and stretching out to soar above the people, carts, and animals on the road to the bridge. Her flight dipped, she flapped again and rose with a 'wheep, wheep' sound.

Aha! There was Wymark Honfleur, her cherry red gown glowing in the light of the watery sun, half running, half walking, towards the London Road. Every few paces she looked over her shoulder. 'Afraid there's a wolf following eh?'

Honfleur began the ascent up the hill.

'I thought that's where she'd go.'

Now she was certain she knew what Honfleur was up to, she turned her beak towards the castle and flew along the High Street, over the castle wall and up onto the roof of the King's House.

She thought about dropping the bag through the smoke flue but that wasn't a good idea as the fire was now lit and burning well.

But she had to get the jewels back into the building.

Turning three times withershynnes, Mabel said, "I wish to be a magpie."

The grey plumage disappeared to be replaced by glossy iridescent, blue black, green and bright white.

Glancing quickly to make sure no one saw her pigeon self vanish and her magpie self emerge, she dipped into the bag with her long, strong beak. Out came the gold chain with its ruby pendant.

Leaving the bag on the roof, carefully wedged against the tiles, Mabel lifted off and, the pendant swinging with her flight, she made for the main door of the King's House.

There were two soldiers standing on the steps.

Mabel alighted and as bold as a bawd, walked between them. She made sure that they'd seen her.

"Ere!" said one of the soldiers. "You see that bird?" He flapped his hands "Shoo... off you go!"

""Maggoty pies... I hate maggoty pies!" said the other.

The first soldier made the sign against the evil eye.

"Bad luck they are."

"Hello Master Magpie... I hope you're having a good day," said the second soldier stepping back. Then he realised that the bird had something in its beak.

"Oi!"

"What?"

"Ain't that what they said the King lost?"

"Jewels, they said. Red rubies."

"Well... those are jewels, ain't they?"

Mabel disappeared into the darkness of the doorway.

The soldiers peered into the hall.

"Magpies like to steal things, don't they?"

"So I've heard."

"I ain't never heard of the bird bringing things back."

Mabel chuckled and carried on walking.

"Perhaps it wants to hide things in the hall?"

Once in that hall, she flew up quickly and passing over one of the tables, she let go of the jewel. It fell with a clunk onto the surface of the white damask tablecloth laid out for the King's dinner.

A couple of servitors leaned over to see what had made the noise. They looked up.

But Mabel was streaking out through the door, suppressing the urge to cackle in her magpie voice.

Next she took out the ring and carefully held onto it. She hoped she could get the two brooches and the ring into her beak at the same time.

Grasping them tightly, she flew up and this time made a quick entrance, swerving to miss a member of the kitchen staff with a large pot of soup.

"Bloody bird!" shouted the man.

"Aw..." said another man following him with a basket of bread, "You mustn't shout at a magpie like that. It's bad news!"

Mabel smiled a birdish smile. It was fun being a bird people feared.

She deposited the jewels on the table and quickly flew up to the rafters.

They were immediately spotted on the white tablecloth and whoops of glee went up from John's staff.

Now he wouldn't be in such a bad mood.

She really didn't like to think of that nice old man, Petit, who was body servant to the King, being berated for losing the jewels.

She sped out of the King's House, up over the castle wall and into the trees of the edge of the Forest of Savernake.

*****

She landed on the top of a yew tree and craned her magpie neck to see if she could find Gabriel.

Smoke came from the central flue in the large hall on Turnabout Lane. Someone had lit the fire but she doubted it was Wymark Honfleur. It was probably her servant Hugo. Mabel scouted round for Gabriel and Bertran. She couldn't see them.

Perhaps he'd had difficulty retrieving his horse from the livery stables? No, why would that be, surely she would have seen him riding up the hill as she'd flown, for she'd travelled over the London Road, the road Gabriel would have ridden. A worm of dis-ease started to crawl around her heart.

She took a pass around the glade in which the house was situated to see if she could find Bertran.

Ah, at last! There he was hidden in the trees, cropping the grasses a few yards to the south; so Gabriel had made it to the house.

She rose up into the top of the highest tree and filled her bird lungs.

"Gabriel!" she cried. It came out as a tinny rattle. "Gabriel!" This time she squawked for all she was worth. Surely he would not be as stupid as to go into the house alone? He made no answer. He had gone into the house alone.

Mabel flew down, turned three times deosil and shook her hair which had come undone from the plait in which she'd worn it that morning. Rapidly she plaited it again and threw it over her shoulder.

She stood and listened carefully. Her human ears could pick up no sound apart from the cheeping of the sparrows on the roof.

Slowly she approached the door and opened it. There was no one in the hall.

Mabel knew that Wymark would be collecting the ill-gotten gains stored at this house and would plan to leave as quickly as possible before the body of Scrivens was discovered.

She crept towards the inner room where she and Gabriel had seen the chests of money and jewels.

Here was Gabriel, his knife in his hand leaning up against the door with his ear to the wood. He hadn't heard her approach.

"Pssst."

Gabriel turned rapidly and pointed the knife at her.

"Oh Mabel! I could have skewered you," he whispered loudly.

"I told you to meet me here. I didn't mean right here," she said breathily.

"Well, we're here now." He nodded to the door. "She's in there stuffing things into a pack or two. She's sent Hugo to saddle her horse."

"We can't let her get away."

"What do you suggest?"

Mabel took her lower lip in her teeth and agonised over what to do.

"We have to stop her. But we have to have witnesses to her crimes. See if we can get her to confess. Our word alone won't be enough."

"A woman like that? Confess? Never. She's as hard as a hog's head!"

"I have an idea." Mabel pulled him away from the door. "Go and find Master Barbflet and a few of his men. Bring them back here..."

"That will take me too much time. She'll be gone before..."

"Alright then. Take them to ... to my house?"

"What?"

"Please Gabriel... just do it!"

"Why would she go to your house?"

"She will, I promise."

"What do I tell the town reeve?"

"The truth, that you have found the person who has killed Scarepath and everyone else."

"I can't mention you and your..."

"You may tell them that I have followed her. That's all."

"And they'll believe me?"

"You'll just have to be convincing. Oh and..."

"There's more?"

"The horse which the woman keeps here. Let it loose, take it away. She mustn't be able to get to it."

"What?"

"And deal with her servant Hugo. He mustn't be around either."

He ran his hand through his hair, "Oh Mabel, what are you planning? I know you. It's bound to be dangerous."

She smiled and kissed him quickly on the cheek. And yes, it was as soft as she had imagined.

"You'll see."

*****

Gabriel had gone.

She felt very alone and her heart was thumping under her ribcage.

She needed to conserve her energies for what she wished to do and so chose not to turn withershynnes into any animal. One quick glance at the door told her that it was open anyway and she'd no need to change to an animal small enough to squeeze underneath it. Silently she opened the door.

As Gabriel had said, Wymark Honfleur was collecting together bags of clothes, jewels and money from the large chest and stuffing them hurriedly into a pannier or two.

"Where are you planning to go then?" asked Mabel to the woman's back?

Wymark spun around. "You!"

"It started with me and it will end with me."

The knife Wymark had carried was lying on the bed. Mabel flashed a quick look at it. Casually she came further into the room. "It's just you now. Now you have killed your second lover."

"You have no proof that I killed either of them."

"Perhaps I'll get it."

"Pah!" Wymark waved an admonishing finger at her.

"You are an interfering imbecile who doesn't understand what you have got yourself into."

"I understand much more than you realise. I know how many people you have killed... or have had killed and that you stole from the King."

"That was Scrivens!"

"Oh yes. And he killed Sweetcheeks, I think and he tried to kill me but my head is a hard one. He killed Master Stoneford and the scribe who lived at your house and even his own wife. To make way for you, I suspect. Poor man. He thought you'd marry him."

"I've killed no one... and Scrivens deserved to die. It wasn't murder it was justice." The woman attempted to look innocent.

"He killed Aimée. We know that because my friend, Sir Gabriel saw him."

"Where is he by the way? Your lovely knight?" Wymark moved her hands to her waist confidently. Arms akimbo, she looked rather silly.

"Busy..."

"As am I. Now go away, there's a good girl. Go away and you won't get hurt."

Mabel turned to leave.

"This isn't the last you'll see of me... just so you know."

Wymark Honfleur licked her lips. What did this woman mean by that? Should she kill her now?

She buckled her pannier and turned back to the door, having picked up the knife but Mabel had gone.

Honfleur ran through the building and out the back door to the stables.

Hugo was nowhere to be seen. Her lovely roan horse, Petal, was nowhere to be seen either.

"Argh!" she cried out in frustration.

She pulled her panniers to her breast and ran around the building. Then she heard the whinny of a horse. Yes! Hugo had already saddled Petal and had her waiting at the front door.

When she rounded the gable end of the house, she slowed. This was not her horse. Where was her horse?

There on the grass, cropping its edge, was a beautifully elegant pale dun horse. She had certainly never seen this one before. In a moment she'd decided. There was no time to wait. She couldn't see her own horse, so this one would do.

With a nervous look around she dropped her panniers and rushed back to the stable for tack and saddle. She was all fingers and thumbs as she threw it onto the horse and attached the panniers, in haste.

The pretty pale horse was docile and sweet natured and never once gave her trouble. It must belong to one of the more wealthy clients who frequented her house, she thought. Ah well... it was hers now.

She mounted and thundered off down the track to the main road.

It wasn't long before this docile and good natured horse started to become difficult.

Wymark wanted it to go straight along the King's Road. She was making for Newbury, Reading and ultimately London.

The horse had other ideas. It veered off from the main road and raced along a track leading further into the forest.

Wymark was forced to cling on tight to keep her seat. No matter what she did, the horse went where it wanted. She pulled the reins, she kicked the beast's side in anger in order to bring it to its senses. It bolted forwards.

Onward it galloped, turning to right and then left. Honfleur was abysmally lost. She had never been so deep off the main road into Savernake before. Scrivens might be at home here. She was not.

The trees flashed by in a blur. If she fell off, would the horse stop? She fiddled at her waist for the knife she'd taken with her. One hand was not enough to keep her on the horse's back and she quickly grabbed at the mane. She wasn't a good rider at the best of times, but this horse was impossible to control.

They seemed to have covered miles. Where was the beast taking her? She was out of breath and unstable in the saddle and she leaned forward, grasping the horse around its neck in desperation. Should she try to take out her knife again and perhaps stick the horse in the neck. Surely that would stop its onward dash!

Then she thought again.

Many miles had been eaten up by this horse's hooves. Wymark was a good distance from the town now; she was safe. No one would follow. She might not know where she was. But neither did anyone else.

The forest was passing by in a bleary and confused blur; trees, glades, small cottages. Wymark had seen no one; all she heard was the thudding of the hooves on the track, the blowing of the beast's breath and the whistling of the air as they sped along. The horse didn't seem to have tired but Wymark knew it had slowed a little and she could hear it was blowing.

As if the horse knew that the woman was suddenly resigned to go wherever it took her, it changed its gait from gallop to trot.

They were now passing fields where there were people out tending to their crops. Some looked up. Others kept their heads down. One man with a drift of hogs who was knocking down acorns from the oak trees surrounding the fields with a long stick, watched carefully as they passed.

They came to a village and the horse changed its gait yet again and walked down the road. Its head began to dip. It turned left onto a track where there were several cottages in small plots and Wymark counted two dwellings on the corner and then strips of cultivated garden and two more houses.

The horse stopped in front of the last cottage with a garden at the front, filled with seed heads of herbs and flowers. She could see a bothy which seemed to house hens at the back of the cott and a well, with a pump handle in a silvery wood leaning over the side. Where the Hell was she?

Well, she was glad to dismount and catch her breath. Oh, she could do with a drink.

No one was around. With a quick look at the horse whose head was bowed and whose sides were heaving, she walked round the cottage.

*****

Mabel knew that Wymark had never been to her house before. She stood outside the front door, her breath steadying, her legs shaky with the headlong dash through Savernake. Eventually she was able to raise her head and put her left front hoof over her right. In this way she turned deosil three times. "I wish to be a woman again."

Mabel's body shrank. Her hooves turned to hands; her mane became her usual plait of hair. Her elegant nose retracted and became the attractive snub which Gabriel found so beguiling. The saddle and panniers evaporated and then appeared on the ground. Mabel hid them under a bush.

She took a deep breath. Her human lungs expanded; no longer did she breathe like a horse.

She lifted her chin. Time to catch this evil woman out. Time to get her to confess to her crimes.

She felt much more safe at home. She knew every corner, every wall, every roof beam. If she was to make Wymark admit to her crimes, she needed her wits about her and her wits were much better employed here at home, than in that unknown house near the town. Mabel was in Savernake, her home. Wymark was completely lost in the forest. And there was no chance of help here, no clients from the house on Turnabout Lane, no Hugo. They were alone. She fervently hoped that Gabriel had managed to convince Master Barbflet that they could apprehend Honfleur for her crimes, if they came with him to Bedwyn.

She stepped through the front garden gate and walking to the rear pulled on the handle of the well. Up came the small bucket and Mabel cupped her hands to take a drink. After her fast run through the forest as a horse, she was parched.

She looked up to see Wymark Honfleur staring at her. "Got any of that for me?"

Mabel backed away. "Be my guest. There's plenty."

Wymark dipped her head and drank.

"This is your cottage, right?"

"Yes, it is."

"So this must be Bedwyn?"

"That's right."

"How did you get here so quickly?"

Mabel walked nearer to her back door. "I ran as fast as I could."

"How did you know I'd come here?" The woman was genuinely perplexed.

"Would you believe me if I said that I made you come here?"

"No one... makes me... do anything!" said Honfleur bitterly. "Least of all an ugly, scruffy, useless creature like you."

"Well, now I know what you think of me. Shall we go inside and take some ale perhaps and you can tell me everything from the beginning."

"Why should I do that?"

"It's comfortable. I could light the fire. You could take your ease before…"

"Before?"

"Before you move on to wherever you are moving on to," said Mabel.

Wymark came a little closer. "You think I shall let you go—alive?"

"I know you will."

"Are you a seer that you know so much?"

Mabel opened the back door. "Something like that, yes."

Wymark's interest was kindled. What was this strange girl on about?

Mabel, making sure she had a good view of her enemy, put down the locking bar on the back door, uncovered the turves of the fire and blew the flames gently. She fed the resultant glow with twigs. Then she touched a small lamp with a piece of kindling and the inner house came into view.

"Goodness me. Not what I'm used to," said Wymark nastily. "It's very basic isn't it?"

"It suits me. For now."

Honfleur looked her up and down. "Well you're a churl. What do you expect?"

"Whereas you're… what?"

"A townswoman of property and wealth."

"Wealth obtained through the prostitution firstly of your own body and then of young girls whom you terrified and bullied."

"The strong exploit the weak… it's a rule of life."

Mabel sat on her stool and gestured for Wymark to sit on her bench. "Tell me about that life."

"Why do you want to know?"

"You're leaving the area, I take it? There'll be a space for someone with foresight, brains and daring."

"YOU?"

"Don't underestimate me."

Wymark's forehead wrinkled with genuine puzzlement. "You and your little knight?"

"Ah no... not him. I'll be leaving him behind. He's a liability." As she said this she felt a little pang of sadness. She hoped that Gabriel would understand, if he'd managed to get near and overhear.

Then there was a whinny of a horse. Bertran?

Wymark, panicked, looked to the front door.

"The horse on which you came here," said Mabel. Another lie.

"And the horse on which I shall leave."

"It won't be much use for a while. Best you rest it."

"You have a good head."

"It has been said."

"So where's the ale you promised?"

Mabel took up a jug and two horn cups.

"To show you there's no trickery, I'll pour both so you can see and I'll drink the same," said Mabel.

"You better had."

A cup was handed to Mabel's guest.

"It's probably not what you're used to but it will serve."

Wymark Honfleur upended the cup and looked around Mabel's home.

"I wanted to better myself too."

"And so you took up with Scarepath?"

"He was flattered that a young and good looking woman like me would attach herself to him. I knew I had to play a waiting game."

"Sadly you waited a bit too long didn't you?"

The woman laughed. "I wasn't getting any younger."

"And Scarepath was getting older."

"It took me a long while to gain his trust... enough to get him to leave the properties to me."

"Once he was dead."

"It's odd..." Wymark crossed her ankles and relaxed. "He almost knew that he was going to die."

"The attempt on his life?"

"He had a lot of enemies," said Wymark. "And at last he became so worried, that he disappeared into Savernake for safety, whilst I carried on."

"He expected you to join him didn't he?"

"Sooner than I wanted."

"So, you killed him."

"He was a wealthy man—dead."

"And, he made you a wealthy woman—dead," said Mabel, annoyed that Wymark hadn't actually, in her own words, admitted to his murder.

"You know, he had no idea I was betraying him."

"With Scrivens?"

"I recruited him..."

"Because he worked at the castle. And you needed someone to steal the King's jewels."

"The first man got cold feet," said Wymark. "He lived in my house. Another stupid clerk. He'd heard us plotting and he was going to go to the authorities. Scrivens offered to get rid of him for me."

"So, Scrivens killed him and more or less took his identity at your house."

"It was easy to convince folk that he was just a lowly scribe."

"Well, he certainly took me in. For a while."

"I've no regrets about any of them. One thing you'll learn, young lady, is that men are stupid. We can use them and discard them as we wish. No one ever gives us credit for what we do... alone, as women."

Mabel smiled. "It is strange that men seem to think that we need them, when all the while..."

"It's really they who need us."

Wymark leaned back and made herself comfortable.

"I was already successful and running my houses, the one on Figgins Lane and the House of the Dairymaids when Simon Scarepath came into my life. He was a petty little thief until I organised him and showed him the path to riches."

"Well, now you'll be leaving the houses behind."

"I'll be back."

"Someone else might have moved in."

"YOU? Don't make me laugh!"

"Perhaps, the town reeve will get wind of your little 'empire.'"

"They are a bunch of grass-munching rabbits confused by the ferret. You think any of them could best me?"

"Not on their own... no. Although they had you under surveillance, they failed to understand what you were up to."

"Only you and your tame knight seem to have been able to grasp that particular nettle."

"We were lucky. And now it's just me," said Mabel with feeling.

Wymark jutted her chin. "You remind me of myself a few years ago."

"Oh no... I couldn't possibly be like you." Mabel stood. "I'll go and feed and water your horse. You stay here and rest yourself."

"Ah no..."

"I promise there's nothing untoward. I shall merely water and feed your horse. Then you can be on your way."

Mabel scurried through the front door leaving it open and quickly ran round the house. Her back door was closed and there was no window on that face of the cottage. Unless she was followed, she couldn't be seen. She scanned the trees. Was Gabriel there? Had he brought help?

She approached the well and pumped it a few times just to make it seem as if she was drawing water for Honfleur's horse.

"Psst."

"Gabriel!"

"Quickly. One man is on the roof. Another by the midden at the side and Barbflet is at the other end of the cottage gable." Gabriel was crouching by the well.

"The horses are hidden in the trees."

She nodded.

"She's talking busily to me."

"Good... keep her going."

Mabel crossed her garth and turned withershynnes once more. She was very tired but she had to make Wymark think that her horse was still close by.

She clopped past the house front slowly and made a play of being seen cropping the grass. She saw Honfleur look out at her.

After a while she ambled over to the trees and disappeared.

She reappeared a moment later further along the track, as Mabel, and made her way back to the cottage.

"There. She's a happy horse now and is beginning to be well rested."

Wymark had her knife in her hand. "Whom did you speak to?"

"Why?"

"I heard voices."

"Oh, that was my neighbour, Master Farmer. He was admiring the horse you rode in on. She is a fine beast."

Mabel was treated to a disbelieving stare and then Honfleur relaxed again.

"I have to go."

"Just a little longer. Your horse will carry you further and quicker if you let her rest a little longer."

"Why? Why are you helping me?"

"I admire you. That's why." The words almost stuck in Mabel's throat. "A successful woman, besting so many men. That's admirable."

Honfleur laughed. "You're serious aren't you?"

"Why would I not be? I don't want to sit here in poverty and moulder all my life."

"That I can believe," said Honfleur. "I was the same. I once lived in a hovel like this near Newbury, with an abusive father. Rather than run away, I killed him. I was thirteen. No one thought that a young woman of thirteen could kill her father by cutting his throat. But I did. I'd had a lot of practice with his pigs." She laughed, a sound full

211

of contempt. "Then it was easy to disappear and reappear as another woman."

"Ah, so that's why you cut Scarepath's throat?"

"He trusted me, the idiot. You should have seen his face as he was drowning in his own blood. Especially since I was dressed as a man."

Ah at last! A confession in the woman's own words. So that was why the town reeve's men could never find her. They were looking for a woman.

Mabel smiled to give her encouragement. "You didn't go on cutting throats though did you?"

"I might have cut Scrivens' throat as he slept if he hadn't got in the way today."

"Instead you stabbed him in the heart"

"Your knight saw me... yes. And just for a change I strangled and strung up Sweetcheeks."

"I thought Scrivens killed him."

"Nooo. Though I sent him to deal with you."

"Ah well... he failed."

"I don't accept failures," said Wymark Honfleur coldly.

There was a scrabbling on the roof. 'No!' thought Mabel. 'One of Master Barbflet's men is going to give us away.'

"What's that?" Honfleur jumped up.

"You're very jumpy."

"You would be if you watched a dog turn into a wolf, just like that!" She clicked her fingers. "I just about escaped with my life."

"A wolf!" Mabel chuckled. "There are no wolves around here."

"That's not what your Sir Gabriel says."

The noise came again. Mabel had to think quickly.

"It's probably my cat. She loves to prowl the roof. She's a very efficient birder."

"Have I met your cat?"

"She goes everywhere I go." Mabel giggled. "She's a fantastic mouser. Good job as we are rather overrun in this village at this season. All the grain, you see."

"What? Mice?"

"Oh yes. We have veritable hordes of them."

"Ah… I have to go."

"Just when I thought we were getting on so well."

"Erm... have you any food I could take with me?"

"Of course. Wait, I'll be right back. I have a small outhouse at the rear."

Mabel exited the cottage by the front door. 'Have I enough evidence now to convince Master Barbflet that Honfleur is guilty of murder?' she said to herself.

She scanned the garth. Where were they, Master Barbflet and his men? She looked up on the roof. It looked as if the man there had slid down the front.

Out of sight, she turned withershynnes three times and said under her breath, 'I wish to be a large mouse.'

Mabel had the idea, a feeling in her bones that the woman would try to use her as a hostage or a shield if she returned to the cott as herself. She couldn't have that. She had to get her out of the house and into the authorities' hands.

Mabel mouse scurried bravely into the cottage and skipped across the floor.

WITHERSHYNNES 2: CAT'S CRADLE

CHAPTER FIFTEEN
~ FLIGHT! ~

Gabriel was watching from up on a large branch of the old oak tree in Mabel's garth. He sat entranced as she turned herself into a horse and clopped gently over the grass to the perimeter trees. How beautiful she'd become. Then he saw Mabel as a woman slowly return to the cottage and, jumping down and creeping forward, heard the conversation between Wymark and Mabel. He desperately hoped that the town reeve and his men dotted about the small cott, had heard the confession too; that Honfleur had killed Scarepath, Sweetcheeks and others.

What was Mabel planning?

Suddenly there was an horrendous shriek.

"Argh! No... no... get out. Shoo. Away! Argh!"

What on earth was happening? Gabriel knew that this wasn't Mabel's voice. It was Wymark Honfleur and she sounded very panicked. He made himself scarce and climbed the tree again.

Suddenly the back door opened with a jerk and Honfleur momentarily silhouetted in the door hole, picked up her skirts and ran at a speed which surprised Gabriel.

He saw her look round for her horse.

"Where are you?" she yelled in frustration.

Gabriel had to chuckle. She had no idea the horse which had

brought her to Bedwyn, had been Mabel.

He had been so busy chuckling that he had failed to follow the woman and she disappeared into the woodland trees to the north of the garth. For Heaven's sake, where were the town reeve's men? It was their job to lay hands on her.

Gabriel scrambled down from his perch just as Master Barbflet and his men rounded the cottage.

"What's going on Sir Gabriel?" shouted the town reeve.

"The woman has flown but she won't get far, I'm sure."

"For goodness sake, why couldn't you have stopped her?"

"Why didn't you…?"

The town reeve looked annoyed. "We mustn't let her obtain her horse again."

"Ah no... that won't be possible, trust me," said Gabriel jogging backwards towards the trees. "I'll find her!"

Before he turned he managed to see Mabel just inside the doorway, turning withershynnes to become a pigeon again.

Thank goodness she was alright. He'd worked out that Mabel had become a mouse in order to corner the damnable woman but that her plan had not been successful. Wymark was so afraid of mice, she couldn't even stay in the cottage with one. They just hadn't been ready for her leaving so quickly and from the back.

Mabel squawked and lifted off over the highest trees and Gabriel followed.

The townsmen followed him.

The men were soon hopelessly entangled in the thick vegetation which was Barr Field Coppice.

But Gabriel forged on, protected by his trusty gambeson and maille, looking up now and again at the patches of sky where flew a solitary grey wood pigeon.

*****

Mabel had been unprepared for Wymark's reaction to the mouse.

The woman screamed, ran to the back door, lifted the locking bar and was out before anyone could know she'd gone.

Mabel swore.

Now she'd have to follow and somehow corner her so that the pursuers could arrest her. She really had thought that Master Barbflet and his men would have apprehended her by the cottage.

She kept her eye on Honfleur as the woman madly travelled the gaps between the trees, tore her kirtle from the brambles and tripped over the roots hidden in the bracken.

She'd give her her due; Wymark Honfleur didn't give up. On she pressed, at speed, breathing heavily and distancing herself from the townsmen whom she had no idea were following her. Only Gabriel knew where she'd gone and he only knew that because he was following Mabel.

At last they came to a glade where the trees had thinned. Someone had pollarded the beeches here and they grew close together and their upright branches were huge and straight rising from thick trunks in which there were several hiding places. These trees were lapsed pollards, given up years ago, perhaps as many as one hundred years; great stately denizens of Savernake. Honfleur disappeared amongst them.

Mabel alighted on the out-thrust branch of an oak tree and waited. Her keen eye picked out the pollarded trees with their lichened trunks and their dense leaves held at the top branches. Autumn was here and the leaves were just turning.

Mabel watched a squirrel low down in the vegetation searching for a good place to hide the beech mast he'd been gathering.

She turned her head right and left.

Where was Gabriel? Surely he'd seen her dive into the glade?

Then she heard "Coo cooo cooo coocoo."

At the end of her branch a large, fat male wood pigeon was dipping his head and fanning out his tail. His handsome body was a silky, metal grey and his breast a grey-lavender shade. The stripe at his neck was bright white and his head the grey blue of a dull summer's day. He hopped towards her.

"Well… who have we here?" he was saying. "I haven't seen you before." Or at least that was what Mabel thought he was saying.

"Er no... go away. I'm on official business," said Mabel with haughty grandeur, backing off and fluffing up her breast feathers.

The male wood pigeon strutted a little closer and began to preen his feathers.

"Look, go away and do that somewhere else. It's very distracting."

The pigeon jumped forward and Mabel was startled.

"Ooh! That was unkind." She flew off to another branch. He followed.

Again he bowed graciously, fanned his black tail feathers upwards towards his head and once again preened the feathers under his wings, making snapping noises with his beak.

"I'm not interested, I'm not!" said Mabel. "I'm sure you're a really fine bird in your own way but I have no desire to…"

Suddenly the male leapt at her and began to grab her beak and try to force it open.

"Ahhh!" said Mabel, flapping her wings in panic. "Get off!"

Once again she took off and landed on another tree. From this tree she could see Wymark Honfleur recovering her breath and looking around, trying to work out where the devil she was.

But Mabel's suitor would not be put off.

Once more he followed, ducked and fanned. Once more he came close, puffing out his breast feathers, hopping and bowing.

Now, if this male pigeon were a young man of Bedwyn and Mabel didn't want his attention, she'd turn her back on him and huff and fold her arms over her chest. She'd ignore him, not make eye contact and not speak.

But this suitor was not a man.

Turning her back was just the signal the bird wanted. With a slight purr, he launched himself at her and tried to stand on her back. She knew what he was up to! Oh yes! It took all her willpower not to yell, 'rape!'

She tore herself away with a shriek and half fell, half flew onto the next branch.

"Get away... you... fiend. Don't you know when to take no for an answer?"

The male pigeon fluffed up his feathers and turned an evil eye on her.

Then he began the courtship all over again.

Mabel had had enough.

She summoned up all her strength and flew at him, with a great flapping of wings and raking of claws.

The poor male was forced from the branch and dropped to a lower one in great shock and a noisy clatter.

"And stay there!" yelled Mabel.

Honfleur looked up and took in the pair through narrowed eyes. 'Ah... it was only a pair of silly pigeons! Nothing to worry about.'

Gabriel chose that moment to enter the glade.

Slowly he approached Wymark Honfleur and slowly she turned to meet him.

*****

"You?"

He bowed low. "Madam. Can I be of assistance?"

"You can get me out of this God forsaken place."

"We are many miles into Savernake. That will not be accomplished easily."

"You must have a horse somewhere. A knight is never far from his horse. Or so they tell me."

"And have you knife me in the back as we rode? I think not."

"Why would I kill you, Sir Gabriel?"

"Because you can kill as easily as you can snap your fingers, madam."

"Aw.... Sir Gabriel. You don't really believe that?" simpered the woman. " It was Scrivens who was the violent one. I'd never hurt you."

"I suspect Master Scrivens thought you'd never hurt him."

"Pah... He was a black-hearted devil. Not to be trusted."

"Takes one to know one, mistress," said Gabriel glibly.

The woman fell down onto a large projecting root and sat looking disconsolate. "I'm sure you know a way out. Even if it's back to the town. What about Hungerford? That can't be far."

"No, it's not far. But it's not far enough for you to escape the law."

"I had a horse... if we could find it I could…"

"Ah no... I'm afraid your horse was... not all it seemed."

"Look, you paltry apology for a knight, find that horse or I'll…"

"You'll do what?"

The woman stood and tried to look extra alluring. "I have some amazing jewels in my pack, if you just help me find my horse, " she smiled. "More money than you've ever seen in your life."

"You are offering me money to help you get away?"

"Why not?"

"Even if I could help you, I'm telling you that your horse... well... it wasn't exactly a horse."

"I know a horse when I see one. I rode here on it. Of course it was a horse."

"Just like you saw a wolf, eh?"

"What?"

"And a tabby cat and oh yes, a mouse." Gabriel chuckled.

The woman turned the terrible shade of uncooked pastry and backed away.

*****

Fifty feet, five inches and a smidgen over five eighths away, Mabel sat on her branch and took a few calming deep breaths.

She heard Gabriel laugh and Wymark back away, a look of horror on her face.

"The horse...?"

"That's why you couldn't make her do as you wanted. The horse was actually a shapeshifter."

Wymark's head turned from side to side in denial.

"And from the very beginning this shapeshifter has had you under surveillance, you and your lover. Oh and yes... the little cat at the House on Turnabout Lane..."

"NO!"

"That was the shapeshifter, and of course, the wolf."

"NO!"

"So if you are wise, you'll come back to Bedwyn with me and I'll get the town reeve of Marlborough to arrest you."

Wymark looked around the glade. Gabriel wasn't sure if she was looking for a way out, or for this mythical shapeshifter.

"I don't believe you."

He drew his sword.

"Come on now. You really don't have any choice."

Honfleur started to breathe heavily in panic. "No... no."

"I suspect that this shapeshifter is around somewhere... pretty close. It would be in your best interests to come with me. And I'm really sorry, but displays of this sort are not going to work with me. Now come on."

Wymark began to cry. She howled and fell down to her knees with an imploring gesture. "Ah no. I can't go back. I can't!"

She inched nearer to him. "Help me... kill me now. Just thrust your sword into me... that would be the best thing."

Gabriel was rather taken aback.

Mabel on the other hand was not fooled for a heartbeat.

"Pah!" She clacked her beak together. "Be careful Gabriel. Don't relax your guard for a moment. I know her game." She hopped down a few branches.

Wymark was now prostrate on the ground, wailing and thrashing.

"Mistress Honfleur, please. Just stand up. There is no way I can kill you. It would not be justice."

"I can't stand trial... I can't."

'You can and you will,' said Mabel to herself, watching through her squinting pale pigeon eyes. 'And you'll hang.'

"Take off my head. One sweep. You can do it," the woman pleaded.

Mabel's pigeon eyes rose in her head. 'Oh really! Come on! So overacted!'

"No. I won't. Now. Come on. Rise up." Gabriel leaned forward to grab her hand to help her to rise.

Mabel from her lofty perch saw Honfleur jump up and make a play for Gabriel's sword.

"Here... Just here! Strike at the heart, here." She had hold of the end of the blade seemingly oblivious to its sharpness and Mabel saw drops of bright blood appear on the grass where she stood.

"Let go!"

Honfleur pulled the sword towards her breast. Gabriel was taken by surprise. She really did mean to thrust the weapon into her own breast, he thought. Mabel, up above them, watched as Honfleur partially wrested the sword pommel from Gabriel's grip and turned it on him. However, she did not strike. She knew that was going to be an impossible task, for Gabriel wore maille beneath his cotte and any pass she might make was doomed to failure. Gabriel's hand still holding the sword, she rose up on tiptoe, and with great strength struck him hard on the side of the head with the pommel.

He went down in a heap with a groan.

Mabel gasped. Gabriel was now extremely vulnerable. The woman could easily find the soft part of the neck and thrust in the sword or her knife. She could see her thinking about it.

Mabel flew down to the ground and speedily turned withershynnes three times.

*****

Honfleur's laughter echoed around the glade.

"Men! They are so...." She never finished her statement for, from behind her there came an unearthly growl.

She now had the sword in two hands and was just about to stick Sir Gabriel in the neck with it, when she paused and turned.

Gabriel groaned and began to come round. "What the...?"

"GRoarargh!" was his answer.

Honfleur was completely transfixed. Time had stopped for a heartbeat.

Then, "Call it off... call it off!" yelled Honfleur and put the end of the sword to Gabriel's throat once more.

He moved himself to one elbow and blinked.

"The beast will be a lot quicker than you. You might manage to injure me but I'm telling you, you won't get away from here. Well, not in one piece anyway."

Honfleur dithered.

Mabel growled low in her wolf throat again and the huge fangs became visible as she pulled back her lips.

One paw came forward. Then another. Closer and closer.

"I'm warning you. There's no stopping her."

"Her?"

She looked from Gabriel to Mabel. "Your girlfriend eh?"

"Mistress Cat... Yes." Gabriel didn't want to use Mabel's real name.

"Then you're going to see her die, Sir Knight," she said, as she swivelled and took a swipe two handed at the wolf, who was paused and ready to strike.

*****

Gabriel screeched and dived sideways grabbing Honfleur by the legs and pulling her down.

Mabel sprang and sunk her fangs into the woman's upper arm. Honfleur released the sword with a scream.

Gabriel scrabbled for it as Mabel drew off and growled again.

However, Honfleur was not as badly wounded as they would have liked, nor was she even rattled. She sprang for the sword again, her hand closing around the pommel a moment before the knight.

She screamed triumphantly and swiped for Gabriel again. This time it made contact with his maille and although it didn't wound him, it did wind him.

Mabel had had enough. With a huge roaring growl she sprang and raked the woman's face with her sharp claws.

Honfleur collapsed, releasing the sword and throwing her hands to her bloodied forehead and cheek.

Gabriel rose up to his knees and, with battered breath he said, "Well now madam... we are a matched pair. Both bested by a shapeshifting wolf."

Honfluer babbled and gibbered.

Unsteadily Gabriel stood and wavered a little, smiling at the now quiet wolf.

His brow furrowed. "Mabel? Mabel are you..."

Mabel's right back leg collapsed and Gabriel saw blood on the fur of it.

"Oh, no. Mabel. You are injured!"

CHAPTER SIXTEEN
~ THE NET ~

One quick look at Honfleur and Gabriel sprang towards Mabel wolf. She made a groan low in her throat.

"Oh Mabel... We have to get you back to yourself."

He tried to lift the creature but it wasn't an easy task and he was still a little befuddled himself from the blows he'd taken.

Swiftly he looked round for his sword and grabbed it before Honfleur recovered from her injury. He jammed it back into the scabbard.

"Mabel can you turn... Can you?"

The wolf struggled to four feet with a whine.

Honfleur was watching through a swollen eye, made blurry with blood. She began to back away, her hand clamped to her face.

"I'll help you," said Gabriel.

Mabel whined again and her teeth were bared once more as she saw Honfleur making her escape from the glade.

"My major concern is for you now, Mabel," said Gabriel. "We'll recover her later. We'll catch her, I promise."

Mabel turned slowly in a circle.

The transformation took some time to accomplish, for she was very wobbly.

And when Mabel was fully a woman again, Gabriel could see that she had a wound to her right side. Blood began to soak her kirtle. It was obvious she bore a sword slash to her right thigh.

He took off his cotte and, raising her kirtle…

"Oh Mabel don't be so foolish! I must staunch the blood flow."

Mabel had tried to stop him, but eventually fell back and he pressed the fabric to her wound.

"Wait!"

He drew off his hauberk and then his gambeson. He tore off his shirt and made strips of it as quickly as he could.

Mabel was breathing fast but she was saying nothing. She closed her eyes. Not only was she wounded, but so tired with all her transformations.

Gabriel bound the wound with his linen shirt and then drew his gambeson back over his head. He picked up his shirt of maille and slung it over his shoulder.

"Now, we must get you home."

Leaving Mabel to press the bloodied cotte to her bound thigh as extra protection, he took her arm over his shoulder and began to half walk, half drag her to the path.

*****

It was an agonising journey back through the trees.

Gabriel jollied Mabel along as much as he could and when she grew faint, carried her across his shoulders, murmuring words of encouragement.

He was so glad when he saw the thatch of Mabel's cott come into sight through the trees.

"You lie here for a moment, I'll get Mistress Little."

Mabel grabbed his hand as he passed.

"Gabriel, don't tell her… not… what really happened."

"No… No. Of course not."

Mabel's head turned to the side and she fell into an exhausted sleep.

He was back quickly and Mistress Little managed to make the wound clean and safe.

"It's not as bad as it looks, sir," she said. "It's a long skin wound, just the surface. There's no major muscle damage. She will be fine in a while. I have stitched it and as long as we keep it clean, it should begin to heal in five days or six."

Gabriel nodded and pressed a coin into her hand.

"Bless you, sir. Mistress Mabel has helped me more times than I can remember. There is no charge." And she pressed the coin back into his palm. "How did it happen?"

"Ah, we were out in the forest and we must have disturbed the lair of a pig."

"Ah yes, wild porkers are vicious at this time of year."

"Ah… Yes, they are."

"Especially with their second farrow of young only a few months old. Nothing worse than a she pig defending her young."

"Yes… They can be very dangerous."

"Shall I look in tomorrow, to see how poor Mabel is, sir?"

"That would be good, mistress."

"She didn't believe us," said Mabel from the shadow of her bed in the corner.

"Whether she did or didn't… it matters not. That's what she'll repeat around the village and that's what matters," said Gabriel with a sigh.

"But we lost Honfleur."

"Perhaps we did. I'll go out later to try to find her. She has no idea where she is. She'll be going round in circles."

"She has a wicked knife. I can see her using it on some poor unsuspecting villein in the woods. She has no conscience. She'll do whatever is needful for her to survive."

"We'll hear about anything happening in the forest and then we'll apprehend her."

Suddenly there was a scratch at the door and a voice shouted, "Mistress Wetherspring, Sir Gabriel."

"Ah... the authorities."

In came Master Barbflet.

"No luck?"

"No luck."

"Oh, Mistress Wetherspring, we are so sorry we failed to catch the miscreant."

"But you heard everything?" said Gabriel nervously.

"Enough to get her to trial."

"We shall continue to search as long as the light holds," said Greaves.

"Did you recover the pannier of jewels and money?" asked Mabel.

"Ay yes... it lay where you left it."

"Thank you."

"No, thank you for your... participation. We are only sorry you had to be injured."

"Ah… do you think, Master Barbflet, that you might keep that a secret? We are letting it be known that this was an injury from a wild pig."

"Why do you need…?"

"We don't wish to give the woman Honfleur any credit… if you see what I mean?"

"Ah… right." His face wore a puzzled expression. "As you wish."

Mabel smiled at him. "The woman is over confident as it is, sir. We don't wish to let her think she has vanquished us, should she hear any tales."

"Ah, yes of course." He bowed his way out.

"Now what Gabriel?"

"Now you rest."

*****

228

Mabel did rest. She had no choice, for she was exhausted. She was in and out of dreams the whole time; dreams which were none too pleasant and at last a huge peal of thunder woke her from a dream about a large feral pig.

Gabriel was sitting by the fire polishing his sword. "Ah... you have been a bit restless. How do you feel now?"

"Sore and tired."

"It's raining hogs and dogs!"

Mabel chuckled. "Aw... poor Honfleur out in this."

"My heart truly aches for her," said Gabriel, his tongue firmly in his cheek.

Suddenly there was a great blast of wind which rattled the doors and shutters.

"Autumn storms are early this year," said Gabriel looking up at the inner thatch.

"Have you...?" began Mabel.

"Yes, the chicks and geese are locked up and your goat is happily chewing the cud in Master Farmer's barn. Bertran is there too, tucking in to some hay."

"Thank you, Gabriel. We'll make a husbandman of you yet."

They listened to the rain and the thunder rolling around the heavens.

"Will they catch her, do you think?"

He sighed. "I truly don't know. But if there is any justice in the world... she'll be found and stand trial and hang for her crimes."

"I have a feeling she's not done yet."

Gabriel patted her arm. "Pottage, my dear?'

"Don't mind if I do," said Mabel.

Gabriel ladled the pottage from the pot over the fire and they ate in companionable silence.

Mabel looked at the bread in her hand.

"You managed to make pottage? And you managed to get fresh

bread?"

"Ah well... Mistress Small came round and she brought bread so..."

"She's a good woman."

"There are still some about," said Gabriel pointedly.

Mabel smiled. Gabriel's heart constricted. She knew what he'd meant.

Gradually over the next few hours the wind subsided and the rain diminished to a drip. The thunder rolled away over the forest in the direction of Hungerford to torment others.

Mabel slept and Gabriel polished his maille and when it came time for him to sleep, he moved the spare palliasse to the side of Mabel's bed and covered himself over with his cloak.

The next morning dawned dull and dripping. The plants in Mabel's garden had been flattened by the wind and rain and everything looked sad and forlorn.

Gabriel opened the back door onto the sad sight of Mabel's garth sodden and windswept. He drew water from the well into a bucket.

"It will soon recover," said a voice behind him, "don't worry." Mabel had hopped from her bed to stare out at the morning. "It always looks worse than it is."

"Does it?" said Gabriel sadly. "Worse? Honfleur has evaded us and we are no nearer bringing her to justice."

"Perhaps the town reeve recovered her last night?"

"If so, he'll send us a message today."

Mabel hopped over to the table grimacing at the pain in her leg.

"Here... go and fill the jug with milk."

"What? I don't know how to milk a goat! It wasn't one of the things I learned when I was a squire," chuckled Gabriel.

"It's not difficult."

"Ah well..."

Mabel laughed at him. "Go and ask little Johnny Chatterwell to do it and give him these." She picked up a few small cakes wrapped in a large dock leaf.

"He lives where?"

"Next door... that way."

"Right."

"Ah... Gabriel... the jug?"

"Ah yes."

He went off in his clean shirt and braies with his cloak around his shoulders, leaving his weapons in the cottage.

Half way back to the cottage he began to feel uneasy.

"I'm sure that I didn't leave the back door open," he said aloud to himself.

He hadn't. He was sure.

He peered around the door post.

"Come in Sir Gabriel and close the door."

Wymark Honfleur lounged on the stool by the table and she had hold of his sword once more.

"You have polished it, I see."

"I don't have the equipment here to do a proper job," he said. "But it's still sharp."

"Ah yes, I know." She pointed it at Mabel who was sitting on her bed.

"Do you know what it's like out in the forest, in the dark, with thunder rolling around you and rain coming down like a bucket was being poured over you? Eh? Do you?"

Mabel and Gabriel looked at each other.

"Not to mention the wind! Oh the wind!"

Mabel looked the woman over. She certainly looked as if she'd spent the night in the trees.

Her curly red golden tresses were sodden and lank and hung around her face like a soggy haystack. Her cherry red kirtle was soaked through, heavy and muddy at the hem. She looked like she'd been sleeping in a ditch, for leaves and twigs were stuck both to her clothes and in her hair. Her eyes were dull and there were bags beneath them. She wasn't the alluring woman she had been, by any means.

"I got no sleep at all, whilst you two were comfortably cuddling up here in the warm and dry!" Her expression was one of anger made even more pronounced by the red slash which Mabel had given her across her cheek.

"I hope the sword cut I gave you hurts like Hell," spat Honfleur.

"It did. It's not so bad now," said Mabel bravely. "I hope the wound I gave you will disfigure you for what's left of your short life. Not so pretty now, are we?"

Wymark Honfleur screeched and stood, making for Mabel with the sword.

Gabriel stepped in front of her.

"Punish me, not Mabel, if you must punish anyone," he said.

"Always the chivalrous knight," Wymark sneered. "Here's what we'll do. You let me go—take me to safety and recover my pack—and I'll see about forgetting all about this little episode."

"Why should I do that?"

"Because if you don't, I'll tell everyone all about your little friend here and what she can do."

Gabriel sniggered and then gave a full laugh. "You genuinely think you'll be believed, don't you?"

"In front of witnesses, with this sword to your neck, I think maybe she'll be encouraged to show how clever she is."

"No. Wymark. No, she won't."

"Gabriel…" began Mabel.

"She won't. For a start, she doesn't care that much for me. She won't jeopardise her own safety and her secret simply for me."

"She'll let you die then?"

"Yes… If it means laying hands on you."

Honfleur dithered. Gabriel had noticed that now and again she wasn't as confident as she seemed. But she recovered quickly.

"Well then, we shall see, shall we?" She gestured with her knife.

"Your neighbours... Get them here."

"I have two nearest neighbours," said Mabel matter of factly. "The Farmers, across the way and the Chatterwells to the south. But neither households will be in now. They'll be out at their jobs or in the fields. The nearest neighbour who will be of use to you... is Mistress Peabody. She lives close by, near the river."

"Ah..."

"And luckily for you, she's the village gossip."

"Even better."

Honfleur marched to the back door which was still open, "Out you both go. I have a sword and a knife."

"I can't walk well."

"Well then, your courtly knight here will have to aid you."

Staggering on Gabriel's arm, Mabel moved slowly to the corner of her garth and yelling across the intervening garden, she called for Mistress Peabody.

There was a little delay before the woman realised she'd been called. "Is that you Mistress Wetherspring?"

"It is Emelia. Might you just come to the edge of your garth?"

"Certainly I can... What's the matter?"

Wymark prodded Gabriel in the back with his own sword. "Do you think that you might come into Mistress Wetherspring's house for a moment, there's something we'd like you to see," he said.

"Oh... well... all right, sir. I'll just be a moment."

"The back door is open," said Mabel. Her eyes slid to Gabriel's and she blinked pointedly several times.

His brow furrowed but he trusted her enough, to know she'd probably have a plan, for he knew her to be a very imaginative woman.

Back in the cottage they waited for Mistress Peabody.

"Shut the door," said Honfleur rudely.

"Oh... we haven't been introduced..." said the rather sweet and artless Mistress Peabody, screwing up her eyes.

"And we shan't be. You're here to witness something. Nothing more."

"Oh my dear lady..."

"Shut up."

It was quite dark in the cottage for the day was dull and the shutters were still over the windows. With the doors closed, the corners of the room lay in gloom.

Mabel staggered to the bed and sat.

"It's all right Emelia. Just do as she says. She has a sword to Sir Gabriel's back and a knife in the other hand. If we do as she says, nothing nasty will happen."

"Oh!" said Mistress Peabody, paling, her hand going to her lips.

Honfleur grinned. "I will allow you to live and you will take me away from here, Sir Gabriel. If Mistress Wetherspring will do one thing for me."

Emelia Peabody looked from one to the other in total confusion. "Oh my!"

"Well, let's see you be a cat again, eh?"

"A cat...? Are you mad?" said Mabel.

"A cat."

"You want Mabel to become a cat?" Gabriel said with the semblance of utter perplexity on his brow.

"A tabby cat with a long tail. If you want to save Sir Gabriel's life, you'll do it and do it now." The sword tip prodded Gabriel's back more firmly.

Mistress Peabody wrung her hands.

"Oh... oh... I don't understand..."

"It's all right Emelia. The woman is mad. No doubt a devil has invaded her brain."

Honfleur prodded Gabriel once more, most cruelly. "Just do it."

"Oooh," said a frightened Emelia Peabody, once more screwing up her eyes.

Mabel stood and slowly moved into the shadow of the corner of the room where she had space.

"Quickly... we haven't all day," said Honfleur. She had to admit, this was something she really wanted to see. "And no wolves... do you hear... or he will die. Slowly."

"Certainly. No wolves."

Mabel lifted her arms from her sides. Her wound tweaked badly. One turn, she groaned with the pain. Two turns, "I wish to be a..."

Three turns and her body disappeared into the darkness.

Honfleur stepped forward, the sword coming away from Sir Gabriel's back. He sighed.

"Where's she gone?" cried Honfleur.

Without warning, a large mouse scurried from the gloom and ran over Honfleur's foot.

"Argh!" she screamed loudly. "No! Argh!"

She lifted her foot and staggered back, dropping the knife. Mabel mouse pursued her. Gabriel grabbed Mistress Peabody and turned her to the back door.

"Please, go and find Master Farmer and your son and any other men you can find."

"Oh...oh..." Emelia Peabody fled the scene.

Honfleur was still screaming. The mouse, hopping around her, Honfleur was attempting to swipe it with the sword. Suddenly it crawled up the outside of her kirtle.

Honfleur now dropped the sword with a clatter on the beaten earth floor and patted her clothing screaming at the full capacity of her lungs.

Once she was sure the mouse had fallen to the floor, she leapt to the front door, threw off the locking bar and opened the door.

No sooner had she exited than there were further screams.

"No! Argh!"

The hempen thread which Mabel had made into a net and fixed to the daub of her wall by the door, had come loose in the fierce winds of the night.

It dangled over the doorway like a spider's web.

235

And Mistress Honfleur had become hopelessly entangled in it.

Before she could extricate herself, Gabriel had drawn his own knife, cut the whole thing from the wall and wrapped it around her, further entrapping her.

The woman wailed and screeched, promising dire punishments on Sir Gabriel.

"Too late! Too late. Your secret is out! And the village busybody, too." She yelled at Mabel as she saw her coming up as a woman, to stand in the garden.

Mabel chuckled.

"Aw, Mistress Honfleur. I am so sorry. That will do you no good at all."

"You'll see... you'll see..." Her mouth was flecked with foam like a mad woman in a fit.

"It will be all around the village. Mabel Wetherspring is a..."

"Ah no... It won't. You see, Emelia Peabody is as blind as a bat! (Though Mabel knew that bats were far from blind.) "She sees very little at close quarters and even less further away. And in the dark, she's very blind!"

*****

"Aaaaaah!" Honfleur was screaming at the top of her voice.

"All that will happen is you will be thought a madwoman," said Gabriel. "Our word against yours."

Master Farmer now appeared with two of his sons and Master Hogman. Mabel could see the village reeve approaching with the manor steward, and Mistress Peabody trailing behind with her son, Thomas.

Mabel's job was done. She sighed and fell to the earth in an exhausted swoon .

*****

Master Buttermere sat with a mug of ale on Mabel's log before the door. The hempen net up which Mabel had hoped to twine a honeysuckle dug up from the forest, lay forlornly in a heap close by.

"And so she claimed that you changed yourself into a wolf!" The steward gave a hearty chuckle, "And she said that she'd been wounded by you."

"Really? Oh, dear," said Mabel.

"And she kept saying that Emelia had seen you change into... a cat was it... or maybe a mouse?"

"And what did Emelia say?"

"Well, of course that she'd seen nothing of the kind."

"And Sir Gabriel, what did he say?"

Master Buttermere drained his pot. "Well naturally he said the woman was raving, for he'd been here all the time and seen nothing of the sort."

"The woman is deranged and dangerous."

"Indeed she is." He stood. "The warden will be giving you his thanks personally, I'm told."

"Oh... There's no need."

"No... No. He's very pleased you've managed to rid the area of such a villainous creature. And her lover."

He took her shoulder and squeezed. "I hope the leg is mending well?"

"It's fine. I should still be able to do my job. Two or three more days and I'll be up and limping about."

"Good. Good."

He nodded and ambled off up the garden path.

Sir Gabriel came out of the shadows, pulled down his cotte and fiddled with his belt.

"You knew, didn't you, that Mistress Peabody couldn't see well?"

"After the last time she tried to tell us she could see well and our Lord Stokke proved that she couldn't, of course I knew she'd be just the person to witness my 'transformation.'"

"And you knew that Honfleur hated mice."

Mabel giggled. "The bigger, the better!"

Gabriel took a toe to the heap of netting lying on the ground.

"And the trap? Your cat's cradle?"

"Ah, that was an act of God, I think. The wind had loosened it. I knew that it had come down and made sure all the toing and froing was done through the back door. I knew she'd fall foul of it eventually if she went through that door."

"Will you make another?"

"Of course."

They looked at each other not quite knowing what to say. Mabel broke the silence. "You'll be back off to the Lord Stokke to let him know how it all played out?"

"I must. You know that."

"Yes, I know."

"Where do you go after, Rutishall?"

"Ah... We spend Christmas at Great Chalfield with the Lord Stokke's friend. The rest of the winter at Stockley."

"Ah..."

"But we shall be back here in the spring."

"Have a nice time at Christmas."

Gabriel nodded. "And you too."

"And you will write?"

"I will try to do better than last time."

"You didn't write at all last time."

"I am sure I did."

"Well, if you did, you never sent it here to this manor."

Gabriel took her shoulders in his hands.

"You take great care. When I return I want to see you running on that leg."

"Like a hare," she said.

"Yes... like a hare," he chuckled.

"I think that might be a good animal to turn to, to exercise my poorly leg."

"Ah yes."

He kissed her on the forehead. "And no more jackdaws."

"I shall be a jackdaw, if I wish."

"I will not be here to rescue you from a roof full of angry daws."

"Nor a moat full of water."

Gabriel laughed. "You can look after yourself... remember?"

"I can."

"Admit it... you can't..."

"I can..."

"Can't."

"Can."

"Can't." They were walking towards his horse.

"And when you return you can teach me to play cat's cradle properly and I shall best you at it."

"You won't."

"I will!"

"You won't."

"I will!"

Gabriel lifted her chin to him and kissed her tenderly on the lips.

"That, Mabel Wetherspring... is a challenge which will not go unanswered."

*****

Gabriel rode out of the village on the road east. He looked up to the sky. It was dull and grey and just how he felt.

There was an uncomfortable constriction around his heart which he supposed was a feeling of loss.

Most unpleasant.

He'd really thought that Mabel would accompany him as far as she could but, he supposed, her wound was preventing her. He mentally shrugged and spurred Bertran on.

He was sure it felt like rain.

He looked up again at the clouds which he thought were filled with a downpour. Like tears.

There high in the sky, riding the windy clouds was a large brown bird. A kite. Ah... Mabel was there after all.

"Squee-wee-wee-wee-weeoop, ' came the call on the wind.

"Squee-wee-wee-wee-weeoop, to you too," answered Gabriel chuckling, at the top of his voice.

~~FIN~~

GLOSSARY

Adamant - A compass

Agister - An officer who works for the Warden and looks after all animals in the forest be they wild or belonging to commoners who are allowed to graze their beasts on the common ground.

Bailiff - The men who were superintendents; they collected fines and rents, served as accountants, and were, in general, in charge of the land and buildings on the estate of a manor. Also see Steward.

Bog Iron - iron ore found in peat bogs.

Bow - In falconry a semicircular perch with ends able to be stuck into the ground.

Buttery - A storeroom for beverages, the name being derived from the Latin and French words for bottle .

Braies - A man's underwear.

Cods - Genitals.

Coif - A close fitting cap worn by both men and women.

Constable - An officer of the crown responsible for a county or part of a county whose job, amongst other things, is to look into felonies.

Cotte - A long, sleeved garment worn by men and women.

Crenellations - The battlements of a castle

Crespinette - A hairnet to contain long hair.

Cuckold - A man whose wife is having an affair.

Cunning Woman - A healer.

Dais - A raised platform upon which a lord dines and hears pleas in his manor court.

Daub - A mixture of mud, dung and chalk which is used to make walls.

Deosil - The direction of the sun's path. Left to right. Clockwise.

Dis-ease - Anxiety.

Doxie - Woman of ill repute.

Faggotty Coppice - the name given to a stand of trees used to grow coppiced wood for burning on fires.

Gambeson - a padded jacket of quilted wool stuffed with wool worn under the maille.

Garth - An open space with trees and vegetables planted. An enclosed garden.

Half Tester - A length of material or a wooden hood above a bed suspended from the ceiling upon which are hung curtains.

Hauberk - A coat of maille.

Hose - Stockings.

Husbandman - a person who cultivates the land; a farmer.

Jesses - a thin strap, made from leather, used to tether a bird in falconry. Jesses allow a falconer to keep control of a bird while it is on the glove or in training, and allow a bird to be secured on a perch outside its aviary.

Keep - The tower of a castle on its mound.

Kirtle - A woman's long dress made of wool or for nobles, silk.

Maille - Links of metal formed into a garment worn by knights and fighting men.

Matins - A church service tradtionally sung at midnight. The first service of the day.

Mesnie - A medieval household with a feudal lord. More narrowly, a group of knights who travel closely and fight in tourney and war with a feudal lord.

Napery - Tablecloths and other domestic dining cloths.

Nones - Church service at the ninth hour of the day (3pm.)

Pallet - A straw or hair stuffed mattress.

Paten - A dish used in the church for communion bread.

Pattens - Wooden outer shoes to lift you above the mud of the street.

Paunch - Disembowel

Pollard - Cut off the top and branches of a tree to encourage new growth at the top.

Pope's prohibition - The Interdict - pronounced in 1208 till 1214; a sentence debarring a person or place from ecclesiastical functions and privileges.

Pottage - A stew made mostly of vegetables and pulses. Staple diet of a Mediaeval peasant.

Preaching Cross - A stone cross set up in a churchyard where priests could talk to the congregation.

Privy - Primitive toilet.

Reeve - A man of lower rank chosen by the village who takes care of all business which affects all the peasant inhabitants of a manor.

Seer - Someone who can see into the future.

Scrip - a large pouch sometimes worn on the belt, sometimes carried like a bag.

Scriptorium - a place where scribes work.

Scullion - A lowly kitchen worker.

Shift - The underclothes of a woman; a long linen dress.

Skillet - Frying pan

Steward - A man who is in charge of the finances and general running of a lord's manor.

Stoop - In falconry - flying high in the sky folding back the wings and dropping quickly at a bird or the lure.

Strike-a Light - A stone of flint for striking a flame to create fire.

Supertunic - A sleeveless garment, usually of wool or silk, which adds another layer to Mediaeval clothing worn by men and women.

Tallow - Candles made of sheep fat.

Town Reeve - Mayor.

Tumbler's cureall - A mixture of herbs which was applied to bruises and scrapes. Named mainly for entertainers who were often hurting themselves.

Unguent - A lotion which helps with pain and swelling.

Vespers - Last church service of the day. Evening prayer.

Villein - A feudal tenant entirely subject to a lord or manor to whom he paid dues and services in return for land. He is not able to move from the place he lives.

Withershynnes - Sometimes in modern spelling Widdershins, turning against the path of the sun, anticlockwise.

Wolfshead - An outlaw whose head may be taken and presented to the authorities for money.

AUTHOR'S NOTE

Most Mediaeval people believed in magic and in magical beings of all kinds. Werewolves and vampires are just two types often discovered in the pages of manuscripts and in legends.

Shapeshifters are people who are able, simply by wishing it to be so, to change into any animal they wish and back into human form and this change must be voluntary for them to be considered true shapeshifters. Transformation must not be accidental and it must not be subject to any particular rule or set of circumstances. They must retain their human mind.

This series of books came about by me watching a fly land on my car windscreen when I was sat in a traffic jam. Moments later I had the germ of the idea for Withershynnes: In the Dark, Book 1.

I had long wanted to write another series of Mediaeval books where my 'detective' is female and not noble.

There are, of course, other writers whose tales have female investigators at their heart. I loved some of those books but they just never quite ring true for me, for it's highly unlikely that a woman could do the things they are allowed to do in those centuries before emancipation. Women were at the beck and call of men and would never be allowed to roam freely gathering information about crimes. I wanted a woman who could come and go at will, never be beholden to anyone (except her lord, at times) and be free to investigate when and how she wished.

So Mabel Wetherspring was born; an independent, clever, literate, practical, woman who is from common stock, and with a special skill which proves extremely useful.

The Mediaeval year began in March, not January as it does today and so the calendar is counted differently in these books.

I am at heart a murder mystery writer. I am a Mediaevalist.

And so I chose to set Mabel down at a time I am interested in, the beginning of the thirteenth century, in a place I know well, Savernake Forest. Mabel has been taken to the hearts of fantasy readers all over and so Mabel will go on to solve other crimes, with her sidekick Sir Gabriel Warrener, in a fantastical way.

Sue Newstead. July 2021

WITHERSHYNNES BOOK 3: CHEATING THE WIND

WILL BE OUT SOON.

SAMPLE CHAPTERS AND MORE CAN BE FOUND AT SUSANNAMNEWSTEAD.CO.UK

USE QR CODE FOR SUSANNA'S SITE
JOIN HER EMAIL LIST FOR NEWS & BONUSES

ABOUT THE AUTHOR

Susanna, like Mabel has known the Forest of Savernake all her life. After a period at the University of Wales studying Speech Therapy, she returned to Wiltshire and then moved to Hampshire to work, not so very far from her forest. Susanna developed an interest in English history, particularly that of the 12th and 13th centuries, early in life and began to write about it in her twenties. She now lives in Northamptonshire with her husband and a small wire haired fox terrier called Tabor.

Susanna hopes to return fairly soon to her beloved Wiltshire downs where she will continue to write the Withershynnes series, the Savernake Medieval murder series and her Kennet Valley medieval romances set in the area around Marlborough, Wiltshire.

ALSO BY SUSANNA M. NEWSTEAD

Please visit her website for further information
https://susannamnewstead.co.uk/

Milton Keynes UK
Ingram Content Group UK Ltd.
UKHW011311210923
429112UK00004B/142